JETTISON

STORIES

NATHANIEL G. MOORE

OTHER BOOKS BY NATHANIEL G. MOORE

Savage: 1986-2011 (Anvil Press, 2013)
Pastels Are Pretty Much the Polar Opposite of Chalk (DC Books, 2009)
Wrong Bar (Tightrope Books, 2009)
Let's Pretend We Never Met (Pedlar Press, 2007)
Bowlbrawl (Conundrum Press, 2005)

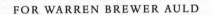
FOR WARREN BREWER AULD

Acknowledgments

Thank you to Amber McMillan and my daughter Finnian; Brian Kaufman, Karen Green, and Anastasia Scherders from Anvil Press; Marisa Alps, Howard White, and everyone at Harbour Publishing; plus Dina Del Bucchia, Warren Auld, Spencer Gordon, Grace Cheung, Nicholas Stedman, Jennifer MacDonald and Kerry Segal. Thanks also to *Sad Magazine* in Vancouver, *The Puritan* in Toronto, *Broken Pencil* in Toronto (especially Alison, Tara, Adam, and Hal). Thanks also to Brian Lee at the Harbour Spiel in Pender Harbour. Thanks to my blurbing author friends who you met before each story in this collection— please read their books, they are all great. Thanks as well to *Forget Magazine* and *Pine Magazine* (BC) for publishing an early version of "Jaws" back in September 30, 2002 as "The Nightmare Lover."

For more on Proper Concern's music, please visit proper-concern.tumblr.com or email properconcern@gmail.com or download the free *Jettison* album at www.jettison.ca and own a limited edition online bootleg of this beloved and seminal Canadian electro-folk band.

TABLE OF CONTENTS

"Of course Nathaniel G. Moore's 'The Catullus Chainsaw Massacre' is absurd, surreal, magical realist, speculative, and any other adjective you wish to apply to a story about things that have never happened and are unlikely to ever do so but it's the demonic logic he applies to the story's unwinding that grabs you by the love handles. This is fiction for people who love the make-believe best when it is perfectly, jarringly reasonable. On its own terms."

—RM Vaughan, author of *Troubled*

The Catullus Chainsaw Massacre

Humans don't have one pose, one image or one reflection. They can bend and crystallize, endure, fossilize and decay. They can prune, spoil, initiate and decline. Floral arrangements announce their arrival and departure. When a man loses himself to objects, when a man destroys his own ability to simplify his lust and solve the build-up with release, when he invents danger and fools beauty into ugliness he goes blunt. As young boys, some men sharpen their dicks in the sand under playground dirt. When the sun hits the school brick wall and the flowers sniff the air on a new spring day, a boy can feel it right through his pants, feel himself become part predator. To sharpen their dicks against this world is all that boys want; it is what they need, it is all they're good for. When this is taken away they become a place for worms to dance. They sit in an underworld of clay and dirt and madness.

For weeks now it snows all night and snows all evening. Still more snow still, well into mid-morning the next day—which is today. A commonwealth of white shellac one might suggest. Or a magnificent de-skinning of snow clouds. Like a snake, another metaphor, Henry thinks, an out of season snake, now very tired from yesterday, a day of books and luminous fluorescent lights bleating down on him in his incubator of pedagogical realism.

And Henry sits up in his temporary hermitage in one robe or another. In his student life he stares blankly at pages, he stares the same way at his patrician roommate. But right now it's the dullness of early morning and his open bedroom door and the hallway in which he casts his gaze. This, he thinks, is the life of a bug in a jar, waiting for someone to feed him a leaf and fly away forever and die somewhere else. Wine bottles lay gathering morning lint along the hallway like a bunch of toy boats. A headache pierces his temple. He barely notices until he sits up a few seconds later.

He remembers a conversation. He was drunk and began to shout. He pointed and with cocky pizzazz said, "Your sad man-made sparrow-themed murder ballads are not the panty removers you think they are."

And Catullus replied, his eyes flecked with candlelight and disappointment, "Is that an anyways for friendships spoken?"

His mind, Henry thinks is too much like a fan of peacock feathers, his sensibility non-existent, and the way Catullus speaks is at times fatuous, but amusing all the same. He's too thin. Too harsh, broken and antique: an antique contraction. Priceless and worthless.

Henry wants to tell Claudia all about Catullus: how harrowing it is to sit through another snack or meal with the guy. He takes off his bathrobe and walks softly, with baby goat steps towards the bathroom as a winter static follows close behind.

❋　❋　❋

Henry Shaw enters the kitchen and begins to remove his hat when he sees the callow man facing him, shucking corn.

"How many to eat?" the man says, his English broken, his eyes growing both impatient and lost simultaneously.

"I don't want any corn."

"Oh. What to eat?"

"Let's go get pizza."

"Yes."

And so the man with the stalks of corn cleans up as best he can manage and finds his winter clothing and follows Henry out the door into the blustering late afternoon.

"Sometimes people just don't know when to die," Henry snaps as a cab splashes his left side.

❋　❋　❋

"My woman says that she prefers to be married to no one other than me, not even if Jupiter himself should seek her," This is what the poet Catullus used to say to the gods, giving them a graffiti-like middle finger as he and others from his day ushered in an entirely subjective movement in ancient literature. While great wars and corruption were abounding in Catullus' world, the poet chose to write almost exclusively in gossip tropes about those in his immediate circle. But all Henry Shaw knows right now is that this man named Catullus is not dead, academic or archived, but has tomato sauce all over his chin. He sits across from Henry and, with his mouth open wide, is eating a hot slice of Hawaiian pizza. This barrel-chested individual with the long jaw and dark olive eyes has been following Henry around town now for months. Catullus blows hard across a slice with protruding pineapple.

On this blusteringly cold afternoon Henry sits in discomfort in the full gauze of winter gear he's grown accustomed to since birth. The men are at a loud pizza parlor at a Ms. Pac-Man table-top. Napkins are everywhere, stained in varying shades of red. The men chew and sip as their boots cry dirty tears of salt and snow. Their laces begin to thaw, breathing the warmer air with all the gratitude of a living thing. Henry begins to clean his glasses with a Kleenex then discards it into the disgusting pile of food crap manifesting at the table.

Catullus is asking Henry about the video game and its neon beacons of light and distraction.

"After you get the pellet you have to eat the ghosts."

"Are they coldening ghosts? How can me eating ghosts?"

"It's just a game," Henry says, edging a greasy slice of pepperoni into his mouth. Catullus' crude version of English has grown on him over the last few weeks; he almost always knows what the old dead man wants to say. The men eat two more slices teeming with heavy goat's cheese and slurp back their root beers.

"It's a really old game no one really plays anymore."

"Then why do we see here?"

"To be ironic, I guess."

＊ ＊ ＊

This is all happening in Waterloo, Ontario and it's the middle of December. Henry blows what he perceives to be hot air over his bare hands. He huffs in a long, drawn-out note of agitation as he leads them down the brutal road.

"Damn bus," Henry says, eating a mouthful of snow. "Always late."

The bus in question has just passed them and as it does they are both hit by a foul wave of winter slop. "This city just shits all over us," he barks. Henry's pants get the lion's share of sludge.

They walk snail-speed past the brewery museum where a forty-foot stack of barrels rests; an eyesore landmark, Henry has always thought, for the King and Erb district.

A few steps behind, Catullus never looks up. He is about as tall as Henry, grudgingly wrapped in scarves and mittens as they move east on Erb towards Fischer-Halman where a giant grocery complex sits.

"My feet are soaked," Henry says in a now familiar tone of complaint. This parlance is absorbed into Catullus, along with all the cruel icy temperament of nature itself.

The men reach a tiny strip mall featuring a discount video store, pet store, fish and chips restaurant, a gas station and a luminous convenience store which keeps irregular hours. Stopping midway along the row of commerce, they cross the road and head south on Amos Avenue.

"It's too cold to get groceries."

For the most part the homes are brick bungalows or semi-detached family units, fitted with small hedges and bulb flowers. Now, however, every property is blanketed in similar depths of white. Walking in silence, their breath wraps around fire hydrants and frozen telephone poles as the mutual freezing continues.

At a simple bungalow twenty houses in from Erb, Henry stops first.

"OK. So just in and out, no snooping," Henry says to Catullus who remains stiff, saying nothing. "I'm picking up a book from Claudia's place."

There is crispness to Henry's words, outlined in the icy fog breath from beneath his scarf and Catullus always appreciates his lucidity. They head up the front stairs and, as they do so, Henry glances across the street to the house where he's rented his room for the past six months. It's a modest room in a house; but, as a student, it's all Henry can afford. Catullus sleeps in the double bed in the basement next to the laundry room where, upon first using the washing machines with Henry, he had asked if the white flakes in the box were in fact snow.

As for Claudia, well, Henry met her at school about a month ago. She had just transferred to finish her final year at the University of Waterloo, studying biology and they'd been seeing each other: mostly movie dates, lunches and snowy walks to bakeries and bars.

A school bus lulls a few houses down the street letting off grade-school kids suited up for the storm in bright coats and pom-pom toques.

Henry coughs in Catullus' direction as if the noise alone contains instruction. His stomach gurgles unevenly, reminding both men that the spectre of hunger hovers like a permanent incubus toying with them in this middleweight city. Catullus' stomach grumbles as well.

"Pizza never really does it for me; I'm still hungry," Henry says as he takes Claudia's keys from his pocket. "Either that or we have stomach cancer."

Henry tongues his gums as he jostles the key into the door. "I just want to pick up a book and go. We aren't staying." The rooms in Claudia's house are rented out to three students: two on the main floor and one downstairs. Claudia's room is the furthest back and is decorated entirely in dark green. "She'll be home from class in about an hour."

Henry is often astonished at the way Catullus has learned to adapt to cold on his own, just as he once learned to curl his toes over hot sand, dodge a bloody cloth or outrun a whore haggling over the bill in Verona. Catullus' every pace is punctuated with a determined stomp, inches from the heel of Henry, his host and only friend.

The men walk down a dark hallway until reaching Claudia's room and Catullus immediately begins to trample over the bed. Despite the temperature outside, Claudia's window is open a crack.

"What the hell! Can't you behave for a minute?" Henry smacks the back of his head.

"I have to find that book."

Catullus sails into silence and anger and tries to put his head out the window. He presses his fingers against the pane until they redden. He inhales softly at the winter air.

"Stop it!" Henry says with a clenched fist, resuming his book hunt.

On the main wall of the bedroom hangs an Egyptian print of a woman holding an unsheathed knife. Beside it hangs a black-and-white poster of Grand Central Station. Above her bed is a small window with a maroon venetian blind, which Henry has drawn. On the floor are scattered bits of clothing and an Elvis bust, immortalizing the King in his late career, complete with rhinestone collar.

Catullus stands up and moves towards Claudia's open closet. He touches her hanging clothes. "You mention green dress and Claudia wearing it at party young time ago. But not now days right?"

Henry ignores his friend.

"The dress Henry, Claudia not wear it now I stand, but why not she wear?"

Catullus sits on her bed, the dress is in his hands. As he spreads it out on the bed, he asks Henry for a third time, enunciating each word with acuity.

"Henry, I ask again it. Claudia never say why kept her green dress so long a while?" He says this but never takes his eyes off the dress which he's taken from her sparse closet. His fingers brush against the vintage fabric in a slow, rhythmic way while Henry's move through the surfaces: a small photo frame that is empty, a pile of textbook receipts, several magazines and a grocery list. "I'm looking for a book. That's all I want. Then we're leaving."

"Why keep dress?"

"She never said. She hasn't worn it in seven years, OK?" The green dress worn to parties with a bright green bra underneath. That's how she described it.

"Never why say dress green keep but never wear," Catullus says to himself now, shaking his head and running his finger across the neckline.

When Henry sees the dress lying on Claudia's bed, he swats the back of Catullus' neck with a magazine.

"No! Put it away."

"She not talk of it more?"

"Put it away." Henry snarls, putting Claudia's room back in order, trying to remove Catullus' touch from the moment.

"No!" Catullus protests, his arms now tight up against his chest. He positions himself as a wedge between Henry and the green tea dress. Catullus grabs it, pushing his head through the bottom of the nearly see-through tea dress.

Henry peers through the crack of Claudia's bedroom door down the quiet hallway.

"Claudia's gonna be home soon. I don't want her coming home from class seeing me and you in some fashion show dressed up like her at seventeen."

Henry grinds his teeth and breathes in a rush as if the air itself is rich with Claudia's scent and he is holding a reed in his mouth deep underwater to preserve her smell, her great smell of apple juice. He wants to send his friend home. To duct tape Catullus to a toilet without dinner. Catullus now has the dress on, and adjusts his body within its limits.

"Take it off!"

Distraction, he needs to distract him. There isn't a tabletop Ms. Pac-Man within twenty minutes. A headline spittoons into his dirty mind before he continues his struggle with the man from sand and lust: micro-skirted pizzeria waitress covered in flour tells all.

"Can we put this away now? I should just chain you to a fence or something."

Catullus sniffs the dress and sighs. Henry looks at his watch.

"All right. I like a dress a lot you know. I've got to go place."

He watches Henry hang the dress in the closet a second

time, brushing out the creases, making it perfect. Henry gets it just right.

"Where are you going?"

"Badman-tan."

"Badminton?"

"Yes I go to play game, I taking new bike."

"You got a bike?"

"Several dollars by policeman auction."

"Where did you get the money?" Henry moves his body along her made bed.

"I sold music discs yours." Catullus says calmly, smiling so big his whole face almost changes its appearance completely. "It in driveway."

Without light or warmth of skin, modern air touches the green fibres. In the closet it sleeps behind the closed door.

Henry grabs the book and stuffs it in his coat. Near the front door he puts on his dripping boots.

Catullus is ahead of him, almost out the door. He turns to Henry, "I'll be home nine and six minutes five eighths." Outside Henry walks past Catullus, nearly shoving him aside and a breeze of gas station cologne from Catullus lunges at him. He stares at Catullus' face and notices for the first time this week that a tiny constellation of black hairs is growing on the lower quarters of his jaw. Halfway across the road Catullus stops and Henry pulls him as if the grown man is a toy waiting for traffic. Catullus tugs down on his toque.

"Seeing you laters!"

Henry pads his pockets for his own house key while watching Catullus attempt to ride a bike in three feet of snow.

The streets are blank with sullen colours of gray and white

and black. Catullus pushes his ten-speed like a plow along the street until both he and his shadows slip into the early evening. Henry shuts his front door. A sense of relief rushes through him—due in part by the end of cold and the fact that he and Catullus are no longer burglarizing Claudia's home.

Henry unzips his winter garb and checks the clock. The refrigerator hums, the heartbeat of the kitchen clock menaces, each individual pulse teems out of his ear in slow motion. He is enlarging the scene, the contents of the house, the still plant beside the brass vent at the top of the small stairwell separating the front door, the main floor and the basement. He flips through the book he plucked from Claudia's bedroom, which contains several handwritten notes. He takes one of them out and places it on the kitchen counter. *Cocoa, vanilla ice cream, strawberries, kiwi, etc.*

On the counter lay three tube socks that appear to be bleeding. Henry examines the socks and makes an alarming noise (intolerance, shudder, disgust in a single syllable of wordless air) when he realizes they contain cooked ground beef with tomato sauce. At least they aren't human feet. *That's all I need: an insane roommate who dabbles in decapitation.*

Still, Henry has lapses in judgment. His faculties unfurl into doubt. Like just last night he thought: *Who's that guy laying on my couch? Tapping the window to get the attention of a hick squirrel on the front lawn? He's always here.* Or walking home after the final week of Henry's Roman Civilization course: *I heard he stalked this chick and he was a rich guy and made fun of Caesar. I heard that he was in love with a teenage boy to make some chick jealous. I heard it didn't work. I heard he killed her pet sparrow.*

The toaster clicks from its holster of convention and the heated bread soars inches into the air before returning to the metal slots. Henry ignores the toast and tends to his forearm which has a small cut on it. Washing it out and applying a medium-sized Band-Aid. It seemed to Henry that it had been snowing for a month straight now with breaks of momentary reprieve, which led to short-lived flood warnings in the nearby rivers that gutted the small city like icy veins. The toast's odour minced with the ground beef that remained in the sports socks: one large and new disgusting bouquet.

At the kitchen counter he reads a book about ancient Greek medicine, in particular the Greek physician Claudius Galen (A.D. C.130-C.20), a native of Pergamum considered by many to be the most important ancient writer on medicine. The section is called "On the Natural Faculties." Henry reads page 155: "Suppose you should fill any animal whatsoever with liquid food—an experiment I have often carried out in pigs, to whom I give a sort of mess of wheaten flour and water, thereafter cutting them open after three or four hours; if you will do this yourself, you will find the food still in the stomach. For it is not chylification which determines the length of its stay here, since this can also be effected outside the stomach; the determining factor is digestion, which is a different thing from chylification."

A jostling of metal and wood knocks Henry from the page and he sees Claudia walking in through the front door; the stark darkness of night outlining her white ski jacket with its fake fur trim is a welcome change. She shakes the frigid elements off her torso and speaks in a whispering cough, almost tongue-tied.

"You must be frozen!" Henry says, attempting to soothe her,

and puts on the kettle. Claudia's face unbundles from wet scarf and hat, all runny red and glistening with the cold, wet world. The snow is done with her face for now and the weather's ghastly hiss is quarantined to the outside.

"Ahhhhhh!" Claudia cries, exhaling loudly, her mouth forming and holding a silent "O" shape.

Henry tosses two bags into the teapot and notices a shift in his stomach; perhaps the oil and cheese and fountain pop's convergence has awoken since leaving the great winter behind him and now, like a horrible dinosaur, thawing out to destroy all of...

"So cold!" Henry fills up the teapot and sets the kettle back down on the stove.

Henry looks out the window, almost anticipating the sight of a pixilated image of Catullus on his new ten-speed, ringing the bell waving like an idiot. But he's not there. Henry poses at the window for a while longer, eventually turning back to Claudia who is leaning against a wall while trying to undo a boot; her mitten in her mouth, big toothy smile.

Henry thinks about the time he first told Catullus about Claudia, when it seemed like there was a very good chance she was becoming his girlfriend, a role she may now in fact be playing.

"She's a friend of a friend I know from class and then I asked her out. I don't know what else to tell you. We just started seeing each other a few weeks ago."

"Sight?"

"She says she saw us on the bus once."

"That time we were do the food buyer?"

"She has honey hair..."

MOORE » *23*

"And full lamb blood lips? She knows of me? That I am a one?"

"She perceives you to be my friend and roommate."

"And you met me on Halloweens because I am ghost, a truly ghoul friend!"

"Yeah, something like that."

"Claudia she were fun, when can I greet?"

"I don't know," Henry says, adding, "you aren't confused are you? You know this isn't Lesbia, like when you thought Leslie was Lesbia, remember? This isn't Clodia Metelli, OK Catullus? this is Claudia Martchenko. Different names for different people, OK?"

"Lesbia and Clodia are same person Henry."

"I know. But Lesbia, Leslie, Clodia and Claudia are all different people as well."

"As well," Catullus repeats and nods his head.

Henry has a theory that Catullus hides in line at the library, the grocery store, buying videotape. He believes the students at school are talking about his new friend. Out of the corner of his gray eyes flares random acts of Catullus graffiti. He sees the poet's disheveled lines inside his own pupils, minced with commercial voiceovers and dialogue in terrible worlds of words: Show her you'd fuck her on the first date all over again, give her Ass Pony jeans. Next time you lose a mutual mistress to one of your muggy male friends, go mutant-mean on your male mate and tell her you'd do her all over again once your gout is gone and remind her that the fella she's fondling smells like a goat. Like she doesn't already know. Calvin, it was so good to see you the other night with that girl and, of course, when I fucked you as you were fucking her at that club, it was like we were one big greasy piston, jeans eschewed, skin-skewered in desire and friendship!

Henry brings Claudia a mug of tea. He pours some for himself and puts the toast back into the bag of bread and grabs his wallet and keys.

"We should get going soon," Claudia suggests, blowing over her mug. "What's that smell?"

"My roommate was cooking his garbage, I think," Henry says, joining Claudia in the foyer.

"Gross."

"It's freezing," Henry says, putting his boots on slowly. "We should take a cab."

"Yeah, but let's walk to the store; I need to go to the ATM."

When a young man can't lift himself up out of his bed grave, when his pants and head mesh and become madness, a madness that is unwilling to dissolve for relief in the mouth of a candy-happy stranger: there is only desire.

The primal urge Catullus has to leap out and claw at the air we walk through is strong. This sensation plagues him with a contrasting sense of numbness and curiosity. In what he feels are endless days and nights of wander, where he bides his time dulling eyeteeth against uneven sides of concrete and trees, park benches and exposed copper pipes—he feels incomplete, missing parts of a full life.

It's like he's a young animal teething. This shameful desire is raw, fluorescent—a homemade bruise kept in midnight drawers next to his bed. He tries to describe this sensation to Henry as a slow river of lovesick gravy hardening inside a lonely condom. But his words don't match up, instead he says, "a slow ribbon of lump chick gray stoning inside a lovely coffin." Or "show liver of lovestick graves stiffing inside lone sock."

Back from badminton, Catullus parks his bike against Claudia's house and finds the side door open. He quietly roams to her bedroom where he runs his hands across the light green tea dress she wore with loud dark green underwear so long ago.

He rubs the dress where Claudia's breasts would rest and imagines her going to a party, her hair tied back in a long ponytail dangling down to her ass. Her pale Gothic makeup coupled with the weak material of the dress, shifting across the bright green rayon solids of her bra. Slipping out of her suburban home to a teenage calibre backyard handgun party... One time she shot a gun; it was her boyfriend's, years ago.

The shot she fired into the woods ruffled that dress, all part of a gunpowder lullaby before the party sex, the car sex, the continuous sex. Catullus imagines all of it.

He stares at the hem intensely until the background changes to a summer backyard party with music and youthful noises. Catullus cranes his neck away from the dress and begins to howl into the party mirage, howling mindlessly into the hot summer sky which curves around Claudia's bedroom. His howl is shrill and brutal, and bounces all over the empty house, but outside no one bolts out onto the street. No one sits up from their couch and opens the curtain.

The mirage dissipates and Catullus notices Claudia's bedroom window is cracked open slightly and fresh air touches his lips. He closes his eyes and lies beside the dress. A black-and-white photograph of Henry and Claudia rests on a book. It is unframed and collecting sparse dust. She wears his bowler hat. He's in her sweater and the whites of their eyes appear startled.

His stomach growls out a multi-second gurgle and the sensation of hunger splashes around inside him. It must be the dinner hour, Catullus thinks, and hastily changes gears. Time must go home, to make eating.

He notices the bathroom light is on across the hall and walks towards the glowing distraction, now clutching the green dress. He shuts her bedroom door behind him and enters the bathroom stealthily. Evidence of grooming and a recent bath are in abundance: towels, underwear, lipstick, Q-tips and cotton balls. He looks in the mirror and sees a frosted glaze in his own eyes.

❋   ❋   ❋

In Catullus' recent nightmare, one he only shares in part to Henry, he and Lesbia (the real Lesbia from his real life) meet at a busy intersection in this new hellish urbanized world in which he's been thrown. However, it's a warm season and not the cold he's struggling to acclimatize to in his waking life with Henry. Catullus has but three dollars. The greeting she gives him is cold, cordial and rapid. No mention of his lengthy letters or the golden birdcage gift: a gift his consciousness, in the dream at least, knows and tells him he's given her. Where you are taking me?, she asked after a few words. And the dream really begins…

Catullus is foaming on the inside: a real werewolf in the making. Women in yoga pants sway by the new couple now in slow motion but Catullus feels paralyzed and falls deeper into an insane silence, which Lesbia will surely never forgive. In the dream he deposits the missed opportunity of women and their tight exercise equipment into a tomb of unnecessary preoccupation which grows throughout the seventy minutes of subconscious mind terror. Remembering his poverty, Catullus cannot fathom a reasonable suggestion to the posit "Where are you taking me?" Finally she proposes the public library. They take a cab. Lesbia (5'2", 102 lbs.) sinks into his lap then rolls her ass over his legs onto the empty seat, overwhelmed by the strong smell of onions. Catullus makes no attempt at dialogue with the driver, willing his psychic dreamstate abilities to conjure up a conduit between them and the driver. The mere fact this is happening, Catullus believes, is absolutely fantastic. The onions are heated, the scent erotic and out of left field. He just knows it's onions and so does Lesbia. They never say the word.

Lesbia hands the cab driver money and they exit. They spend the entire afternoon flipping through magazines, art books and newspapers. Catullus learns nothing more about Lesbia's desires, feelings and emotional landscape. She is withholding but present. Again, Catullus knows it's a dream, and he has no choice in the matter. The moment feels like he is inside a painting without words or animation. Language itself and its consequences seem unimportant. A problem arrives when Lesbia's desire arrives to eat food in a wave of beautiful famine, Catullus nearly faints. (6'1", 192 lbs.) He explains that he has no way to pay for a meal. That his friends won't lend him anymore money and that he has been robbed nightly since his arrival several days ago. Into another cab, this time lightning and shadows, the dream is not steady, they embrace. She mounts him and he recalls her familiar scent. "Wait, wait," Lesbia moans and kisses, the letters in her words remain inside and out of her lips and he can't stop staring into her big dessert-plate-sized eyes, covered in creamy syrup and he begs the moment to never end—imagines her begging for it to extend into a long-playing loop of flesh and grip and animalistic panting with furious precision and familiarity. "Please, Catullus," she begs him, as though whatever she is hinting at is a matter of life and death. The scent of hot and sour soup is potent for a while. Suddenly he puts it all together in the backseat, this wild sweat, this pain in his side—"I'm in love with a maniac, dominatrix, ghostly sex addict, the most gorgeous thing imaginable...I should quit her now, immediately, without another pulse...get out at once...jump...save yourself! Become stone!" Breathing returns.

Catullus feels her hand on his leg, arousing him to fevered states of heart-bleating chaos. Her face is relaxed; her eyes wide open, full, shining with curiosity. "That's better," she says, "I'm fine now." They near his home. She has the cab driver park around the corner. Facing one another, hands clasped, knees to knees. He holds her for several more minutes, as if returning to the earlier mention of an oil painting, the silence broken now only by the phantom howls of nocturnal vermin. Lesbia will call tomorrow from her aunt's place. In his ear she whispers, "I will always be in love with you so long as water runs through Blithe." Lesbia has made Catullus newborn. Renders him new and empty headed, full of wonder. Days pass. Catullus hears nothing from this renewed secret lover. When he can escape sleep he thinks of long poems to write but doesn't write them. How long will she be in town, he wonders.

After Catullus posts a letter to Lesbia's aunt he goes for a walk in the park. It is early spring and the mud smells strong and the air is cold and crisp. Later that day, still running as best he can throughout the narrative framework of his nightmare, Catullus returns to the library. There's a message. It's from Lesbia. The sight of her handwriting makes Catullus feel like he's about to pee. She will meet him tomorrow at midnight. But he must not contact her at her aunt's place. This is where he wakes up.

❋   ❋   ❋

At dinner Henry orders chilled carrot soup and the most inexpensive entrée. "So Claudia tells me you're studying fine art?" Henry wrinkles his nose, attempting to repress his dramatic mask of anxiety remover, and explains he's studying history, adding "I hope to teach it someday." He's twisting a napkin with one hand as he continues speaking in, at first, a nearly monotone voice until he refreshes his cadence with a liberal sip of wine.

"And this is your last year of studies?"

He nods in agreement, more or less to continue the focus on his diatribe, never bothering to make eye contact with either of Claudia's parents—or, for that matter, Claudia herself. These figures at the table are but sparkling periphery for the time being and Henry can hear himself babbling, "I've come to the conclusion that ancient man who helped foster literature and moral high-grounds suffered almost exclusively from ecstatic hallucinations which in turn they claim to have heard voices and committed heinous acts on their loved ones, acts they committed because they were told to, but not by gods, but from their own messed up subconscious. Those who survived kept these myths going, never sharing with anyone what really went on, at least not in the form of stories and ledgers. But someone must have known the truth about all these decapitating maniacs who gouged eyes and stretched limbs and Narcissus, that myth bugs me the most because we don't even care about the myth anymore just the word, of course, to describe someone who is self-obsessed. I'm sure it wasn't stone that someone turned into after gazing at their reflection in a stream. They were probably beaten to death or drowned. But for whatever reason, those who know what really went into the making of the Greek myths—and all that other horseshit—thought that a culture of fear was more important than one of rational thought. Head injuries could have easily led to moments in which the patient—and, let's face it, doctors on the site or not, these people were patients in the most sensible use of the term—the patient believed he or she could speak to gods or a group of immortals, and during these conversations he or she could be told something by these higher-ups which, of course, over centuries becomes a malleable myth that defines history and a bunch of generations of people who are supposedly responsible for shaping the modern world. Fables, Bible passages, or a fully developed character like Zeus or Jupiter or Hades, you know all come from some idiot hitting their head on a rusty pot. All designed by the person experiencing these interactions to tell everyone how special they now are because they were chosen as a vessel of intellect by a divine, made-up celebrity, right? Then someone finds a highly edited version of what really happened from this made-up headache of an account, right, in some bushel 300 years later and it's manicured into myth."

Henry again can hear himself babbling and feels charged.

He has another glass of wine and notices a sludge forming in his guts; it's a slow oozing sensation like hardening batter or something.

✳   ✳   ✳

Claudia walks in gusty strides, her boots kicking up the snow in frantic steps. The road seems haunted in tinsel as reflective garbage and recycling tins wink in their temporary cemetery. Henry eyes Claudia's hand, which is just out of reach. Each step he takes he gets closer to its precarious position amongst the chaos of snow.

"It's like walking inside of a snow globe," Henry says, half a chuckling trailing off into night.

"So why were you so weird at dinner? It was kind of aggressive."

"I was nervous, maybe I had too much wine, I rambled on," Henry offers, eyeing her movements as she slows down through a patch of unshovelled snow.

"It was a bit much for a first impression: more like ten first impressions or like impression one through fourteen in one sitting," Claudia says, her face a scowl of snow and Maybelline and fog breath.

"And what happened to dessert? I thought you were going to allude to that somehow and we'd invite them back for coffee," Claudia says, synching her purse up over her bunchy shoulder. "But you didn't even offer."

"I felt like it wasn't the right time," Henry says, the sting of tonight's assignation now tingling and loud.

"What set you off on that rampage?"

"I guess, school, the pressure and the what the fuck am I doing with my life, all of it, you know. I sit in class and half the time I don't even know what the fuck the students are talking about or how they come up with these impromptu speeches for the teacher. So I guess, I just, I dunno . . . wanted to sound like I was benefiting from an education."

"None of those ideas were yours?"

"Mostly, uh, you know, things we discuss in class or other people come up with, yeah I guess none mine. So you worked at that restaurant when you were a teenager?"

"Yes, I already told you that. Don't try and change the subject."

"Oh shit," he says under his breath. Ahead in the distance, a familiar figure looms. He stops, and Claudia notices, "What?" Henry's heart pounds in recognition, he coughs out a combination of Oh Shit! Oh Fuck! Shit! Oh Shit, Shit, Shit!

Pirouetting in the middle of street is Catullus.

"What?" Claudia asks.

But just as quickly as Henry catches him in his eyes, Catullus has completely disappeared and the animated snow that plumes hard continues a seasonal dance.

"Nothing, come on," Henry says.

Claudia pauses along his driveway, "Why is your front door open?"

"Roommates must be home I guess." A friction noise is coming from the house and shadows crash against available light.

"What the hell is that?"

"I don't know," Henry says, touching the doorknob slowly, as a new percussive triple thud is heard.

Claudia lets out a half-scream, cut off by her woolen hand across her mouth. Henry opens the front door and his eyes can do nothing but focus on small birds, a half dozen or so, milling about the kitchen in panicked flight.

Then Claudia really screams. The sound ping-pongs up and down the street. And she falls. Henry takes his eyes off the livestock and turns around. Claudia is sprawled on the porch against the metal railings, holding her head. "What happened? Ice?"

"Something pulled me backwards."

Henry helps her up, "You OK?"

"Uh, no!" He brings her inside.

Claudia reaches for the door. "I'm going home!"

Catullus seizes her arm.

"No!" Henry shouts. The lights go out and Henry senses a hand over his mouth, and then an additional sensation, that of a moist cloth. The birds are still making a racket. Claudia's screams fill the room. "Are you trying to scare me Henry?!"

"Stop!" Henry shouts, but is pushed through the darkened living room and thrust onto the couch where he's struck across the jaw and crudely blindfolded and tied up. The way his head feels now reminds him of fainting during school assemblies as a child: hour-long presentations on cancer, anti-drug campaigns or leukemia. The combination of topic and enclosure always had the same effect: blacking out. He can no longer hear Claudia. It's like he's falling asleep.

❃   ❃   ❃

The living room is perfumed in hot chocolate and cabbage soup, a disgusting medley of domestic aromas. Henry's blindfold is partially drooping and he notices Claudia is bound and hogtied but not blindfolded. She is eye-bulging towards Henry in spastic gestures of pure fear.

Blinking and nose-breathing, Henry, equally fettered, attempts to hop his chair towards her. He's tonguing and biting away at his gag and demonstrates a strong desire to speak to her.

As he lunges towards her, he thinks about her behaviour at the restaurant; she did nothing to stop him from his elongated lecture. He can't even remember what he ordered. Maybe a burger covered in beige sauce, some type of meat pie? Her parents were quiet and withholding. He's thirsty. His mouth tastes of cough syrup. What will happen if they survive? At least one of them will get hurt, perhaps not badly. Maybe there's a way to get out of this one. Maybe not. And Claudia will complain that the evening just got worse, even if it ends up getting better. Claudia always complains. She will complain about this forever. Henry hates that personality type and likes to tell Claudia she's too cynical for his tastes sometimes ... but the truth is this has happened before, with Leslie. Poor women. He does this to all of them. Last time it was Leslie: he spent hours trying to catch any sparrow that hopped on the front lawn. Thought her name was Lesbia. Now this one, Claudia; he must think I said Clodia. Henry digs deep and almost has his left hand free. Poor women: all of them, really. All suffering in his poetic discourse, headed into the final stanzas of pain and regret.

Catullus is plugging in a blender; his movements throughout the kitchen are loquacious. He's wearing Claudia's now infamous green tea dress and is cutting a large piece of cardboard. Fewer birds flutter; some now lay still, possibly dead on the floor. From the living room where they are bound, both are audience to his menacing noise. Henry sees but a fragment of what this man is about to do. He is lighting a candle now and glances over at them without a word.

Scissor sounds take centre stage now and it is entirely possible that Catullus is trimming his pubic hair in the kitchen. Henry wants to tell Claudia about his new roommate's strange habits. He has seen Catullus do this before, placing the short clumps of antique curly hair into an empty soup can he had forgotten to add to the recycling earlier in the day. The cream of celery label wearing thin from hot water abuse.

Catullus blows out the candle, inhaling the strong familiar gray streams and holds up a crude chainsaw fashioned from the cardboard. Henry hisses at Claudia to get her attention. "Don't worry; his name is Catull…(he's about to sneeze)…us, he'll start to cry any moment now and pass out. This happened a while ago." In proximity to her now Henry begins to pick away at her knots with a free hand.

The blender sounds off and sends a bolt of hostile energy into everyone. Henry's got her hands loose now and pushes his own fetters off with his feet. As she lowers her gag and blindfold, she screams, "What the hell do you think you're doing?! I'm getting out of here!" She stands up and grabs her backpack and as she does, turns around, clocking Henry in the head with her heavy load. "This isn't funny!"

Henry watches Catullus move the chainsaw limply into the air, mimicking the actions of a real chainsaw as the blender's metallic symphony continues.

"Don't worry, watch: he'll start sobbing now and moan himself to sleep."

"What are you talking about, you psycho!"

Henry rubs his head. He watches Claudia sprint across the street and enter her car, which is parked in her driveway. The backlights glow and it backs out at a jittery, uneven speed.

He turns to Catullus who has since put down his makeshift chainsaw (he has even drawn some buttons and outlined the jagged teeth that run around its intense chain) and is drinking from a large mug of wine.

"I told you what would happen if you did that again," Henry says, looking up the stairwell from the hall. "You were in my room again. You saw the box with the chainsaw in it. That's how you knew how to draw one and cut it out. You are so retarded."

Catullus is silent. Henry walks towards the hallway mirror and in it continues his dialogue with Catullus who he sees slouched over at the kitchen counter. The blender roars on.

Henry rolls up his sleeve. "Now real fear and sorry begins my plucky friend," Henry says, staring into the mirror and meeting his own icy stare. "That wine you have been drinking is laced with sleeping pills."

He walks menacingly towards the hallway and opens the closet door and gets out a small blue power drill.

"A simple quarter inch hole in your skull, some soft lighting, music, more merlot, muriatic acid gently tearing into the frontal lobe…"

Henry plugs in the drill near the mirror and stares blankly at himself once more. He guns the drill—the sound filling the cold air—and with a dented smile, pulls the noisy tool up towards his skull.

"'Son of Zodiac' depicts a life haunted by meat, decay, poverty and one man's efforts to survive the legacy left to him by his absentee serial killer father. Like the cryptic messages sent to the media by the real Zodiac Killer, Nathaniel G. Moore's story is neither safe nor sorry."

—Ashley Little, author of *Anatomy of a Girl Gang*

Son of Zodiac

Most people just die and leave you a box of cigars and letters and a gold watch or perhaps a chalet in some remote geographic trope. Fine wines, a horse, a car or a condominium make nice after-I-die gifts to leave folks! I have this story to leave whoever might be interested in who The Zodiac left alive by abandoning them all together: me, my brother and my grandparents.

Our house was simple, our lifestyle too was, in a way, straightforward. On a lanky street in a small urban community, a quiet pair of disconnected bungalows sank slowly with weeds along a gum-smeared sidewalk. The street was a washed-out river of brick as far as the eye could see and this is where I spent most of my early teen years.

From far enough away, the week-old chicken bones and late autumn leaves look exactly the same in the late-October morning light. Both possess involuntary arthritic composure: a flimsy blow-away predictability.

When I was a wee lad some sixty or seventy years ago, I was raised by my grandma and my grandfather. My own father Arthur had abandoned us all (me and my brother Jim) years earlier. Things were different back then and life was what you made it. This underlying struggle (the unspoken paranoia of financial woes, the stubbornness of the meat we tried to cut with our crummy knives, the whereabouts of our biological parents, the strong smell of bleach that permeated the house) was making our weird generational gap of a family into something of a bomb shelter, a prop family streamlined in design for survival. Also we had this grotesque neighbour named Derek who I tried to make money off of by selling tickets to watch him eat six different kinds of meat and cheese in a diaper. Ok, well not entirely that gross but this man was the foulest thing on two legs you'd ever see. This was when I was a full-fledged teenager and money was scarce. My grandma was now in her eighties and my grandfather was on his last few months of life.

Grandma's dressing gown was a sexless pink tea cozy in which she lived out her prescribed daily rituals of maintenance and dominance in our sparse bungalow. Her feet were covered in wet tinsel and sports socks, which combined for a rotting gauze effect in terms of aesthetical presentation. As she moved like radiant fuzz from room to room—the tinsel dulling with every carpet stride—I stared straight ahead at the television, unable to breathe. I was not afraid of Grandma; I simply didn't want to believe she was the only thing that separated me from infinite loneliness, starvation, and a general destitute existence.

"Are you going to get dressed?" she would ask me.

"Yes Grandma, of course."

I guess I found it degrading the way she spoke, as if I was nothing more than a backwoods, lice-munching mute with two fingers on each hand.

When Grandma wasn't wheelbarrowing me to school next to
a pile of dirty laundry in three feet of snow and scowling
"Goodbye Jack!" (showing me her yellow and copper teeth as
the morning sun's tyrannical glint blinded us all), she'd be
knee deep in chaos within the house's inner workings, tend-
ing to the heavily stained couch cushions (mostly thick gravy
and mustard), controlling the build-up of excess newsprint,
watering the wooden floors in our bedrooms, or in the
kitchen chainsawing slabs of half frozen meat for our treacherous dinner hour.

School was a whole other bag of hammers altogether as I
was short, anxious, half blind and an amateur masturbator: a
true crime teen dweeb generally incoherent to anyone my own
age. The mass-produced lowbrow props stinking up my
bedroom collection during those days: stale board games,
worn-out comic books, ceramic garage sale commemorative
dishes and the torn plastic sheen from the binding of expired
bikini calendars is now handsome landfill or has been recycled
into a pregnant-looking cashier's bra. These are the sorts of
memories I fashion from the crude remainder here in my
fermentation centre of an old age home. More on my present
state later; while I'm lucid, I want to share more important
biological history.

My grandma raised me after my father Arthur Lee Allen
took off with my mother, a college student of sorts but mostly
a diner waitress. They were never heard from again—by us anyway. I was five or six at the time.

Right now, here on the seventh floor the air now seems to

fill my head with water-into-a-pipe kind of pressure, you know, and I am riddled with all these tiny scenes and sensations from long ago. Someone must have died because a few windows are open. It's usually the same consistent level of heat and smog in here. Not smog, but you know what I mean. Now, sixty-eight years later as I sit here in rubble, my tenth year in this urine-fresh senior's asylum, hours from the hot porridge-like swamp known as Lake Ohio, not a day goes by that I don't think of my father's crimes.

Grandma had once told me of my father Arthur's love of trapping game, scuba diving and camping, deep sea fishing, carpentry and crossword puzzles. So, one day after school, she had left me a cruel note on the kitchen table. The usual pre-pared meal was gone, the plate empty in the fridge. The note read: "Supper had to be eaten, there will be more ... I'm out doing my busy bee work..." but it didn't look like my grandma's handwriting, come to think of it. I suspect my father had been in town and visited while I was at school and had eaten my supper.

For many years after my grandma's death I was convinced somehow that she never died. I believed her to be undead, hap-pily toiling away in a basement with a niece or two, living hand to mouth through a hole in a wall, being fed bits of Kodak paper while wearing a senior's discount diaper, showing whoever will look her way terrible Polaroids of me semi-dressed in my hockey outfit for the last time before eating the jagged cellu-loid image. Perhaps she'd finish her snack with some ginger ale and crackers.

To be fair to her, grandma never wanted a knife swallowing family of crybabies (which is what we were); she wanted a

lovely symphony of life playing in the background with
little drama, purposeful plot points, redemptive characters,
hard workers and morally clean perspectives.

Ever since I could remember I have spoken in an odd, borrowed, garage-sale-like dialect, unique to my species. I push
these depraved sentences out like long magician scarves and feel
sick. In the spirit of cinematic properties in which two young
girls who meet each other only to reconnect sixty years later on
death's door and perhaps another type of film with a spooky—
the earth is going to be raped and realigned because of a single shift in global weather or computer code plot—I have
reached my limits in basic, day-to-day survival and need now
to reconnect with the truth about my father before I die, in the
greatest sense of those words.

Yes, I too followed in the family's odorous footprints of
neglect, abandon and shame. At least I never had any children; however, I say that with a bitter-edged sword. I'm igno-
rant and will die as such, having never known the experience,
and what I would imagine to be joy of, raising and admiring off-
spring. Oh but how I didn't want to repeat my father's pattern,
follow in his footsteps; the self-righteous path of his rolling
stone, cardboard box, and couch-crashing trajectory. It is for this
reason that I'm telling someone (anyone, really) as much as I
can about the father I had and how sorry I am that I never knew
the joys of being a parent.

❋   ❋   ❋

I always thought that a hard find is a good luck charm. I was
into garbage picking in those days. Digging deeper, I retrieved

a whole slew of great finds: a lounge chair, two forks, a calendar not yet expired and a spark plug. I rolled the spark plug handle in my left palm, feeling the metal pinch my soft skin.

Earnestly researching debris, I grabbed at a spark plug handle and thought about dinner: how I didn't want scrambled, how I wanted to eat organic bread. More specifically, I wanted to eat twenty-grain bread, seven Siskonmakkara sausages served in a basket of sour dough with free range portabella mushrooms suspended over melted Havarti or tama cheese dripping over broccoli spears.

For months I carved out a routine in which my rummaging had led to ample harvest; however, I saw these jigsaw pieces for what they were: I was missing something in my life, something I couldn't find in a heap of garbage. Our home was not in unison, no connective spiritual tissue in the cosmos connecting the, well, everything. I dodged the normative patterns being tunneled out by my contemporaries. This was the beginning of the false world. I could feel it.

I stood calmly in front of two major heaps, gravitating and judging. The street was swamped in noises. I looked up and a nearby tavern was fashioned with two convivial relics outside, gyrating in top form and singing.

At first, I thought this was an impromptu Heimlich session between two choking friends—it was not.

"Oh Lordy, won't you buy me a Mercedes..." and as they sang, the two chain-smoking senior citizens were pirouetting non-stop. The dive bar was no more than a flimsy shack with a few stools inside and a cigarette machine, possibly a toilet. I laughed to myself, fantasizing the men were moments away from being gang-beaten. So many reports of elderly abuse had cropped up on the news lately with the word "justice" being used over and over again in each reporter's sober message.

"That's some terrible dancing!" I shouted from my garbage. "Awful! You're awful!" I hated the sinewy sunset, the overwhelming colours in the sky pushing forth, the swarm of foul car fumes phantoming the men's depraved twirls and coughing fits.

Finally they stopped their abject dance of death and looked up, spitting cancerous lung wads onto the ground.

"Shithead!"

"Fuck you!" I yelled at one of the seniors in mid-pirouette. "You're hurting my eyes!"

"Fuck off!"

A half block from my house more garbage appeared on my after-school horizon. I zoned in on a particularly dense patch of refuse. In spite of the wasps, I stretched deeper into the puddle of lonely mildew to find exhaust pipes, worn stockings and a chair.

"Legs are all right," I noticed, lugging the remainder home, recognizing my perilous lifestyle in every car window, puddle, or gawking pedestrian's never subtle sneer.

"Hi Mary Beth," I said, waving at our neighbour in possession of one such sneer.

From across the street I eyed her angling a discarded vacuum on the curb with all the dramatics of an action hero. It kept falling over, back into the driveway. On its handle, a crummy sign rendered in pencil crayon (light blue) read "FREE."

✳   ✳   ✳

At this time of great youth and hope, I spent countless hours on my bed fully clothed plotting out "get rich" schemes because I never had any faith that I'd have a regular working-class job of any sorts. Perhaps it was my disenchantment with the educational system or the simple struggle with two senior citizens trying to raise my brother and me.

Cut open with anxiety at the mid-brain upon each arrival home, the economic weakness and pain my family exuded did not go unnoticed. I was born into their economic fantasy world. I was born with cheese powder on my toes and processed cheese splayed across my screaming red scalp.

I was born an Allen and had the plaid pants to prove it. This Kodachrome realism had us all enduring a thousand worrisome weekends, tantrums with weak-lunged grandparents and solemn movie nights. Reality? I knew nothing else. I merged complete into the anomaly of unmade dinners, quarter-vacuumed rugs, singed library books, impromptu games of Bridge going into sudden death overtime on a school night and disastrous plaster jobs where chair legs had accidentally penetrated walls during wanton evenings of social invasion. "Get a chair for so-and-so," was a popular command. I remained dutiful to a point.

The dryness in the house was not human, not even close. The house was simply a skeletal host in an ongoing domestic experiment in its eleventh brutal season. Despite being balls-deep in *National Enquirer* charades, (a colossal twist on the popular family couch game) everyone at the table on this afternoon was enjoying the hefty leftovers of shepherd's pie, while throats were splashed in cold skim milk, ousting any temporary over-heated swallows which could, of course, aggravate consumption.

The bones in my grandma's cooking, especially the fish, took hours to pry from our thankless gums, sweaters, even fingernails. Some nights she'd only be able to prepare half the dinner, the rest was guesswork. Bread could be toasted but the meat sitting in the sink would have to be restored somehow. But the fish reeked for days. And we could have taken turns deboning one another's gums on the couch if we were cozy close.

If fish were the cause of odours from, let's say, a greasy casserole for example, the meal's dense potency would include the most inefficient bones from the deepest parts of Lake Ohio where all nutrients went to die. Sometimes our eating experience was like picking bits of plastic from a bowl of mushy cheese.

This one day the crisp autumn afternoon held a threat of rain. We had been released from school early that day because of a bomb threat. Attempts to vacuum the semi-detached home had taken its toll on my frustrated grandparents. They sauntered around, prison-like, in matching red rayon crépe pants. The all-day kind. My brother Jim was wearing a tank top and sporty shorts. In addition to skim milk, a shared can of cream soda drenched our palates, and with energetic limbs we all reached for the day-old dinner rolls purchased for under a buck from the local corner store.

Determination abounded on all fronts: love, digestion, the appearance of a grandparent's smile, or gas, a family member's head about to detach from its spine were all possibilities; physical gestures appropriated from a song about the connecting body parts, the one that over-uses the word "connected."

Still, the family moved and digested with a machine's intent. Each cog had a unique demonic fury to it, part of a system.

A letter lay unopened down an uneven hall. It was sitting there by the bathroom door, waiting (in government handwriting no doubt) to embarrass us all.

"Are you going to have lunch?" my grandfather asked me. Jim was on the phone with a classmate and we all witnessed the spectacle of him speaking in tongues, "What do you think? You're lucky I don't come over there with two guzzling chainsaws and my lawyer! I hate that shitty school!"

Grandpa walked past me, motioning towards Grandma, and as he passed her, nearly passing out and collapsing into the wall, "Did you get a chance to look at that letter?"

"No," Grandma stopped momentarily, the casserole in her oven-mitted hands, and glanced down the hall at the letter. "Lunch boys," she said, placing the heated-up leftovers on the table.

"I'll read it after lunch," Grandma answered, taking a glob of food that fell off my plate with her spoon and sticking it into her mouth before putting the spoon into her apron pocket.

We were getting by on my grandparents' social security but had just applied for a type of welfare for families with old people with kids in them. That's how my brother explained it to me. We would take turns worrying about our grandparents keeling over while raking leaves or pulling out meat pies from the oven and us having to deal with a slew of government nannies and well-wishers baking us zucchini bread and offering to breastfeed us.

When we arrived home from school that day, the letter was

lying in the hallway, perhaps a breeze had sent it from a more secure location. Upon closer inspection, I noticed it had a return label from the state government of Ohio. I knew it! My grandparents moved around it like it was a landmine. The letter was sparsely talked about as lunch was being digested but neither my grandma nor grandpa seemed inclined in any way to touch it. Jim didn't seem curious either, but I was as mail to the house was usually nothing remarkable beyond a political flyer or the odd postcard from one of my illiterate pen pals from Camp Chrysler.

As the oven's door made that horrific castle drawbridge sound, the cicadas turned up the dial full blast. The sun was now so bright inside the house it looked as though the walls and floor were being brightened by some magic domestic cleaning product. The government envelope was nicely lit where it rested along the broadloom, showcasing it as a puzzling piece of postal samizdat for all to see.

The sink stunk as I passed it en route to lunch and Jim was still howling on the phone which hung on a wall in the musty kitchen. He began to jump up and down as he cried into the beige mouthpiece, "She's a total sex offender!"

"May I be excused?" I insisted. "I'll eat in my room."

"Yes Jack, you may," Grandma answered, taking my plate from the table and scraping it into her mouth before rinsing it. "OK, I gotta go. Yeah, I think that bitch has stigmata or something. She bled all over someone at lunch. OK, see you tomorrow. Later, dickwad."

Jim was now off the phone and was scraping a large pot into his mouth when he remembered something.

"Oh yeah, I forgot to tell you guys something!"

As Jim blabbed to Grandpa about his heroics as a fledging idiot of track and field, Grandma opened the letter and began to pace up and down the hall. Turns out, the letter stated that we qualified for a special family benefit because our legal guardians were so old and couldn't earn as much money as a normal-aged set of parents.

I could hear Jim who was all, "Totally forgot to tell you guys, so, for seniors, like I beat almost a hundred kids this morning in the four-hundred-metre dash." I could see Jim jogging on the spot, in slow motion, raising his hands triumphantly in victory like a clueless cartoon kid about to be nuked.

"For track, we had qualifying races today, three cities," Jim added, pretending to be out of breath. He then raised his hands again in the air as if celebrating a lobotomy.

I was edging myself back towards the kitchen, eavesdropping on my own life. Jim was now pretend boxing with Grandpa—"I beat them all." He was doing jumping jacks now and scraped a spoonful of food matter into his mouth from that big pot, while Grandpa did the same, only he was louder, the small sloppy sounds orchestrated unevenly in his mouth made me want to vomit. I pulled away from the kitchen.

"It's too bad you didn't just keep running Jim," I said with a loaded laugh, which led to a coughing fit. I noticed how out of breath our family was, myself included.

"Grandma, I think we need to change the asbestos in the walls."

"Grandma, Jack didn't get his flu shot today, he skipped it. The nurse called me to her office to let me know."

"Rat," I said. "You undercover? CIA?"

The more perfect Jim seemed, the more I wanted him to

suffer, for he knew he would never be his father's daughter, never be prom queen, or the first brain surgeon in space, or anything he used to go on and on about. It was as if he knew that somehow, the pecking order was a prearranged constellation of woe but that didn't matter. He could fake just about anything. We never talked about it but I got the feeling we both knew we would end up with no living family members by the time high school was over.

Despite the phone conversation I just described Jim having with his classmate and his overall hyperactive disorder that day, he was the good child: a great athlete who had a chip on his shoulder. He was a real beauty, and all his friends were like, "You should totally model."

Grandma then explained to Grandpa the details outlined in the letter from the government. Jim of course was listening and eye-popping and groaning with every sentence.

"This will help us out a lot," Grandma said, waving the freshly opened letter up and down by the sink. Jim, standing on a chair, chimed in with a vaguely aphoristic nugget, "The Allens have graduated to Legends of Welfare," adding, "Do we get fitted ball caps?"

I grabbed the brochure Jim had been guarding at his hips until letting it fall to the ground. He was furious and possessed a look of absolute betrayal and hurt. After growling, he raised his voice and Grandma—caught entirely off guard—had a look I had, up to that point, never witnessed. Like a weak dove sipping a thimble of lukewarm tea, she backed away from her grandson's booming alto voice.

"Look at this! For God's sake! It's disgraceful!"

I finally had a chance to scan the material: in the glossy pamphlet a family sat in front of a giant vending machine with a clear front to it which contained swirling macaroni and cheese. The family sat before the monstrosity as if it were a fireplace.

I was standing near my brother as he unraveled, then piped up, "Don't worry family, I got this one!"

"What," Jim said, mouth full of what appeared to be scrambled eggs, "your latest get-poor-quick scheme?"

And so I dashed past the bathroom clutter and a towel disaster down the hall and into my bedroom and began cackling. I had work to do.

"They just want to know how we spend our time. A lot of their studies show that families spend far too much time cooking, so there is less time to work on job searches, cleaning the house and school work. It's really clever when you think about it."

"Well, clearly Grandma, you're not thinking about it. How am I supposed to have friends over with that stupid thing in our living room?"

I knew we had no money, no accumulation of funds. That time was wearing down our brick and mortar nest thin and fast. I needed a real life plan—and fast. Paper routes and leaf raking wouldn't do it. I was worried about my mind: how it led me into tangled veins and malicious social incisions. I thought perhaps the military would call on me at some point, and that I'd jump at the chance to mean something to the world, to shoot things, wade through swamps and seek a living target. Or come up with a great way to overturn a small, half-dead under-armed Third World village and escape my adolescent mildewed laundry hamper state of mind.

Anyhow, that neighbour of ours—Derek. He was quickly

becoming my salvation, in a way, and I guess, for a few months, my obsession. He was an odious human being I didn't conjure up from nightmares after a foul fish casserole. Burping Derek, cackling Derek, topless Derek with his gut draped over the elastic waistband of his pyjama bottoms as he scratched himself like a deranged scarecrow was all to real a tableau on constant display next door.

Derek was a short, round, down-and-out real-life bar singer—a country-and-western singer to be specific, with shoulder-length dyed black hair and a big stomach that looked as though he'd swallowed several roasted turkeys whole. His legs were thin and his voice sounded like something you'd hear coming from the basement telling you everything was going to be all right while your entire family was picked apart by amateur dentists from the Deep South, plucking comforting banjos and washboards.

I drew the crude venetian blinds (yellowing, desperate, fungus-ready) and peered into Derek's malicious backyard where all sorts of unrecorded activities took place. A series of primitive smoke streams and barbed dialogue weaved from a crappy grill, and a mindless dog followed the round man, a man who paced back and forth from the small garage to the back porch. The big, black dog was named Blew and would co-star in sanitary depravity scenarios such as Derek dropping cheese on his bare foot and Blew eating it. To anyone within earshot he would say something gross like, "Blew ate some cheese off ma toe," as he wobbled up and down the driveway half-naked playing his guitar.

"All right, Fatty! You are my golden harpoon! And I'm coming for you!" I said in a frenzied whisper, remembering the film my grandma had taken me to about the guy who hunted the giant whale. Thanksgiving was fast approaching. As I digested what tasted like bits of sawdust and hamburger meat, I closed my eyes and imagined myself in a room full of golden objects: vases, lamps, globes, cups, beds, statues, chairs and chests of drawers.

I lay on my thin teen bed, imagining Derek's burps breaking up a beam of dust in his living room. Adding to the Satanic constellation of bungalow bliss was his bleach-blond wife Masha (her hair as thick as seven looms of oily yellow thread, skin the colour of lightly barbecued chicken), who smiled awkwardly, awaiting the perfect moment to tell her husband something like "I made tuna fish sandwiches for lunch ... my sister has bronchitis ... we have to take the dog to the vet."

According to my early surveillances in which I'd stealthily moved along our mutual driveway, Derek was fond of hand soap, six-cheese lasagna and barbecued lamb. Chicken and pork chops, barbecue chips, corn on the cob and the Greek meat his Greek neighbour would hand over the fence in the backyard. He'd have moose meat mailed to him for the holidays and would constantly harass the postal carriers about the whereabouts of his crepe paper carcasses.

This husky stay-at-home musician with tiny black bean eyes and a big greasy brown moustache had a lot of recording equipment and a penchant for Newfoundland moose meat. The hairs on his chest stood alert, reaching out for another host, only to falter moments later, to cover his bulky body like a suggestive layer of soil, encouraging his inevitable death.

❋   ❋   ❋

Thanksgiving weekend arrived. Derek, as he usually did during cluttered occasions, once again positioned himself beside the activated television so everyone in the room couldn't help but catch a glimpse of his entirety. I was standing on their front porch looking through the large window in a very obvious way when a few relatives spotted me. I moved towards the front door which was open save for the closed screen door.

As plates filled with turkey, cranberry sauce, potatoes and bread, Masha passed Derek his big steamy plate, which came with extra moose meat just for him. She eyed me and motioned in her static-filled gestures (those electrocuted eyes, that straw-coloured blond hair, that fresh-from-surgery smile of sobering tenderness) that she was heading towards the front door.

I heard Derek talking to some poor cousin or sister-in-law on the couch, "Oh, man, it's so the moose meat, so fuckin' good. Clyde sent us this, all the way from Newfoundland! You sure you don't want none?"

"Yes?" Masha said at the door, her face creased in a stressful smile of sorts, (and yes, as far as I can recall, her name was Masha, that is what Derek continually referred to her as...)

"Hi, I'm Jack, your next door neighbour." I was acting nervous and quiet, not the jerky kid I truly was. I wanted it to be a complete con. "Is Derek home?"

Of course, I knew Derek was home, but wanted to appear as a complete and utter stranger. Fresh from the curb. All the moose meat, potatoes, turkey, gravy and metallic clinking of forks and tongues colliding as the hot parts dissolved deep into his sandpaper throat: a big wet cave full of loud echoes. On the television a video was playing featuring Derek and some of his friends clubbing baby seals back home in Newfoundland.

Derek took a huge serving spoon full of food and shoveled it into his mouth.

"Derek, be careful," Masha said, watching her husband's eyes bulge with venom.

"I'VE BEEN EATING MY WHOLE GODDAMN LIFE!" Derek shouted as he came towards the doorway.

"Derek, it's for you." Marsha said, making way for her husband to see me. "Just a minute Jack," Masha said.

"Hi, I'm Jack from next door. The Allens?"

"Yeah, we're eating supper. It's Thanksgiving!" Derek said. "What's up kid?"

"Well this won't take long." I said, holding the screen door open with my knee. "I want to get shots of you, like ah, you performing," I said. "I've heard some of your stuff, from next door. I know you're a singer and I thought I could make a short film and—"

I was marvelous at convincing Derek that I'd heard him play a couple of gigs at local bars, or even humming a horrific chorus on the way to the musician's own studio in the insolated garage.

Derek returned to his gross-out duties: caveman lips pressed against piping hot offerings. The family had lived through the ten-minute viewing of a seal hunt featuring local hunters and their caustic pirate cackles, bouncing along the video's spine like a terrible treble. Pointing the video camera at the head of an innocent piece of life crushed and smeared red in the Newfoundland snow.

Meat. Death.

And Derek, trying to get a second cousin's attention, "We dug into that pup later, with gravy, oh so good."

"Um," I continued, fighting off the wind, "so I have this Uncle, Peter he's in the meat business and would really love to get you to record something for us, like a commercial."

"What?"

"I'd pay you."

"Uh huh," Derek said.

"I can pay you two hundred dollars, plus all the beef you could ever want," I said. I knew I could borrow my friend's dad's Super 8 camera if I really needed to. There was such a rush in just being there and asking Derek if I could film him. I figured a monster movie or some weird hillbilly film about a man who couldn't stop eating would surely make some money.

"For life?"

"For your whole life, sure!"

"OK, well, come by tomorrow afternoon and you can tell me more. See ya," Derek said.

I pretended I was a fractured potato chip lodged in his navel, trapped under a web of body hair. His stomach's girth as if expecting a dolphin would give a rumble and I would be jettisoned to salvation.

Using the finest pencil crayons known to humanity, a handful of his gig posters I'd taken from his garage, I stayed up until the next morning drawing many diagrams of Derek dancing in cooked ground beef. At first I imagined a malicious snuff film, similar in plot and box office intent. Then I thought of a children's book like Jack and the Beanstalk, but instead Jack makes an educational film shown at public schools about obesity and illiteracy and vocational error prevention. Then a monstrous record album, repackaging Derek as country music's answer to Alice Cooper. The ideas came far too often and with such rapidity that I almost couldn't contain the think tank as it oozed through the morning. When the sun's beams broke through my stale curtains, I knew I had stayed up all night.

I even drew up a rough draft of a contract between my fake Uncle Peter's meat company and Derek, saying we'd pay him in cash and beef. When my grandma found me at six in the morning, she noticed the insane tribute to our next-door neighbour.

My brother, sensing that I was about to be humiliated somehow burst into my bedroom to examine my art risqué. "Holy shit Jack! This is the neighbour? That country singer? Man you've gone off the deep end!"

My grandma felt that I should make it up to both Derek and our family without of course revealing my retrospective multimedia tribute to the man in question by saying I was misinformed about the opportunity to "sponsor" (as my grandma called it) Derek's music, but would like to offer to cut his lawn all spring for free. Over the summer I awkwardly mowed Derek's lawn, trying to put my depraved film aspirations behind me, always feeling embarrassed about the Thanksgiving meat promises I made to that man in front of his family.

I don't remember the moment I noticed my parents were gone but I do remember a scattering of visitors at the house and my brother and I continuously lurking from the hallway as we tried to piece together what was going on. What I am going to tell you about now is the moment in time I realized my father was The Zodiac Killer.

This was also around the time when I first understood that my grandma was very, very old. She began to complain of stomach pains, and would also be overcome with bouts of vertigo. When she was laid up in bed with illness I became hypnotized by the palpable void in the house. It had this cosmic sensation to it, like a closed factory or a forest plucked of life. Then, all of a sudden, Grandma would be back on her feet, baking lasagna or cookies, asking me to help take pails of water out of the basement from the leaky tub. "It's not too much Jack," she said. "If you can take a few buckets out to the garden or driveway and dump them, that'd be a real help." The basement was a place I never enjoyed visiting, it smelled funky and made odd noises as if it were being woken up by my presence.

When I was eleven, Grandma took me to see *Charlie Chan At Treasure Island* telling me it was my dad's favourite film as a kid. Before we left for the theatre that afternoon, I noticed how focused she was on making sure the doors and windows were all locked. We were to go shopping for groceries and a new pair of boots for me after the film as it was getting close to wintertime and she must have said to me a hundred times over and over again, "I've got a little list, I've got a little list," and smiled at me gently, in a slow and deliberate way, as if trying to keep my eyes on her face for more than was necessary.

The film was about a bunch of people who die and a mystic lives in a strange mansion and this mystic who turns out to be the bad guy speaks in riddles and says disturbing things like, "Death is a black camel that kneels unbidden at every gate." I thought of black camels roaming the streets at night outside my window, kneeling on the grass and looking at me. The film scared me a lot, and I became worried for a few weeks that all the doors would unlock and we'd be picked off one by one. "What did you think of the movie Jack?" "It was all right," I told Grandma, not wanting to let on about my fears.

One night Grandma and I were watching TV when the phone rang. She answered it and was gone for half an hour. I kept watching TV so I didn't notice right away, but whenever I did hear her speak she was talking in a low voice way down the hall. I was on my Christmas vacation and had so much to eat that night I couldn't move from the orange carpet. I slowly dragged my ass towards the couch where a side table had another phone resting on it.

Furtively, I picked up the receiver and heard a man's voice. He said something about running errands and having to take side streets to do deliveries. He then shouted, "We had a lot of snow recently and it seems they're too sissy to work in the snow…" I put the receiver back on the cradle and resumed my child-like pantomime until bedtime. Grandma returned and sat down on the couch, occasionally eyeing the front window.

Grandma had a recurring dream before her death in which she was a little girl who was so hungry she wanted to swallow herself by opening her mouth very wide and turning it over her head so that it would eat her whole body and then she'd be this perfect little meaty ball, annihilated by herself. She would tell me the dream over and over again then whisper, "Jack, that is how I see the end of the world."

❄   ❄   ❄

One investigator believed when it came to Darlene, The Zodiac must have been a cop because she had dated cops and because my father used jargon in his letters to newspaper editors. Yet using a flashlight is not staunchly cop behaviour, though it is very cop-like, so is approaching a car from the side, so is being able to see moving targets with a flashlight, not to mention rope, breathing, bullets are all cop emulations. Dad's watch logo namesake was an heirloom in my pocket, and my darling comb-over was about all I ever inherited from this man. The cold dates my father etched on the lifeless car door at Lake Berryessa over the years were so pretty in the setting sun. They add up to only a handful of moments. I've looked at the scrawl on Bryan Hartnell's white 1956 Volkswagen Karmann Ghia and seen the warmth, the cruelty, the endless potential of my father's touch.

Vallejo
12-20-68
7-4-69
Sept 27-69 - 6:30
by knife

One theory I came up with was that my dad must have researched Jack the Ripper because Jack the Ripper sent letters to the press and bits of the victims too, just like the cab driver's shirt tear that Dad sent the papers—in addition to the countless cryptic letters, of course. These are facts that add up to only a handful of moments from an entire life I was never privy to know. I truly never knew the man.

From when he dropped us off at his parents' home when I was five and my brother seven, well, we never did see our father again. We came close, my brother and I. One night Grandma answered the phone and disappeared into her bedroom. Then she spent the entire night on the sofa, peering through the curtains, which were drawn. The phone rang throughout the night, what seemed like thirty times, and in the morning we found two black camels on the mantel. I asked my Grandma where they came from and she froze, stone-cold and turned her gaze past me to the front window. She was holding a parcel of some sort, and appeared to be in the midst of tying it up or taping it up; I can't fully remember. She stopped what she was doing and cracked the best smile she could muster. She appeared to have not slept at all the previous night.

"Better get ready for school, Jack. Do you want some money for lunch?"

❋   ❋   ❋

Before our father's death, my brother and I spoke only once about him. Jim began: "One night, I heard a ruckus in the alley behind our house. I tried to fall back asleep but couldn't. I peered out our bedroom curtain and saw a thick man coming from the gate leading to the alley into our backyard. He was holding metal objects. I figured they were metal because whenever he would turn one way or the other the moonlight would follow them and reflect. He wasn't pacing so much as counting steps and looking into other yards. That's how I remember it at least. When I could see him, he was dressed all in black; otherwise it was just the metal and the sound of his footsteps. The next morning I thought I saw faint outlines of big boot prints all through the house leading to the garage. I know my eyes were just playing games with me, that I was inventing the outline of large boot prints as if my eyes themselves had a felt marker. I figured if I tricked myself into seeing Dad's boot prints in our home it'd become real and so would he. It was like a game I played a lot, actually."

I chimed in with my own memory, "I remember whenever Grandma would tell me something about Dad, anything really, you know, from when he was 'a kid, well, I'd see him as I remember him but slowly shrinking from big to small."

We discussed the street we lived on and how there were a couple of cars that didn't seem to move. No one went inside them and it was as if they were staring at us, our house, from some distance.

We gradually changed the subject and fell asleep under the moonlight on his porch—something we usually did back then. We never saw our mother again and, of course, being incredibly old to begin with, our grandparents died when I was about forty-five. Nothing remains. I don't have photo albums or 8mm home movies, crude audio recordings labeled "Thanksgiving 1963." The solitary family tomb is entirely cerebral: one whose protective crust ages with thick wrinkles as I watch the rest of my life come to a full stop.

❊   ❊   ❊

I know now the difference between living and thinking. The voice of my father still climbs the stairs towards my face; his likeness, not as sharp as it once was, fades each day; another mile down those darkening roads.

"I am infuriated by this story because I cry hot blood tears whenever I read it and then realize that I did not write the thing. Fucking Natho."

—RM Vaughan, author of
Bright Eyed

A Higher Power

Hello everyone. My name is Amanda and I'm an alcoholic. My trouble began early on, as I was not a very confident girl in high school, junior high actually, and my self-loathing accelerated into negative attention-seeking morays. Not the typical sexual kind such as hanging upside down in a bikini drinking from a keg with some ape holding onto my ankles. Mine was a greater depravity, one I hope you will at least partially identify with. It started with this clipping I found when I was thirteen, and found fascinating in a negative way.

And then this guy, who the clip is about, right, had the gall to build a six-hole golf course on his family home! At sixteen, I don't know if you remember, but you are really sensitive to injustices in the world, whether they are happening in your own family, in your neighbourhood, or the nation at large. So I'll read you the clipping to get you a sense of how it upset my sixteen-year-old soul to the core. "There won't be an early tee-off time for former prime minister Paul Martin and his family after the Town of Brome Lake ruled this week that a private, six-hole golf course the family wants to build on its Eastern Townships estate has to go through an environmental assessment process like everyone else. 'Look, if I charge people to, um, use my private golf course on my family home, my profits will be divided between a number of tax-deductible charities and causes, some church-related, some artistic, others for conservation and ecology and things like that,' Martin has said in interviews." —*Quebec City Gazette*, May 11, 2007.

He failed the country; he fired the sponsorship fall guy Adam Burtt, the minister responsible for the sponsorship program in the first place, the program that withdrew hundreds of dollars from Ottawa Senator hockey players' bank accounts and put these funds into a Swiss bank account for the Liberal caucus. He coined the phrase, "Don't blow my whistle or I'll blow yours," and promised the public he'd never do it again if they actually voted for him in an election. He said he'd protect those who would help find the rats on the Liberal ship—not punish them. He used academic yardsticks to bury public school budget cuts, insisted on using Dolly Parton's *Jolene* as his re-election song, grossly predicted that "by 2021, Canada will have a population equal to China or India and by 2029 it will have a population of 2 billion; 500 million more than either one at that time."

❋   ❋   ❋

Near Christmas back then, I got an infection in my leg from a school ski trip when someone poured hot wax on me and it got into a shaving cut. I was hospitalized for two weeks and began listening to the radio for long stretches of time and soon discovered a long, drawn-out uncharitable morality play was presenting itself before me, centering around Paul Martin, who was still in the news when his emblematic excess took the country's psyche by storm with that bleeding private golf course. It was all those basic structures of empathy at play: man versus land versus state but in the end, Paul Martin was allowed to build a six-hole golf course on his family's land. Listening to the talk radio shows for hours made me feel a part of things and occasionally I would call in and, until being hung-up on repeatedly, make my points clear: No former prime minister needs their own golf course in a world where Canadian children go hungry before they dot their first "i," where more money is spent on men's hockey advertising than research for anorexia, cancer and smallpox combined. I raised other points, raging on, wasting my young years, nearing carpal tunnel levels of routine in my fingers from hitting redial.

I had to be put in a drug aftercare program for three months following an overdose on painkillers. I must tell you, I looked forward to my late April release from the codeine emporium. Well that's what I called it anyway, but the folks at Norstrom Youth Drug Centre were keen to make sure my addiction to pills—not Paul Martin—had subsided completely. When I left the clinic, I was down from 140 pounds to around 100.

The sound clip that I was proudest of will be played now in its entirety so you can get a sense of my essence back then. My sponsees always laugh when I play it, which I do on special occasions like their birthdays or medallion nights. OK, so here it is: I just need to press play, it's on my phone, one of those mp3's. "Everyone is asking, why is Paul Martin all of a sudden a bad guy? Why is he acting like such a badass with Paul Newman? Why is he doing all these dress-up-your-lettuce-or-else promo spots and showing up to heckle anti-funding aware-r.ess activists like yours truly? Well, ladies and gentlemen, boys and girls, I'm not gonna lie to ya. Paul Martin and I loathe one another. Whether it be at the church picnic, your local bookstore, or in the locker room at the men's clinic, make no mistake about it, Paul Martin hates my guts. And to be perfectly honest, I hate his. Now you see, it's always been this way, we're gonna take the gloves off, he's always been bad. Bad at running the country, a bad cook, a bad dancer, a bad gardener ... he comes on programs like this one and he talks about how the Canadian media exploited his family. Well, I've got news for ya, ladies and gentlemen; Paul Martin is the one that asked the tourists to take the pictures of him and Paul Newman jet skiing together. Paul Martin is the one that drags his sister and his children and wife out on TV with Paul Newman. The Canadian media exploits Paul Martin's family because he allows it. Paul Martin has an obsession with me and the speeches I give at local and out-of-town charity dance-a-thons after I win. Last year I won the Grizzly 'N Bear It Oshawa dance-a-thon fair and square. At the time, because I was so busy dancing my heart out for the unfair treatment of circus bears in Oshawa, I didn't even notice Paul Martin on the dance floor. Nor did I notice that I accidently bumped into him, causing him to knock over the popcorn machine and start a small grease fire. But I want to digress back to three years ago when I first noticed the Canadian government's war on arts funding. The feds suddenly began fostering community charity events such as putt-putt golf, dance-a-thons, karaoke, face-painting, juggling, ice sculpturing and other fringe arts events to almost mock the entire arts industry in Canada as a whole. That's when Paul Martin was the prime minister. Even though I was young and naive, I ran to support him. I told everybody, including Paul and his family, that I supported him. But then, six weeks ago when it came time for Paul Martin to return the favour and send me a recent photo for my collage while I was laid up with a bad wax burn on my leg, oh yeah he did it, but he did it kickin' and screamin' every inch of the way. You see, Paul Martin is obsessed with being in power in some way because he was born into it. If Paul Martin wasn't thought of as a world leader, or someone who has an oak desk with a Canadian flag on it, he would feel like he had fallen short. When he goes home to Ottawa he is still Prime Minister Paul Martin. When I go home, I don't hang my hat on a hook that says "Pilled out dance-a-thon Prime Minister spotlight-stealing maniac." I'm just plain old Amanda. Paul, you are Former Prime Minister Paul Martin twenty-four hours a day. You are the one who stands in front of his house squinting into the sun waiting for your golf ball shipments like they were delicious deep fried llama meatballs covered in confectionary sugar. And the reason for that is Paul Martin cannot separate all of this from his real life. That's why he brings his family in on it, and that's why he's bringing Paul Newman into it. Nobody knows better than me, you have to have a handwritten note from the Lord Almighty to win a dance contest in this country, let alone get a break on a monthly bus pass, no matter how many rats you kill on the tracks. You see, that's fine, blah, blah, blah, Paul, you're a better dancer than me, that's fine, you're tougher than me, you're new buddy Paul Newman and you are going to take the home-based charity golf tour world by storm and invade our country with nationalistically themed salad dressings. You've got more money than me, that's fine; I don't have to be number one! I don't obsess like you do. I dance in this country because I like it. Because charity dance participation is one of the few recognized art forms this country has because of political mind control that was fostered by the likes of you. You do these things Paul because in your mind you really think that all of this is yours. What you need to understand, every time a Canadian reaches into their pockets to watch you dance, or buy Paul Newman's dressing, or buy one of my dance-themed burn-therapy collages, they have the right to buy whatever or do whatever they want. Paul Martin, your obsession with me and my charity dance-a-thon celebrity, will ultimately be, and I want you to read my lips, even though we're on radio, your DE-STRUC-TION."

[applause]

❋   ❋   ❋

For weeks *HELLO! Canada* would run suggestive photographs of Paul Newman and Paul Martin cavorting throughout the Ottawa valley in erotic golf-based attire. Local children would wheelbarrow them through poverty-stricken areas of downtown Ottawa where they'd hand out salad dressing sample packs to underprivileged families. The two spent most of June that year at the former Prime Minister's home where Martin had convinced the sex icon and salad-dressing king that he,

Paul Martin, of all people, should come up with his newest dressing flavour in the divine presence of a six-hole golf course, with a possible lean in flavour towards "something Canadian, or golfy." His words.

At a press conference, Martin was quoted as saying, "So Paul did, and that is where the Free-Range-Potato-salad-dressing-flavour idea came from. Paul Newman was in my house and came up with a creative idea. He was also thinking of a new film idea involving a former politician becoming a golf legend, with the help of an ex-PGA legend. He also said he wants to spend more time in Canada because we have a lot of forests. The Chicoutimi Cucumber Free-Range Potato salad dressing is exclusive to the Canadian market. We feel like this is a great salad dressing for Canadians to enjoy while watching golf or a hockey game or the news."

No one came to this press conference, but Paul Martin posted it on YouTube where a bevy of rude comments spilled out in an honest lacquer of Canadian rebellion.

"Why the hell not!" Paul Martin bragged to the CBC, telling them that Paul Newman was charmed at the cross-border idea.

Paul Martin would go on to say that every Canadian has the right to rush to their nearest salad topping centre or grocery place right now, and enjoy a sampling of this great, new Canadian dressing.

The animosity had been building considerably since April and most definitely had something to do with the St. Patrick's Day radio spot on CBC Radio Zero where I tore into the former prime minister. (It was their highest-rated show ever, I was told.)

Following the Paul Martin golf-ball news junkets and reading countless court transcripts had taken up a lot of my spare time. I did phone-in interviews whenever I could to weigh-in on the minor scandal, and then got a temp job in Ottawa as I wanted to be near the action.

※　　※　　※

At a charity event near the Rideau Canal dubbed Feed the Beasts III to raise money for underused animals in Canadian film productions, I bumped into Paul on the dance floor during the square-dance marathon. Me and Paul closed that dance floor! There was a small fire due to some wiring problems, though many believe it was the indoor barbecue. To take the focus off what was now something like the tenth charity indoor barbecue fire Paul Martin could be linked to, he was advised to turn things around and quick. Salads seemed like a safe bet and when Paul Newman's new line of fantastically economic salad dressings bloomed over Easter weekend, well, someone from inside Paul Martin's office patched a call through. "No one is sure who called whom," *HELLO! Canada* blogger Stephanie Reinhart was quoted as blogging. I offered her my two cents. "Well, look who came out of the woodwork asking to go half-sies on some salad-dressing stand on the King's Highway and start to get the Ottawa Valley all crazed to usher in a new era of salad dressing for Canadians."

In the washroom at the charity dance thing, Paul Martin's security officer was talking to someone and I heard him say that the phone lines were crossed and that Paul Newman was not even trying to phone the former prime minister, so it only looked like Paul Newman's office was calling the former PM all morning. And then the security guard got paranoid and said shit a few times and put his phone back into his pants. The lines were crossed, how do you like that?

Despite being in a lot of dance-a-thon photos with the former prime minister (in our boxers, sweating with the tiny flames just starting their demonic rage behind us), I dodged all the controversy, popped my big tapioca-coloured diet pills and saw things through my dried out pupils. I was starting to believe that being skinny took me further into a netherworld where I could eschew normative degrees of infamy.

I recall, moments before falling asleep soft as a dead birthday balloon, I was dreading the morning I would eventually star in.

The next morning I only had one thing to do, that is have lunch with my sheepish ex-boyfriend Peter Moss. After fifteen minutes of buttering rolls and asking for new cutlery, he said he didn't want to hear about Paul Martin anymore. I asked him if I could tell him one more thing and he agreed.

"When Paul Martin talks it sounds as if he is not even trying to speak about our situation and my blood boils."

"That's enough," he said, and made a face that could have been translated as a complete willingness on his part to leave at that moment. An arrow of a face. I'm going that way, WATCH ME! type of face. And so he did. Thankfully he brought me the photos of Parliament Hill that I requested.

I began to scribble down notes throughout the day until the late evening when I got the strangest phone call suggesting I come and give a speech at an event in Paul Martin's backyard and that perhaps the two of us could settle our big dance-a-thon problem once and for all. "It's a Hall-of-Fame-themed backyard barbecue and Mr. Martin would love for you to be there. You also get a free case of the new Chicoutimi Cucumber Free-Range Potato salad dressing."

The next morning, I stood in a short queue to give a speech. A man approached me and offered me some ecstasy and began to gyrate in front of me. He was tapping his silver belt buckle and dancing to invisible music. It was one of Paul Martin's friends I was sure of it. As we all stood in the heat that Canada Day, Paul Martin's voice played on a loop from a CBC sit-down interview he did in 2003:

"Have you ever, on a cloudless night, looked down from a passing aircraft flying over Canada? Endless, glowing strings of cities, towns, and backyards with only the stars in the distance, and the cool breeze of a million backyard salads being enjoyed with just the right ingredients."

❋   ❋   ❋

More often than not at this time, Paul would send his sexed-up, middle-aged, drug-dealing goons out to wherever I was to entice me and, of course, sexually harass me. They would say things like "How's the dancing going?" and I would answer with, "Does he pay you to act this way?"

Then they'd stop dancing and call me a name and just blurt out, "He really cares about you, ya know!"

The sun bore down on my pimply back and I began to feel faint. Then a man was waving his hand over my mouth and pouring water on my nose and it was all just so many hands and attention and this strange short line I was in disappears and I'm stuffed in a van. I hear a voice "Next stop: Paul Martin's back-yard!"

A security guard named Stanley was wheezing in and out of coherency. He leaned in and said to me, "These types of devilled-egg events go on non-stop in Ottawa."

"Uh huh," I said. He was fiddling with some mints, shaking a big box the size of laundry detergent. He handed me a couple and we got to talking.

"What's your speech on? Paul is curious," Stanley said with a warm, microwaved-Wonder Bread smile. He pawed at me, patted me down, and touched the zipper on my orange shorts.

I was in debt, lacked confidence and had inconsistent hair-styles. I had nineteen inconsistent hairstyles all of which left people with no option but to stare at me intensely on busy streets. I posited that since my name must have started coming up so many times when it came to government inquisitions that Paul's people figured I would make a really great sort of am-bassador for an upcoming home backyard rally for some cause Paul was trying to bandwagon.

Stanley's face was beaming with delight in between song shuffles on the van's stereo. He lit up and, nearly shouting said, "We're so glad you could make it! You don't know how hard it was to track you down!"

It was true; the only reason they had reached me at home was I had just installed a new phone so I could get dial-up Internet. My former school teachers, local ministers, former babysitters and the like would give the government constant updates on my condition, bank account numbers or my physical whereabouts like natural turncoats. Some, like my terrible former babysitters (Linda Everson, now aged fifty-three,

1523 Bayview Avenue, Toronto, 416-544-7355) would often serve banana bread during one of their random government-trolling, information intervention visits.

"They just want to talk," I would hear from those they made contact with. No matter what time of day it was, these turncoats from my storied life were always very cordial, even offering to drive them to one of my alleged hideouts. I resented all of them and wished them malicious ends.

According to Revenue Canada's mail-out PDF surrounding my late-teen activities at the time, I started three hundred arts-related companies, all of which were taxable and subject to administrative abuse. That was the sort of thing they wanted to talk to me about. Their questions read like a high school essayist's thesis statement on society during the days of rum-running:

1. What was with all the lay-offs and closed factories?
2. Are you still a wax burn victim?
3. Are you an artist or a business?
4. Are your employees mentally ill artists?
5. Do you plan on registering for any charities involving dance contests?
6. Are you feeling limber?
7. How many times a week do you use salad dressing?

It didn't help matters of my paranoia when I noticed that these questions were handwritten. The paper also seemed covered in salad-dressing-scented tears. I wanted to tell the Canadian government the whole truth, and that truth was quite simple: my designers and board of directors were not out of work, mentally ill or dancing, but in fact collage-based renderings who all resembled Paul Martin. I knew however, telling anyone in a government level any of those things would get me the electric chair. And no matter how badly I yearned for said current, I had to keep my distance. Especially since Paul was still hot on the trail for me.

We exited the van. The afternoon was a delight of orange and yellow fringe. Fire trucks did donuts in available spaces, and crossing guards led flash mob dance montages. It was just what the city needed after a two-hour bank robbery standoff, with three gunmen wearing Trudeau masks (and one in a Chrétien).

So, in the now very long lineup that ended up leading right into Paul Martin's backyard, I was handed a button and told I was being inducted into the Paul Martin To Build Six-Hole Golf Course At Personal Home Hall Of Fame.

I looked at the button thanked the helper and said, "Catchy name."

At the time I saw the honour of being inducted as an opportunity to network my own counseling centre, and get some of those Chicoutimi-Cucumber-Free-Range-Potato-salad-dressing topped corn on the cobs I'd been hearing so much about.

As I made my way through the line I noticed fourteen seniors in velour tracksuits doing jumping jacks in the driveway, panting, red in the face like a group of abused goats. Several bottles of water were tumbling unevenly down the sloped driveway as one of the elders cried, "Can we please have our water bottles!"

An assistant had me take a photograph with a cardboard cutout of Paul Martin with his hands at his cheeks, his mouth open comically, one eye winking.

Beside the cardboard cutout was another cardboard cutout of Paul Newman surrounded by lettuce that I was later told had been stolen in broad daylight from a local grocery store.

The ceremony got underway after Paul Martin's grandchildren (The Letdowns 613) performed a cover of "The Good Ol' Hockey Game" by Stompin' Tom Connors but they had changed the lyrics considerably to include mentions of the Hall of Fame, Paul Newman, salad dressing and the game of golf.

❋   ❋   ❋

I remembered the words of the *Globe and Mail* columnist who once wrote "the penis is king," and would later in the piece go on to say, something to the effect of: if a woman is ever made to feel as though she has to walk on eggshells or is undermined in any way during a sexual routine with a partner, she'll likely run off with the nearest inflatable (wo)man until her ego is stroked the right way. I was nearing the front of the line and counseling myself. Could I write this off?

On stage the feedback crowed a big macaw sound and someone began to speak incoherently. "Hello, eat up, get a seat, buttons are great too. Thanks for coming everyone! My name is Cate, I am a professional dancer and also work for Canada's War on Cultural Excess, with a part-time job promoting Canada's amateur dance presence at community-organized events. I am also an amateur golfer and am glad-handing—I am happy to be here! But tonight, it's about you, the public, sharing in the moment that Paul Martin is so proud of! The pending construction of a new home-based golf course! Ladies and gentlemen, we would now like to introduce the Paul Martin To Build Six-Hole Golf Course At Personal Home Hall Of Fame inductees. To do so, Mr. Paul Martin!"

Paul Martin finally took the stage and looked out with a squinting paused-like grimace and said, "Ah, it's great to be here, at my house. This is my backyard. Thanks for coming. Cate, back to you."

"Thank you Mr. Martin," Cate said.

This crappy banter went on for another ten minutes or so, with members of the audience throwing half-eaten corn cobs up on the stage. This only enticed the soon-to-be former Prime Minister into catching the discarded cobs in his mouth.

"Don't you know who made the dressing?!" Paul Martin yelled like a banshee from the stage, on his knees, gathering some rolling cobs, then smearing the cobs across his jaw like a prize-winning soap model. Then he tossed the cobs he caught to Cate, barking, "Put these in the fridge, Cate!"

His body language lacked the grace he demonstrated so frequently at charity dance-a-thons; he was desperate, like a stroke victim reaching for his pills, like an astronaut struggling with his electronic will.

I looked down at my cue card: "Winning is great, sharing the honour is a compromise in the ego, my name is Amanda and I'm so thrilled to be here." I felt like an abused goat trying to go on strike, but not knowing how to talk. I popped the mint the security guard had been shaking in front of me and walked towards the microphone.

❉   ❉   ❉

They say you never get over your mother, the first time you tell a joke to a room full of adults, or the first time your teacher spanks you on Valentine's Day, but I'll never forget the time I fell asleep on stage in Paul Martin's backyard.

I must have been drugged because the next thing I knew I was being dragged down the driveway past the guests and thrown somewhere inside his mysterious house.

As you can imagine, once I woke up, hours later in Paul's kitchen, I started screaming. I saw with complete accuracy, Paul Newman's blue eyes staring deeply at me as he shook a large bottle of his new Canadian brand of Chicoutimi Cucumber Free-Range Potato salad dressing. So they tucked me into the basement for a few hours in a room with several hamster cages but no hamsters. I fell asleep twice. I heard the television click on, and the door rattle. The Pauls were standing before me, sweaty, smoking cigars. "Get up and walk up the stairs," Paul Newman said, pushing me towards the back door. Outside, they ushered me towards a large hard tree. It was super early in the morning.

"See, I told you. A living target, Paul," Paul Martin said, steering the other Paul into the backyard with me ahead of both of them. Both wearing matching hunting uniforms, which were pretty decent knock-offs from this fall's fashion week in which the world of popular urban rodents and vermin (raccoons, skunks, pigeons and squirrels) met the hunting fashion world. Paul Newman spat on the ground and glared at me.

"She better not spit that apple out of her mouth, or I'll shoot you too."

"I know, I know, I'm prepared to take that risk," Paul Martin said. It was a Granny Smith, it was salty against my palate.

My pubic region itched. Did they shave me? Did someone from the ceremony get crazy with the scissors down there? Was I the afterbirth sacrifice of yet another US-Canada orgy of brinkmanship?

I couldn't believe this was happening to me; these two guys with hunting gear on were about to snuff me out over some light-hearted and essentially esoteric comments I made about salad dressing and golf courses and indoor fires at charity dance-a-thons. I thought this was the end and that the love I have for the earth and life itself was greater and richer than any lettuce-loving sauce. I screamed from my brain, which could not speak of course, because I had the apple in my mouth: So shoot me Paul-squared; I just can't make you love me. I just can't fight you both anymore!

The Pauls stood there, pointing their arsenal at me; the sun beat down on my baseball hat. "Please," I said, Granny Smith apple still locked in my jaws until I passed out again, hunched over, the ropes nestled tight, allowing me the luxury of discovering and patenting the first vertical hammock. They must have spent a few minutes discussing their plan, for I weaved in and out of coherency like some prehistoric radio station, hearing bits of dialogue and physical gestures.

"Damn, it's getting hot. Let's let this heat tenderize her a bit, come back first thing, nightfall, you know, shoot her then, fry her up with some scrambled eggs."

"Want a salad, Paul? We just have to go pick up some shaved carrots from the store."

"You and your shaved carrots," Paul Newman said. "Such a delicate delicacy! Such a prissy twat you are Paul!"

"It soaks up the dressing."

"Shut up, Paul!" Paul Newman shouted, lifting his rifle up and resting it on his shoulder, a look of comfort caressed his jaw.

The Pauls were awkwardly sharing a large Thermos of coffee as they made their way through the sliding glass door, hissing commands and shushing one another like an old married couple in matching red plaid hunting coats, all wooly. I tried to speak. They wore the typical early morning scowls that all Ontario faces possess, and carried on like a pair of abused goats being startled and hooked up to a lactation-extraction device.

As both Pauls sipped their morning coffees and adjusted their rifle bits, sharing fingers of camouflage zinc with one another, I could feel the wrapper to Stanley's mint in my pant pocket. I could tell someone had retied me in the night, changed my T-shirt to a yellow number with a target on it. (In the television movie produced by CTV, the Pauls attached a milking machine to the character "Amanda" for experiments in their ever-expanding Canadian brand of food toppings. "The crew was just told the day we shot the scene that the electric milk extractors would only be available for three hours, as the machines were in high demand." According to director Atom Egoyan, the microbial-diversity scene was inspired by the delightful inter-religious comedy *The Fuck He's My Son In Law* in which the protagonist named Greg is caught attempting to milk his future father-in-law after taking one too many painkillers after dinner one night, thinking the octagon shaped blue pills were, of course, his anti-hysteria medication. In the interview with Movie Suds, Egoyan suggested that he felt the hyperbolic scene would inspire the salad-dressing king to sponsor the film.

*　*　*

The morning sun insinuated itself, bore down in harsh tones, cracking through the theatrics of pine trees in orange and pink rays, blue was to follow. I was now an angular piece of a Paul-squared jigsaw puzzle, and no matter how I tried to fight it, I wouldn't fit into their demented plans of restitution, of reinvention, of holiday weekend treasured memories: I would be that little piece in the corner by the tree trunk: a blurred white girl with an apple in her mouth, perhaps mounted one day in one of their trophy rooms, perhaps they'd share me, after getting cleaned up and stuffed after the brutal finish: my head impaled by two distinct bullets: one in the throat and one in the right eye. The last thing I recall was my spine against the tree, the two rifles pointing at my face and the sound of sirens.

One of their phones went off. "What time? Sure. I'll be there tonight. Looks like it's your lucky day, Amanda," Paul Newman said in a mirage of rope, Ottawa-hostage drugs and the scent of Irish Cream coffee gobbling away. "That was headquarters, they want me to do a talk show tonight in New York and sing a song as well."

"Can I come?" Paul Martin asked.

"No."

The day was illuminating before me; if I could only reach around in my pockets, I had blunt instruments, like a caveman on the first day of school: elastics, nail file, nail clippers, nail polish, a pencil and six cue cards. I was so parched, tired, couldn't think straight, how would I get home, they would find me, right? Hunters always find me. Crossing guards, baristas, telemarketers. I was fading. People always ask if I saw it coming.

If I could get a finger or two loose, couldn't I just break free? I knew caught or free, I had no idea where I was, and in all likelihood I'd wind up tied to another tree in another backyard.

Three weeks later I awoke in the hospital, the apple never removed from my mouth. To commemorate the ordeal, I had a dyed red cast-iron apple lodged in a steel-octane jaw. Granny Smith, oh the Granny Smith! What a shared history we have now, that deliciously brave fruit and me. My rehabilitation at this time involved large servings of honey, raisins and candy apples with plenty of rest.

Flowers and gift baskets came regularly but without a card or return address. The doctors had no idea what sort of pills to give me so they just took my blood. I wanted Paul Martin to approach me with a Thermos of soup and a rescue blanket and tell me everything will be OK but he left me, much like he did that night at the all-you-can-eat-buffet fundraiser jig-off for an all-you-can-eat buffet. I lived with roommates to absorb the cost of light bulbs. Everything I ate at this time had gristle or fat on it. I found myself chewing on bark and coughing up feathers. The doctors didn't know what to do with me. I spent my days listening to people use blenders or idle their car engines.

It was as if God never wanted my jaw to stop smarting. It was in this state of extreme jaw pain and frustration with all the mistakes I kept making in my life that I thought I'd give the family business a stab. But working as an ambulance attendant, even part-time on weekends, was too morbid for me: I was simply too sensitive. That's why I started my own publicity company. I figured if I could bring awareness to so many lies and faults and develop gossip-based conflict for one former prime minister, working in the opposite direction, I could probably help people discover good things to say about themselves and their businesses. With this newfound ardour in place I moved forward, sober and sensible in my vocational passion. Mine wasn't an easy road to clear away and sure there have been a ton of obstacles to overcome in recovery, but one day at a time I am here and don't need alcohol to fuel my passionate desire for change and justice. And I'm a much better dancer, I've been told, sober than drunk!

By the grace of God I have never been audited, never had to fight for my rights for a GST tax credit, an environmental goodie-two-shoes coupon from the provincial government, or had to return a single overdue library book. I've been given a great life since I emerged from my rather unusual late-teen binging years. While I'll never remember all the dance moves I pulled out in a sweat of vodka funk with the former prime minister, I can tell you this, not a day goes by when a Top 40 song from the early 2000s plays on a radio that I don't cringe in shame. Then, I dust myself off, move forward into the bright reality of modern life and feel a warm gratitude that I survived. This pendant around my neck that dangles from a chain is, of course, a basket of Granny Smith apples. It arrived one morning in the mail, around the time of my dry date, which is coming up on twenty years. I like to think that it was from Paul, but of course, I don't question this. What other people think, do, or believe about me is none of my business. Keep coming back, it works if you work it, and thank you all for being here!

"'The Magic ~~Kingdom~~ Empire' is an imaginative and sad-hearted story about famous people being unkind to each other, fictional people navigating around each other, and all types of persons struggling with the uncomfortable weight of being entranced by a cultural product over which they have no control. As a voice, Nathaniel G. Moore is funny and unusual throughout."

—Jacob McArthur Mooney, author of *Folk* and *Don't Be Interesting*

The Magic ~~Kingdom~~ Empire

"You get all kinds," Mitch Adams tells Lance as he taps the stack of file folders under his arm. According to Mitch, the folders contain the lion's share of this week's legal woes. "We sort based on priority, as set by our supervisors. Some files have helpful stick-it notes, let's see: I mean this one here for example," Mitch stops speaking in his rapid-fire parlance long enough to extend his index finger towards an already-opened green file folder. "This guy is a regular nut job," he grimaces, "sent us twenty letters last fall; I swear he must have quit his job by the amount of time he spends serving us for last year's film *Banjo*, you know the one about the surfing rabbit who gets marooned on a desert island..."

Lance's nostrils flare but not by any noticeable measurement. He's been here all of four minutes and already feels Mickey Mouse's curvy ears against his freshly pressed shirt—the result of a prank chair placed at his desk a few minutes before arriving this morning...

"So Banjo fashions a canoe out of a dead tree and halfway back home realizes he didn't pack any food so he goes back to the desert island and there are new castaways who are in this traveling band..."

Mitch reads Lance the opening statement in the summons, "Wherefore, Plaintiff seeks judgment against Defendants for a cease and desist from any and all sales, distribution and marketing of 'Banjo' in any media format, as well as money damages in the amount of 125 million dollars together with costs of suit, and such other relief as the Court may deem appropriate."

"I mean, the guy wrote a short story in some kids magazine eight years ago and says we stole the whole script idea and likeness and merchandising schematics from him. We get this shit all the time."

According to Mitch, the lawsuit has been getting a ton of attention on book and film media channels on message boards teeming with convivial chatter and gossip.

"Someone on every elevator from here to Paris to Texas is talking about Banjo this morning; I guaran-damn-tee it," Mitch says.

And whether the news has been in the book chatter culture or the popcorn media circles, parents' groups or fan sites of both sides, Disney has had to react the same way Disney has reacted for nearly a century: opaquely. "We don't talk to the press; we cover our asses and check our contracts, our dates, and ask the rights lawyers if we have any holes in our side of things."

✳   ✳   ✳

When Lance asks why no one from Disney talks to the press, Mitch balks and takes a big noisy slurp of coffee and downs two croissants in under half a minute. "Usually the 11th floor handles that shit. But today, buddy guy goes public, his lawyers are publishing PDFs of the summons on his blog, but we have legal guys working on that. Our job today is going to be, Oh Hi Doug, that's Doug, he works with us sometimes; anyway, from what I've heard there's been negative trolling going on about how *Banjo* depicts the local surfers and residents as stoners and airheads. A bunch of us feel like our division is in for major damage control today. My first day was hell too. So welcome."

It's under these strained but typical (according to Mitch) circumstances that Lance Auld begins his first day at Disney's highly clandestine legal wing in the big mouse-ear-shaped offices on 500 S Buena Vista Street in Burbank California, twelve miles northwest of downtown Los Angeles where Lance lives in a small one-bedroom studio apartment.

Who wouldn't wonder—as it relates to the *Banjo* heat-seeking letter writer and the legal futility of it all, the painstaking grandiosity, pompous, histrionic God-like antics—what does his wife and kids think about his litigious obsession? "What's the point?" And, as Mitch continues to flap his 8:00 a.m. gums at Lance about his "pretty decent" Spielberg connection, his cousin's graphic novel and its looming indie film adaptation, his fiancé's condo going up for sale, the new yoga instructor at the gym, the department head Rita Sinclair who hasn't even properly introduced herself to Lance (who is eyeing him every thirteen seconds it seems), who is standing next to several plush Donald Ducks on a long bureau (next to the only entrance this conference room has) with two well-manicured assistants hanging on her every word and she now stands—accessible, open and without a shred of body language mystery—not twenty paces from Lance, who now, it seems, has Mitch (is that even a name?)—Mitchum, Mitchell, what the heck is Mitch short for? Oh right, Mitchanius—pegged as a colossal time waster and seeker in Lance of a sidekick for some chummy bromance, a smothering gender salute pile-up of "us" versus "them" jazz.

And in a world of zero tolerance, a world of firewalls and privacy software, company line-toeing memos, linguistic cleanliness and moral office codes of conduct, Lance can already hear the stiletto whispers in between latté slurps, "Did they know each other from before? They're really tight I think, maybe went to the same college."

Lance puts his finger up, as if to tell Mitch to shut up, but Mitch is indifferent, noticing his new best friend's index finger no more than a fruit fly or passing pixel of light registering against the eggshell wall from passing traffic, interrupting the sun's natural office burn. Lance doesn't know if being too friendly with Mitch is a good career move this early into his first day; who knows what this possible maniac has done or not done properly. Who knows if he got drunk at the last Christmas party and pinched someone's ass, had a racial slur come out when Rita Sinclair's lesbian partner was introduced to the office and things are just now being smoothed over due to Mitch's otherwise flawless record and his innate ability for get-

ting cases thrown out or possessing other cost-saving, grati-
tude-worthy qualities that Disney values. Let's hope Mitch isn't
an established non grata around the water cooler or staff gym
or other animated environs. Let's hope, Lance says to himself,
to his bones and blood as his back accrues sweat. Let's really
hope the sight of this motherfucker each morning isn't grad-
ing against certain minions of minions until there is no choice
but to toss the prick out the window like a piece of earwax
hurtling down the sleek window-washed building with its
comical mouse ear aesthetic, err, architecture.

The Disney corporation home office is located in a downtown carcinogenic region of the city, the brickwork slick with
two-hundred-year-old oil stains waiting to be gentrified. According to Mitch, the building itself is frequented mostly by his
employees or heritage activists who would leave affectionate
messages for him and the others on his floor like, "We're so glad
you're treating the building with the respect she deserves."
They were under the impression Mitch was on the board of
Disney's green initiative Green Mouse. "I'm not in the environmental concern racket; I recycle but that's about all I do,"
he points ahead of him and mouths a word Lance can't tran-
scribe in time. Mitch adds that he felt no need to disrupt their
magnanimous view of him.

His official responses, as Lance is learning, are always written in what he considers to be artistic fonts like Garamond or
Lucinda, and read minimalist things like, "Art is preservation."
Mitch says he could hear their applause as he printed the
memos, alternating colours with each sentence.

Lance is eyeing a fresh stack of Disney-related samples that
appeared on his desk including postcards, erasers and pencil

crayons. "I see you've been privy to the incredible perks of working here," Mitch says smugly. "They make great stocking stuffers."

The team is assembled and Rita Sinclair begins immediately.

"Morning exercise will be to get in groups of three and come up with a solution for our c.o.o. to delineate hope and put out a worry-free vibe for an upcoming shareholder's meeting and at the same time, the solution will be put into effect immediately to swerve the possible damage we might be doing by not saying anything or by not addressing the growing opinion that Disney is slighting the surfing community through its depiction of Banjo, the lovable surfing cat, and his friends. Here is one of three hundred comments. Try to imagine, as you sit with your team of four, that you are taming these respondents in person and then build a wider solution based on our favourite Internet darling IP . . . you know him, you love him, Banjo."

It's a shame that Disney is trying to make the residents of Encinitas, California look bad . . . or like dumb? Am I reading into it too much? I don't know but it almost seems like the company is a propaganda tool of the government.

One of Lance's group members pipes up, a real redhead and red-faced, Nervous Nellie type, but still, despite the obvious jitters presented in his parlance, is ultra-enthusiastic and ready to conquer the world: "This comment board is all fired up; it's making people scrutinize over simple entertainment storylines, like a surfing rabbit with a Californian accent is suddenly now construed as a slight against them, Arnold Schwarzenegger and Hollywood, simply because the story winds up taking place on the Eastern seaboard."

Over the next seventy minutes newly formed cells break off to "think tank all things *Banjo*" in an attempt to swerve the accruing associate press feeds that "are feeding off amateur blogs and Internet viewers and fan comments."

Lance comes up with the idea of the pop-up store and a red herring pop-up store at a neutral location to "humanize" the corporation's seemingly one-track perspective on marketing, that is to soak and drench the public; of course he doesn't word it that way to his co-cell mates, he cleans it up a bit from his shock-rock mindset. So Lance suggests a pop-up: a friendly, free, all-day, double-screen screening thing at a local, cool family-friendly café, bistro or even video store, library!

❋　❋　❋

At lunch Lance sees a woman from grad school; it's been four, maybe five years—Carla Meyers, and instantly a caravan of snapshots parachutes through his caffeinated lens. Carla was always active, unattainable or switching classes, lectures, sometimes highly involved in the pedagogue social causes, other times entirely removed. She has auburn hair, curly, like a mid-1980s slo-mo starlet any red-blooded, hetero underdog protagonist would gush and pine after for ninety-two minutes only to be relived on VHS rental life someday later. He has no idea what she is doing in the lunch room, maybe working for a PR firm, a caterer or she works here too in another sector. She's dressed like a server but he can't solidify exactly her role. Maybe those are executive leggings or tights or stockings.

The lunch room is equipped with a Starbucks and a buffet as well as a sectioned off "quiet room" and Lance wonders why on earth he can solve Disney's problems, putting out their fires at minute seventeen of his first day at work, but can't solve any of his own. Carla had rejected him once, and he doesn't want to go 0-2 but doesn't want to just give up. Doesn't want to act out a popular trajectory in which he can now pick her up because the power imbalance is so obvious (she is a waitress at an executive martini bar, he's a mid-level think tank left-winger or defenseman for Disney—oh haha he thinks: what a terrible pick-up line that would be. But does he even want a relationship or to date or to even talk to this woman? All that has happened now is recognition. He stalls. He goes outside onto the loud street; somehow the noise is so well-vacuumed within the Disney building,

Lance forgets the world has anything to say. It does, and he hastens his steps towards a grocery store, which just happens to be his favourite pastime and franchise. He takes enormous pleasure in grocery shopping. The Whole Foods chain had recently expanded to set-up shop in his neighborhood, and this one he feels is just as fine. Though Lance can't imagine eating most of the products, he does love the countless hours he has totaled watching the emasculated shoppers. He enters the shiny store knowing that his Whole Foods bag that gave him a discount was miles away.

On a visit to his nearby chain several months before, a young Amish boy yelped "shoplifter" just as Lance accidentally walked out with a carton of lactose-free milk and goat-shaped pasta. Though the boy was referring to a man attempting to escape with an armful of leg warmers, the damage was done. Lance was conditioned to feel criminal each time he mysteriously transgressed the ill-defined threshold, the unwitting Pavlov's dog of Whole Foods. That day he simply returned to the cash register, hands outstretched before him with not-yet purchased items in full view. If this weren't enough, he made sure to maintain a sheepish grin that said, "I couldn't possibly be a shoplifter, I have far too much money."

Sometimes in a shopping daze, he would be forced to re-enter, caught up in the tear-duct-shaped pharmaceutical section that fed into a maze of perpetual holiday paraphernalia. He would find himself mysteriously thrown beyond the border of the store, and into a sea of outdated leg warmers.

On this perspiring afternoon of blazing cartoon sun, Lance inhales an eyeful: heaps of bulk goods are situated in an effort to create the impression of the rigors of farm life. Though distasteful, the Whole Foods labyrinth has become old hat.

His thick shock of chestnut hair could easily pass for very expensive plugs. Not yet out of his thirties, his lean body has held on to its elegance. His Nordic bone structure and distant, deep hazel eyes are synthesized with his olive complexion. He has a magnetism whose rewards he never reaped, blinded to his own grace by a childhood of spirited disapproval.

"Have you tried St. John's Wort, sir?" a tartly Whole Foods employee asks as Lance slips into the vitamins region.

Lance responds with a negative headshake, absentmindedly forgetting to speak English aloud. "Always room for mental improvement," the chipper middle-aged sales clerk mutters as Lance passes out of sight.

The agility of mind reminds Lance of Yeti, his suicide coach of a mother. She held an orb about her: a covert disdain for mankind which enabled the chosen few who possessed it to turn a casual experience into a nightmare of self-doubt. Usually these people were restricted to careers in telemarketing.

Once he gets past the persuasive drug corral, he veers towards the prepared-foods section. Though he rarely cooks, he considers himself adept in the gastronomic arena. He inspects the culinary treats, imagining that he can do a much better job. And would if there was someone to enjoy his food.

Making his way along the long tramway of sundried tomatoes, olive tapenades and giant gold blocks of chocolate, Lance nearly collides into a pretty girl—wait, that's Carla Meyers again, she must have popped in when he wasn't looking—kneeling down beside a pile of kernels. It is Lance's belief that for this franchise, shoppers are made to feel they have scavenged their inordinately priced product, and could therefore enjoy their bounty with a sense of conquest. Affable tattooed punks come by and clean up the stray granules, suggesting vapid mineral waters appropriate to the contents of your shopping basket. Where were all the real punks these days? Lance thinks as their trackless forearms force-sample him pink zinfandels.

What am I doing, he thinks, and turns his attention to the humanized Royal Dalton figurine. Looking up from her mini-Babel of popping corn, Carla's face, taken up mostly by giant blue eyes, shook slightly before opening into a hyperbolic grin. Blasphemes flashed through his mind—Oh My Mighty Lord Baby Jesus Christ, Pez Dispenser.

He stands above Carla like an immutable ogre and she becomes aware of his proximity and scuttles into the dairy section, still on her knees. My mother was right, I am an asshole, Lance considers honestly as he continues through with his course to the prepared-foods section. He chooses a selection of chicken and braised magpies, which he assumes was a euphemism for something vegan. He enjoys politically correct food, though this notion usually dissolved into fits of week-long tofu binges. His lack of carbohydrates and other assorted needs have rendered him ghoulish, obtuse and lacking in physical empathy.

Lance wants to get his items and leave before another retina scan envelops him to heights of tabloid shame. Carla's toothy grin, dancer's posture, the personification of antioxidants, makes her look as though she has all the vitamins necessary to make the most energizing power shake. Her skin, both gold and silver, is as supple as a meal replacement, and as illuminating as the most opulent piece of cellophane in his Nixon-obsessed neighbour's collection.

Lance examined her burly sweater and sinewy opaque-stocking legs as her velvet micro-jacket burned orange into his work-swollen eye sockets, while she named the items in the lengthy, steel, imitation fifties freezer.

Ready to elope with a pineapple nearly half her size, Carla hovers near a small platform covered in Astroturf. Lance can hear the faint whisper of the tragic sample lady who resided there in her tea-coloured leotards, "Care to try our new tomatillo and marjoram ravioli? Just heat it up and voila! Dinner!" and Carla responding quickly, "No. Thank you. That sounds nice though." He imagines her voice at fully audible levels is the sound a Dodo bird would have made, had the species endured into the gourmet-grocery era.

With his petite bowl of ready-to-eat cuisine and a juice box he dodges the faux-punk employees and makes his way to the frozen-foods pavilion. He arrives behind Carla, cropping her with his epileptic gaze. Her sheen of copper hair smells like phosphorous alcohol from the "whiskey and eggs" conditioner samples in the shampoo and soup section.

Lance turns around and heads to the cash, never looking back, shaking his head from left to right when asked if he needs a bag for his items.

Back at work, he analyzes his wordless lunch and Carla Meyer sighting as he drives a straw into his infantile juice box. Mitch says something cheesy like "Missed you at lunch big guy," and says that upon being hired sixteen months ago, a human resources rep explained, "It's key to have a few favourite Disney films or characters on your mind at all times. This gets workers more in line with consumer proclivities."

❉   ❉   ❉

Over the afternoon, the winning cell's PR solution was put into action. Lance acts humble and low-fi as the executives single out his group of four's work ethic and ability to think on their feet. Communications teams announce the Encinitas theatre has agreed to the pop-up store treatment to be installed in three days time, early Tuesday morning. By 4:00 p.m. the press releases for local papers, tiny local papers and mom blogs are put into effect, set three days in the future: "The legendary La Paloma Theatre will be turned into the fictional home of Banjo for a day. The Disney character is thought to be an amalgam of personalities from the legendary Encinitas surfing community. Here patrons can not only enjoy an all-day screening of the film but eat the same food Banjo serves at his beach birthday breakfast party, while enjoying live music from the bands that play in the movie itself. (And yes, we're bringing a sandblaster to give Banjo's new temporary digs that beachy vibe.)"

That night, Lance wakes up soggy. His night sweats prove what he always knew; he possesses a certain viscosity in his breath. An intermittent insomniac, he uses his evenings to order his tightly defined apartment, in between pathological bouts of Googling the phrase, "you are not my mother."

He makes sandwiches at Guinness-record speed, which gives him gut rot. He steps out onto his mini-porch, fourteen flights above the vast Los Angeles plane, and thinks of Minnie Mouse's percussive eyes and parched persimmon lips. He thinks of *National Geographic* game-hunting snuff films and how his new strategy with Carla Meyers, if he ever sees her again, is to pretend not to recognize her or to roll over and play dead. As he paces on his balcony he hears a repetitive sound: that of a bunch of dogs being hurdled over backyard fences, miles away.

Lance has no backyard, just a balcony view of a slanted street that ends out into a divide between a big park full of orange trees and a bunch of busy streets. The lack of a backyard makes him feel both old and new. He always had a backyard as a child and would go there for countless hours playing with the water hose, examining bugs or attempting to build a clubhouse. Staring out at his sloping panorama of sparse street lights, he notices a pair of strolling bike enthusiasts who sip hot beverages from one hand while arm-pitting their helmets in the other as they push their bikes along the sidewalk in front of his apartment. He considers the postcard quality of this particular quadrant and deems it heart-wrenchingly more vapid than a trio of sand-kissed, tanned bottoms, the sort of California postcards you'd prank-send to your brother or sister or even girlfriend if you had it in you.

On his street each building is exactly the same as the next: red brick for red brick, olive trellis for olive trellis. The nightly wolf-howl soundtrack put him to sleep, even though tonight's sounded more desperate and disturbed: an orchestrated, late dog-hurtling competition.

✳   ✳   ✳

Seventy-two hours later, *The Encinitas Herald* publishes the story on their homepage with the headline "COME FOR BRUNCH AT BANJO'S TEMPORARY DIGS" accompanied by several "set up" photos and early patrons enjoying the unusual spectacle. The piece was a "home run" according to Lance's bosses, who were impressed with how well-choreographed the entire process seemed to unravel. Jenny Tretheway wrote, "According to reports, residents woke up to theme music and invitations to have breakfast with Banjo and his friends in his kitchen, which included pancakes, eggs and of course pineapple smoothies. Homes along streets in the area awoke with gift baskets full of Disney merchandise on their doorsteps. Chalk drawings of waves with the words "Follow the waves for free breakfast and movies all day" lined the sidewalks, leading the neighbourhood residents to the pop-up location where Disney employees (some in licensed mascot outfits) were waiting."

The mostly positive article fluffs the details and overall made the PR gesture seem on the up and up, organic, cute and full of class. The piece ended with an incentive to those seeking more than just a free breakfast. "All of this is a one day PR stunt by the company to draw attention to the more than 2,000 positions it is trying to fill at Disney World which includes the new *Banjo* water ride which of course you do on a very large surf board. The pop-up outlet will permanently close at noon Tuesday."

This morning, as the articles appear in search engine traffic and the pop-up *Banjo* home is being installed, Lance arrives several minutes early and security has to let him in because there is something wrong with his swipe card. "You need to talk to Helen in resources; she'll straighten your card out." Lance does warm-ups to prepare for Disney's latest naysayers, adjusting the legs and arms of his desk and chair, checking them carefully like they were flotation devices.

❊   ❊   ❊

Mitch steamboats into Lance's periphery. "You're not going to believe this Lance," he says, catching his breath. For all he knows, Mitch was preparing to do a cartwheel or something. Lance positions his facial body language to receive information. Mitch continues now, taking a sip of coffee, "Today is the mother of all days, the rumours are true. We're going to have the best two weeks of our little lives here," he says, handing Lance a memo with what appears to be a missive which begins with the words A LONG TIME FROM NOW IN A CORPO-RATION CLOSE, CLOSE NEARBY and a graphic of Mickey Mouse holding a light saber.

"Disney is doing the next *Star Wars* film!" Mitch beams with the proud enthusiasm you'd see reserved for those accepting praise for inventing green-screen technology. "What I mean is, whatever PR conversion jazz we have to do for the next two, three or even six weeks as it relates to Disney will be *Star Wars*-themed!"

The announcement causes a shift in global Internet usage and key terms such as "Han Solo," "Disney," "Darth Vader Lives," "Carrie Fischer Dead?," "Donald Duck," "Death Star Theme Park," "Mark Hamill's Surgeon," "Part VII," "Pluto R2D2," are but nine of several hundred search terms associated with the pending merger.

By three in the afternoon, other staffers confirm to Mitch and Lance that George Lucas himself has been seen in three different offices wearing plaid under a black sweater and Khakis walking "arm in arm" with Disney brass as they complete the circuit of interviews and confirmations. Lucas disappears an hour and a half later surrounded by Disney security and is shuttled back by limo to Skywalker Ranch.

"Here, read this," Mitch says, handing Lance a printout. Lance scans it quickly, his eyes darting and settling simultaneously, "An investor conference call will take place at approximately 4:30 p.m. EDT/1:30 p.m. PDT today, October 30, 2012. Details for the call are listed in the release." Lance nods. Mitch reads some aloud like it's his favourite lyrics to some Pink Floyd song and he's high, "The Boards of Directors of Disney and Lucasfilm have approved the transaction, which is subject to clearance under the Hart-Scott-Rodino Antitrust Improvements Act, certain non-United States merger control regulations, and other customary closing conditions. The agreement has been approved by the sole shareholder of Lucasfilm."

Throughout the day, Stormtroopers appear outside of hallways and Darth Vader himself is deployed with several of his soldiers to one of many press conferences to answer questions from the press and record Disney-infused clips. The repeating Disney logos behind the Dark Lord's iconic likeness orbit and twinkle in lifeless delight.

❋　　❋　　❋

Over the next two weeks, George Lucas was SPECIAL EDI-TIONING his soundbites to the media—*The New York Post*, *The Atlantic* and *The London Times* respectfully—meticulously osculating his opinion on the sale of *Star Wars* from that of relief, "... so now someone else can worry about cryogenically bringing Darth Vader back as a multiple personality, omni-headed and clinically centenarian, have him be the dusty, withdrawn casualty of war and commerce that he always seemed to be, casually dressed and drinking a blue milky pab-ulum in a spaced-aged food court all by his lonesome..." to the banal, "... and every six-year-old on the planet will be sporting a TIE Fighter tattoo as they wait impatiently in line for *Star Wars VII*, dozens of them extemporaneously swelling to a multi-monotone rendition of John Williams' irrefutable lunch-pail jingle!" to pure rhapsody, "... not long after Mark Hamill is released from Waco County Hospital diagnosed with cirrhosis of the liver and a bad ticker, Carrie Fischer will step up her game and win the Academy Award for best supporting actress, look directly at the camera and say, 'Mark, I know what you are going through, you're at home now with a mouthful of mint-flavoured cotton balls and an apartment refrigerator-sized defibrillator/dialysis machine with a built-in beer cozy by your side, cheering me on while you recover; I just want you to know that you are my brother and I know we'll be swishing our glowy swords together in our next on-screen family adventure...' Then she'll burp and continue after dozens of out-of-sync laughter from the audience and, of course, she'll be all class and blame catering for the oily foods that are 'turning my stomach into the Sarlac Pit,' inciting more laughter from the audience before thanking me, who had a simple dream a long time ago in a galaxy far, far away."

Lance is getting the hang of things; he moves cordially through hallways and responds passionately to memos and Carla Meyers is a bleating asteroid in his sprawling galaxy, slowly dissipating into a single granule of cerebral concern when he finds himself at a work-related function at a nearby bar named Penguin's. He has told himself that he will endure up to forty-seven minutes of camaraderie before jettisoning away to lonelier quarters, sighting that he needs to visit his Aunt at a nearby retirement home because it's her birthday. As it's close enough to Halloween for ridiculous attire (and as Lance has almost convinced himself, using a didactic God-like tone, "Everyday is like Halloween and Christmas combined here at the Disney Corporation," imagining his repetitive co-worker Mitch borrowing the line from his own subconscious) he finds some of his table-mates dressed up as Snow White and various pixies, elves and of course pirates.

No imperial mascots seem to be invading the terrain. He nudges himself with an itch and checks his watch, noting that he's about seventeen minutes into his vaccine for escape when he recognizes Carla Meyers several tables down. He could confirm everything right now with Mitch or Megan or Amy or anyone at the table, casually asking if Carla, of course not using her real name, just casually pointing her out—works at Disney. He uses the vague question, "That whole table work at Disney?" Instead of dragging the cursor of self into everyone's pupil and divulging any form of interest in Carla, Lance counterstrikes his own Death Star destruction mission and has avoided any follow-up water cooler gossip should Carla ever appear again amidst co-workers in his vocational periphery.

Closing his eyes slightly, lowering his head ever so much, he puts together the most comforting image he can muster; his thick gray duvet wrapped around his body, a scented candle and the lulling soft music of clicking bicycles moving up and down his street. He thinks about George Lucas in his Skywalker Ranch, unceremoniously pulling at his beard surrounded by *Star Wars* models and artifacts, the maids dusting them with a deeper curiosity perhaps.

He glances at his watch and copes with any possible accruement of jitters by taking the route of campy rolling credits, hums the tune of *It's A Small World After All* under his breath for the next thirty minutes, never saying a word or looking up from his centre of view.

"Seismic shocks of recognition as Nathaniel G. Moore in his short story 'American Psycho' portrays the mug's game as T.S. Eliot liked to describe the sport of poetry writing. Mr. Moore's Big Smoke slugfest takes place over time (extra rounds) with both combatants thoroughly bloodied."

—Philip Quinn, author of *The Double* and *The Skeleton Dance*

American Psycho

"Do you sometimes look up from the computer and look around the room and know you are alone, I mean really know it, then feel scared?" —Tao Lin, *Shoplifting from American Apparel*

When one is discussing absolute adult-level trauma, the tendency is to put as much distance between one's key opponent—leader of the opposition, monster in the closet, front lawn shadow at midnight—and yourself as is possible.

I've often wondered if it didn't all start with this reader comment in *The Globe and Mail*'s book section in regard to my latest novel—"I picked up *Annex of Evil* last week, and I am glad that this is not regular Canadian Lit fare. Did anyone else feel appalled by the depiction of women in this book? They're either secretaries or half-nude, teen sex toys, flitting around stupidly as the narrator describes their underage bouncing bums at nearly every turn. I found the excessive descriptions of underage female nudity to actually detract from the plot, instead filling the pages with the author's illegal fantasies.

"The writing was often funny, but more often cliché and, to be honest, disgustingly misogynist. I'm not saying that every novel needs a strong woman, but this one really went over the top with its debasement of femininity, along with a completely open objectification and characterization of women as snake-like sex-driven airheads. Perhaps Mr. Benjamin should have cut down the misogyny a notch, and provided a more clear understanding of the 'emotional truth' the book description says it contains. I didn't find any."—because it still makes me wonder just how many little pinpricks against me have come from the exact same hand.

Yet, compared to the grave realism and tortured tome of my all-time darkest hours (new and selected), Susan Malkin's suspected behaviour—cyber stalking and bullying my girlfriends (exes, current, even platonic female friends)—barely stands anywhere near the long list for a greatest hits treatment of my most anxious, terrible and antisocial cruelties suffered. Its uniqueness however, is worthy of a stand-alone, fully charged true-crime story arc, nestled halfway in a book between a story about a mysterious bug bite and one about an artist's nostalgia for Gordon Lightfoot.

Susan has published eight or so books (mostly poetry but some novels too and a book on Paul Bernardo—long before every Toronto writer was writing about him) and is a big deal in the sense that everyone (despite age or genre persuasion) seems to know something about her: how cool she was at a reading they attended or that she is a great teacher. Susan writes about killers with punishing enjambments and is possibly a killer herself, a quality which somehow makes people both fear and admire her from afar.

The electro-attacks on those I love remained a noteworthy mystery for me, and a tight-lipped retinue of friends, to discuss and attempt to solve. Susan Malkin, lead suspect, and her electronic high jinks cosmetically arranged to make me appear depraved to the young and beautiful I mingled with some five years ago, may have been real genuine terror but in all honesty, fell short of her intent. I still got away with dating Sarah, even after Susan (allegedly) tried to paint me as the abject, evil ladies man in a smoking jacket surrounded by pretty heads jutting from the wall in some abject hunting-parlour trophy room.

The psych-outs, threats and alternative universes Susan created while I tried to date someone made it feel as though I was getting away with a major crime.

No one compares in terms of levels of achievement, as it relates to the vindictive arts of anonymity. This unmitigated spy, brilliant super genius, confrontational, irrational, loyalty-testing feminist, vegetarian, journalist, English instructor, celebrated poet overlord Susan Malkin.

❋   ❋   ❋

Over the years, Susan's actions feel as though she's taken a page from Graham Greene's Ida Arnold, the nosy middle-aged woman from *Brighton Rock*, bounding after me at every bar and teahouse, warning doe-eyed stiletto art-scene beauties (who walked like baby goats taking their first steps) of my true nature. That would of course make me, Daniel Benjamin (32), Aquarius, Calgary-raised, amateur novelist, short-story writer,

Van Halen expert, 6'2", 190 lbs., Irish Canadian,) the antagonist, Pinkie Brown.

You might be asking yourself, so what does Susan Malkin do exactly? Acting like a self-appointed boy scout for the arts cultural sex scene in west Toronto, Susan ties her knots and moors in her vintage heels each morning and begins her prowl into the fabric of her well-manicured social proximities. Using saved screenshots of message conversations between herself and another woman in which Susan (the creator) extracts personal information, opinions on other key characters in her virtual-reality psychodrama of invention, Susan then sends those exchanges that may implicate me to, let's say, Sarah, who then confronts me in tears about who this person is, if it's me, if I know them, etc. Sarah begins to form doubts. This was a technique Susan used many times. Sometimes the lion's share of Susan's aggrandizement about my personal life was a simple direct message to a love interest or someone suspected of being my love interest.

To achieve this, Susan of course first has to create a fake profile and begin anonymously probing the women about their relationship with me, calling these friends, exes, etc., names like "silly little sluts" in a cyber-performance, art cruelty piece with hints of Hannibal Lector talking through the walls of his cage until his cell mates chew their tongues off out of fear. She would add little twists such as, "Just seeing if Richard is still fucking young stupid sluts like you . . ."

Watch out Hallmark!

Two things happen when Susan implements this untraceable cyber behaviour: the women question getting involved with me, even friendship-level relationships are put into doubt almost immediately, especially if they are relatively new friendships. Second, a discussion on the validity of this anonymous tipper's claims against me takes place between myself and the person Susan is harassing. What I never comprehend is whom Susan's alter-ego is supposed to be perceived as being? An ex-girlfriend? Scorned lover? Superhero?

For all her white-woman wisdom, *bona fide* education, simultaneously controversial and bestselling-author status, world-weary exhaustion and passion for justice, Susan must have calculated the simplest question coming forth: "Daniel, who is this person?" A question which could inevitably wind up eclipsing the potency of her callous claims about my behaviour.

Susan's electronic shock therapy, (i.e. the loquacious online messages to those I love, care about and trust) is a sadistic feather ruffling, which has extended into spheres I didn't think her capable: trying to hack into my Gmail account, sending me my own unique messages to other people from years earlier: messages that don't exist in any other electronic database but my own.

❋   ❋   ❋

When I first met Susan for drinks after talking to her online, I was trepidatious but mostly curious about becoming friends. I believe the month was October. Susan was then, and still is today, eleven years older than me. We had a couple of drinks at the Cadillac Lounge in Parkdale and went to her house where she insisted I make her Wonder Bread sandwiches with cheese and a side of vegetables and have more to drink. Without explanation, she then ran up to her bedroom where she began calling for me. I walked upstairs (sweating, with trepidation, with anxiety, drunk on panic) and moved towards an open bedroom door. Once inside, I found her lying on her bed under the covers. She said she was dizzy and needed to lie down. She motioned for me to join her. I mumbled something about the food I had to finish preparing and turned around to leave.

Completely terrified and a bit drunk, I ran down the stairs and called my friend who lived around the corner. Only later did I realize doing this would leave a traceable number on Susan's phone. I left a message for my friend indicating I was stopping by immediately and then left the kitchen in a mess and ran the six blocks to temporary sanctuary. Susan wrote the next day apologizing for her state and wanted to make it up to me. We made plans to hang out but a few hours later I cancelled and began dating Sarah a few weeks later in late November. The incident up to me leaving her kitchen in a globby mess would later be transcribed in her award-winning short story collection *The World Is Yours*.

In early 2009 I had been dating Sarah for almost three months when Susan began messaging her for three days straight, letting her know that I was "not a man but a pig" and that I "entertain several women at a time." That week I had no idea who was trying to sabotage my relationship with Sarah as if I was wearing a rainbow-print souvenir T-shirt that read I'M A PIG, DON'T TRUST ME with a pig jerking off in the mud. This non-existent garment was one I'd wear to bed, the tags still on, and those words, sent deep into the heart of my real world with a mystery dagger looped in my brain until I eventually fell asleep.

I, the presumed incubus, thrashed against the throes of Susan's tantrums, her demands, tests of friendship loyalties and the colossal revelations that it was her behind the cruel attacks on my "young sluts," a term she pinned onto any woman she saw me with, interact with online—I still had hope we could sustain a normative plane of existence.

"Don't ever ask Susan if it's her," a playwright warned me. He went on to say, "Look, from what I've gathered over the years, it's best to just pretend you don't know how crazy Susan is and if she's doing something crazy, the last thing you do is question her about it."

So you have this balance right, this split in your life plan: a life you live where you never confront Susan, tell her that you think she's the one behind the anonymous slut tips and defamations of character being left like dead-bird cat gifts on the doorsteps of your caffeinated girlfriends. And then, a life where you imagine you have in fact confronted Susan about this behaviour and of course you are never heard from again. Here were some clues that my associate and I went over behind closed doors, leading me to believe Susan was my secret Santa of love pain and psycho chaos.

1. During the peak of the Sarah fiasco, I was doing a reading with one of Susan's friends. We spoke casually in a group setting before the readings started. My friend told me later that when I went up to read, Susan stood up and with a face of disgust, went out to the back patio for a cigarette. He said she looked angry. **2.** Her use of the words "little sluts" as well is a giveaway. Many friends, both male and female, know her to disapprove of casual sex. She even gave a lecture on it once. **3.** Susan also talked to me at length about how dumb she thinks the girls are in her classes, and suggests that I am in love with these "academic bimbo sex dolls." This is the type of thing we'd discuss as it related to me coming to read to her poetry students as recently as last year.

❋ ❋ ❋

Four years have passed since that first "session" with Susan and the Sarah mind games and a vocational reality rears its ugly butt in my face and so, since August of this year (one marred by Rob Ford, the summer streetcar cop-shooting of eighteen-year-old Sammy Yatim, and the city surpassing Chicago in population) I've been working for American Apparel at their pop-up store at 215 Spadina Avenue, right next to Dark Horse Espresso Bar and the building that houses seventy thousand Canadian media offices.

The intersection of this vocational breakthrough hinges on two unique facts: no one I work with knows I'm a national cultural disaster slash treasure, and no one who knows me as this aforementioned entity outside of American Apparel actually believes I work there. The concept of the store (from what the well-dressed scientists who pay me have said) is to move new and old merchandise (some of which is up to ninety percent off) from others stores all over North America and sell them at our cool two-storey warehouse all the livelong day. During the peak of the Rob Ford scandal (unless this hasn't happened yet, and the ex-mayor is practicing his best Godzilla impersonation and is biding his time in Etobicoke in choreography rehearsals), the LA bosses even had a special Rob Ford shirt made which are now sold out of course.

What is funny however, are the handful of times people from publishing come into the store. It's essentially the same conversation I've had at book launches for the last ten years. I wouldn't trade edging pencil skirts, zipping up corduroy flies or stuffing tightie-whities into plastic sleeves for all the author bios in the world. I feel good about my body and my colour coding. (Yes I wear the clothing; it's part of the job!) I know the release dates for most of the antique Christmas pop music that is played. I know how many $5 T-shirts we have, how many $10 T-shirts we have and how many $8 neon tank tops we have. I know there is a plethora of skirts, dresses, socks and beanies waiting for the right person's body.

At some point however, no matter how covert my age, origin or purpose in a given temporary job might appear to be, my personality always shines or infects a staff like a bad case of nuclear stomach flu.

I tell jokes that the badass cashiers, all dressed up at 9:00 a.m., as if en route to a music award show after work (ten hours later) either enjoy, "Does anyone have any gum, or like, a hamburger?" or result in them telling me to shut up or say things like, "Dude, you are permanently set on random."

I've learned a lot of cool hood slang, like "extra" meaning complicated, or "he's extra" for someone who is, and this is just my take, "extra work" or unnecessarily complicated.

Despite my random jokes I have never been called "extra," since these co-workers seem to like me and I believe the term "extra" is not a good thing.

It's a fun, colourful and vibrant store with high ceilings and a staircase similar to the Emperor's chamber on the posh orbiting killing ball known as the Death Star. I just know it would someday make a great loft for my retirement. But this job is a ruse. In fact, my whole attitude thus far is a bait and switch for a darker existence which pains me to bring up. But I must. But I must also continue this retail-meets-literati charade, so bare with me as I help this customer. [*Muffled sounds of light banter, dead silence and eventual laughter.*]

That was easy. They just wanted to know where the T-shirts were. As I scan the endless sunset of cotton and leather my eyes create the subtle alchemic fusion of two invisible worlds coming together to comfort people's bodies and minds. Clothing and Canadian small-press books. I write the promo copy for this book-marketing panacea at my retail daymare:

How about curling up with *Little Brother* magazine (2-year subscription, $50) in a new pair of leg warmers ($10). With the right shoes, handbag and top, you could have the perfect ensemble by simply adding a striped denim circle skirt ($28) and a copy of Robin Richardson's *Knife Throwing Through Self-Hypnosis* ($18.95) from ECW Press. You'll look like the perfect bastard in a pair of tan classic four-pocket work pants made in heavy and durable cotton canvas, featuring back welt pockets ($28) whilst reading David McGimpsey's classic poetry collection *Asbestos Heights* from Coach House Books ($17.95). Reach for the stars in subdued comfort wearing a cozy plaid cotton twill long-sleeve button-up with pocket ($32) as you read the ever-flashy *Cosmo* by Spencer Gordon also from Coach House Books ($18.95). Or how about two years of *Taddle Creek* delivered to your door ($18). When the first issue arrives, you can answer the door in nothing but your baby rib briefs ($10) comes in all sorts of colours, just like the magazine's covers. The Party Pant (reduced from $82) is perfect for getting your holiday literary party into gear. And before the guests arrive you'll look fabulous in a pair in front of your cat and boyfriend while reading Damian Rogers' *Paper Radio* from ECW Press ($16.95). And if you read your classy literature outside, don't forget to wear a beanie which comes in an array of rainbow colours ($22). And circle scarves, those are on sale, too.

It's honest work, I'm on my feet all day, my biceps and triceps look like those of a senior high school boy for the first time in my life—plus I've lost hundreds of pounds. But like Canadian publishing itself, like a specific book let's say, people simply can't imagine where exactly the store is (geographically, spiritually, etc.) in Toronto.

"It's one block north of Queen on Spadina!" I tell them.

"I can't picture it," they reply, continuing in their lives. After I jaw away and hint towards a few geographic slide shows, YouTube videos, break-dancing mime maneuvers, and institutionalize hyperlinks on their BlackBerrys, some leave my seizure-inducing information session at peace.

✳   ✳   ✳

OK. Back to why I brought you here in the first place. The macabre, sometimes supernatural story of false-bottomed friendship, deception and mind control all coming together in an oozing tale of pain and social injustice impossible to explain in a single sitting. For me, it's just another day in the office, but for you, the sacred reader, it's something more. It's a caveat. You know that old saying you cannot choose your family but you can choose your friends? Well, this little episode wasn't covered in my friendship owner's manual.

I'm still smarting from the ten smart-bomb ransom letters from hell (read: Susan, novelist, poet, age fifty-three, bat-shit insane or as my fiancé says, "stubbornly insane") I received this calendar year as my aging corpse moves from aisle to aisle chasing dust bunnies to appease my twenty-two-year-old boss, Dana Zool. As I trap a ball of dust and plastic bits, I'm reminded of the stress-balancing act I've endured these past several months in the pay-you-never trenches of publishing warfare. As Dana Zool, all five-foot-nothing of her (born during the Quebec referendum, very late twentieth century) glares at the bunnies then to me, saying "I'm watching you," with a dirty, gremlin-in-a-toque-like, gnarly stink eye.

Here in the retail hip-hop you don't shop apocalypse; much how it is in publishing (where the pay stinks), you also meet the most sociopathic, lying jerks you've ever had to endure since you were in the tenth grade and everyone is fucking broke as broke.

Have you ever had the fear of waking up drywalled inside a fake room in the house of Susan, an ex-*Globe and Mail* columnist who keeps getting fired from teaching university kids how to write because she gets in fist fights with other faculty members in the hallways, who toils away fashioning the perfect entomb for any number of unfortunate new friends.

This type of friendship is unique to my species, I believe, and I can tell you about it now as I bend over and pick up another dust bunny while carefully eyeing Dana who is tree-hugging some tall managerial type near the front bank of cash registers like both of them just won a new lawnmower from a radio contest. "I love you!" Dana shouts.

* * *

Susan has a dog named Ted. Ted is her best friend—a terrier that reminded me of that dog from the Son of Sam case, you know the dog that David Berkowitz said told him to kill a bunch of people in New York a few years ago. Even though that dog was a black lab, this dog—Ted—performed the same service for me as it did for Berkowitz. It made me behave in ways I thought I'd never behave. Like buying chicken wire to fix Susan's strange backyard fence for example.

I can still hear the sonic slab of Susan's voice, charging me with another labour, "I need you to fix the fence or else the Dominatrix that lives next door will kill my dog with her Rottweiler," she said, dishing out another commandment of didactic protocol.

On my way out the emergency exit of "Toronto's vibrant literary scene" (Registered Trademark Neilson Chocolate Ball-point Pen Company) towards retail afterlife—which I guess begins by working for $11.25 an hour with teenagers, wearing clothing for people who drink Red Bull for breakfast—I had hoped to do one duet with one writer from Toronto and it was this writer Susan. But the finish line for this three-legged race was a mirage.

We were going to write a poetry collection about a serial killer. Don't forget the blood, I hear Susan adding. Yes, she wanted to put bits of our blood on the pages. There would be no such dream team-up for Susan Malkin and me.

Ours was a trial friendship that could have for all extents and purposes ended up in an actual trial. After a handful of hang-outs with cheese sandwiches and stiff vodka-infused cocktails, discussions about our families, lost loves and creative dreams, all in an attempt to conjure a closeness that I secretly hoped neither of us felt. Strange demands to go to the Dollar Store to buy her fake lawn squares for her living room in the middle of the afternoon were met with texting back, "I'm sorry I'm at a meeting I can't," and Susan screaming at me over texts and emails to the point where I have to run into the nearest washroom to call her.

"What the fuck!? Did you get the grass?"

"Don't yell at me. I'm at work, in a stressful meeting."

"You wrote me," Susan reminded me. "I find you stressful and irritating."

"I just mean right now this second, I'm sorry I annoy you, I have started a new job and am in the Annex."

"Are you Rainman?"

"Probably, I'm working. Uh, I am in the Annex. Sorry if I failed you. I have to concentrate at this job, lest I be destroyed."

Though I can't of course prove this, I chalk all this up to Susan's insane need for me to demonstrate loyalty to her. Like I had to earn the friendship. A friendship I was now equally afraid of leaving and participating in.

Database memories billowing in a metaphoric fire room from the life of a once terribly pathetic, lonely young man. Despite Susan's obvious agenda with terrorism as a background setting for this friendship, I agreed to continue speaking to her on a regular basis.

Levity did exist amongst the harsh tones and battle cries. I called Susan one afternoon to confirm an appointment during a point in time when I didn't own a cellphone and the first thing she said after "Bell Phone" appeared on her caller display was how it reminded her of *Back to the Future*. I smiled as I saw myself in an orange vest, scouring the phonebook in 1955, looking up Doc Brown's phone number. So I told Susan that Ronald Reagan was the president and she laughed. I couldn't really hear anything very well because the café was really loud and the espresso machine was attached to an amplifier, which was then attached to the pay phone—or so it seemed.

And then we'd hang out again, with—at least on my end—an underlying feeling that expectations were being devised, and a large chore chart was becoming legible in the distance.

❋　　❋　　❋

Like a power protein shake we slammed down more additives designed to speedball the getting to know you portion of our benign attempts at civility: long enough phone calls and sandwich and snack planning, poet gossiping and trash talking and who we hated the most.

And you know what? It sounds so dumb to explain it to you now kneeling over here showing phantoms of fashion where the black tights for Halloween are supposed to be, but of course is not. I point towards the racks they've already pawed through, just over there where the brown tights are teeming from the hangers like a mudslide simply because no one wants to dress like dogshit for Halloween. Or ever.

A few months after Susan's book launch, which I dragged as many of my friends to as possible, at which she sat like a regal underworld Queen, she invited me to read poetry and fiction and talk to her class of pup university students about publishing. I was broke and the thought of doing anything as it related to literature for free was not only beneath me but made me want to end it all in one waste of a TTC subway token. The confusion over my payment was self-created: I kept all the money for a while—money my publisher had made selling my own book to students which I delayed sending to its rightful place.

Instead of just acting normal about it and saying something like: I hope you can get the money to the publisher because I trusted you to do it, or I guess I should have not given the money to a student to give to you to pay your publisher and should have just sent a cheque to the publisher because after all, it was my class and my responsibility as a person with a real job unlike you—she began sending emails to the publisher saying she'd call the cops and that I was a criminal.

A few hours after the emails, Susan phoned my cellphone and after twenty rings, my fiancé picked up the phone and Susan was calmly passing on this message: "Tell Richard I'm going to break his legs."

She laughed at Susan and hung up the phone but months later confessed to me she was surprised nothing came of it. "I was sure you'd have a mob hit out on you or some retaliation; she sounded insane."

So the magic of a duet-killer poetry collection with this Frank Sinatra meets Nancy from Sid and Nancy fame ended in a no contest, no fault, it's your fault, it's all your fault, Internet pinching fight draw.

A whole new crop of clean-haired writers are emerging in Toronto's never-ending parade of ISBN numbers with likes, hot links, friend requests and goodreads ratings worn like heavy medals won from prestigious wars. As Susan once described the poetry scene here, "It's a bit like Jonestown."

All I ever really wanted from all this was to write. I knew I'd be poor and have to work at shitty jobs here and there. I knew that I would age and that people born well after the Gulf War/Operation Desert Storm would be my managers and evaluators. I knew I would write about them—sort of, more like write about myself and blur them out in the background; using them as a metaphor for contempt in my own histrionic sad-core pride parade for crowd shots.

Somewhere in the universe a ghastly, low-resolution, pin-thin vapour of my former self exists. He is that journal-writing, paperback-in-the-back-of-his-jeans, anorexic, bowler-wearing, late-nineties-arthouse-pin-up-boy flash you might see while rubbing your eyes as your DVD loads, as you hear the clugging away of a VCR on rewind, as you photocopy something, as you fold bits of paper to make yourself feel important, as you accidentally lick a stamp not realizing for a nanosecond that stamps are now essentially stickers and no longer require human DNA to convey lexical sustenance worldwide. And this glowing clone, this vapour-thin starving bohemian, low-res romantic poet manqué in training, has no idea what is in store for him as he tries to legitimize those infantile pen scrawls he has set his mind on believing in.

"If you were having a great life day, would you really notice if you were having a bad hair day? How long have you been waiting for the novel called 'Jean Coutu'? How will CanLit and Sports Entertainment finally team up to parcel out the national imagination? In this tarot of a short story, this frightening glimpse of what most certainly will be a menagerie of talking heads prop up each forthcoming book by Douglas Coupland, who remains one of the few who continue to practice the debased writing habit. The omission of Margaret Atwood is strange, but the absence of Nathaniel G. Moore himself is shocking. Is this his threat to quit publishing? Au contraire, it reveals that through this cultural skin pricking, this sparkling micro serfdom, he plans to outlast the last literary institution, the last of us."

—Daniel Allen Cox, author
of *Mouthquake*

Also By Douglas Coupland

A t precisely eight o'clock, Clinton Edwards, the provocative, yachtsman-like president of Random House Penguin Canada stands at the lectern and delivers his introductory comments for the evening's affair. The speech goes on to exceed twenty minutes and ends with the promise that the fun is only beginning. The audience cheers, perhaps now elated that there is life after Clinton. "…But that's not why you, our special Random House Penguin Canada readers, are all here today. Some of you already know about the great plans we have in store for Douglas Coupland's upcoming film and the next fifty years of his career. So it's with great pleasure tonight that we take a look back at the prolific half a century of Douglas Coupland! The fifty years of literature, starting of course with *Generation X*, a personal favourite, [audience noise], yes, too true! The fifty years of literature in which he gave us some of his most exciting work including the 2019 Giller Prize-winning, yes, I know I love it too! Yes…thank you. The book, which taps into different themes including forgiveness, raising horses, families dealing with Alzheimer's, dreams and murder, was an international success. It's no wonder Canadian director Sarah Polley, seventy years young bought up the film rights back in 2020 and is spending a lot of time with Doug right now working on the screenplay's final stages. The film, *Goodbye Horses*, will be Polley's final film before she says she'll be going into what her agent calls "semi-retirement." With Canadian senior heartthrobs Rachel McAdams and Ryan Gosling returning together for the first time since 2002's *The Notebook* to portray the present-day leads, we just know a whole new half-generation of *Foot Locker* fans will enjoy the special film-tie-in edition of *Foot Locker*, of course now, for commercial purposes, re-titled *Goodbye Horses*. Sarah is here tonight, so glad you could make it; it's an honour. The material at your seats, which you may take home, are a portal back in time to the original press releases, reviews and jacket promotional copy or as my colleagues call them, hype documents, [holds for laughter] we've culled from our archives and exhausting bowels of preservation. In addition to the materials at your table, we hope you enjoy this thirty-minute multimedia presentation of text, interviews, reviews and more. Please enjoy your meal as you watch the film and join us for cocktails immediately following this presentation. And don't forget your BACK TO THE BACK-LIST tote bag, which is under your cozy chairs! You'll find diamond-encrusted bookmarks, autographed memorabilia and previews of special limited edition aqua-book versions of all fifty Douglas Coupland classics including: *Worst Person Ever, Life After God, Foot Locker, Generation X, Microserfs, Generation A, Player One, All Families Are Psychotic, Girlfriend in a Coma, Back To The Cineplex, Bye-Bye Mon Cowboy, The Gum Thief, Hey Nostradamus!, Shampoo Planet, Eleanor Rigby, Star Wars, 2 ¹/², City of Glass, Miss Wyoming, Zine, Souvenir of Canada, Polaroids from Dead Dreams, God Hates Japan, Kitten Clone: Inside Alcatel-Lucent, Terry*, and so much more!"

※ ※ ※

By 9:15, the gallant host is drunk on the dance floor at the prestigious Silver Fillet banquet hall on Hastings Street in downtown Vancouver and goes into hyperdrive, so to speak. Music warbles and some dance heavily; other corners are pocketed with the who's who of Canadian and international book and film media, including *Entertainment Toronto*'s Ed Broadbent Jr., director Atom Egoyan, *HELLO! Canada*'s editor-in-chief Alanis Morissette, *Zoomer* magazine columnist, screenwriter and author Stacey May Fowles, host of CTV's *Film Wreck* Ray Myers (son of the late Mike Myers), photographer and Tim Hortons' spokesperson Bryan Adams, Indigo Books and Music spokeswoman Shania Twain, CBC Sports Books publisher George Stroumboulopoulos, film director Drake, producer and director Dakota Fanning, Premiere of Quebec and former Canada Council of the Arts vice-president Heather O'Neill, graphic designer Jenna Elfman, MTV Poetry Canada Executive Producer Damian Rogers, children's author Elisha Cuthbert, 2041 CBC Canada Reads judges Todd Mulroney, Shary Boyle, Jen Ackroyd, Jason Bateman, Mark Medley and Emily Keeler, Griffin

Poetry Prize executive producer Ellen Page, *This Magazine* fiction editor Kevin Drew, children's author and Disney voice actor Jonathan Goldstein and *Desperate Housewives of Canada* host and executive producer Paulina Gretzky.

It's the sort of party the Conservative government has condemned for the last thirty or more years citing "unrelatability" and promoting the celebration of the arts which directly alienates and to a degree mocks the hardworking everyday Canadian nine-to-fiver. Clinton Edwards has been stammering now as half the elite crowd of book-worshippers is sliding their tingly feet towards the coat check. Some scatter back for their tote bags which they've left at their assigned seats. Clinton nearly kicks over a stroller full of sleeping children in matching *Generation X* print tees as he yells, "YOU KNOW WHAT I MEAN, RIGHT!!! Oh shit, is he here, oh, right, oh right, no, you know HE IS EVERYWHERE! I love that guy though; and THAT'S WHY WE'RE FUCKIN' HERE!" The sort of behaviour you've imagined might take place after grazing over swank photo-heavy reportages in regional social columns of today's leading newspapers. Of course those photos are always taken before the first glass of merlot is even poured. Hardly the case here as the interns take turns snapping covert Reti-Polis (Retina-Polaroids) to share later. The interns spread like village-invading soldiers, stealthily hidden behind giant, laminated book covers which are temporarily plastered throughout the hall, the invisible belles of the ball, so to speak.

Clinton is now remixing the speech he delivered earlier with impromptu stand-up and a purging of mixed emotions. Fortunately everyone here (save the interns) is equally intoxicated. The speech, (which is peppered with cribbed lines from the speech he'd spewed out earlier on live television to millions of book lovers worldwide) is "like watching someone try to do yoga while hoolahooping." That's how one intern explains it in a whisper to another. So Clinton ends his comment (as the next song gears up) with a big belly-roar and says, "When severed feet in sneakers, complete with sport socks, kept washing up on the shores of British Columbia way back in 2010, Timmy Mulligan's parents had no idea the severed feet belonged to their teenage son. Nor did they know he'd run away from home hours earlier because they took away his Xbox because he had bad grades and they'd found these severed feet, right—oh, wait! Is this a fucking Coupland novel or what? Am I right or am I right?" [holds for room laughter] Clinton falls into his chair before being swooped up by two vice-presidents and carted off into the shadows.

"I'm surprised they didn't ham it up a bit and dead-hand wave for him, you know when you wave someone's hand and they're dead or whatever?"

"I think you mean asleep," an intern says, popping a handful of bean-sized Echinacea pills.

❋   ❋   ❋

The party fizzles out and janitors and publishing interns are left with the dusting remains of merlot burp clouds and cold carrots drowning in tributaries of rich gravy. They wade in the aftermath. This story's crux is based almost entirely on the barbed conversations the interns have as they clean up the massive promotional material with wine glass ring stains and mustard fingerprints. Each gallant table is a gluttony of Douglas-focused group hysteria.

As the interns polish off half-empty bottles of red wine and mingle with the janitorial artists, the interns (Samantha Ironside, twenty-three, short, bubbly, has fierce bangs, tonight she wears Invisible-brand eyeglasses with gold lenses, yellow tights and musical note print twinsets with Avril Lavigne's fall 2039 series prison shoes Kellblock Kool, plays the ukulele, graduate of Ryerson's publishing program and former summer intern at *Nylon, Jettison, The Believer* and *Quill & Quire* and currently works part-time at a big-box book chain in Milton at their Bayer Street location; Jackie Munday, twenty-four, tall, wears power suits and loves hoop earrings, tonight she's wearing a fuchsia-infused power suit with Geisha-styled makeup, thick hoop earrings her mom says would look at home in a bird cage, and Claire Danes' Cinderella-brand slippers, is addicted to fire-skiing, is an aspiring novelist and is ex-intern at *Maclean's*, BookThug, Soft Skull Press, *The Kingston-Whig Standard* and *Zoomer*; Phil Donovan, twenty-five, Bard College graduate with honours, currently moonlighting as an intern at *The Beaver* and bartends four nights a week at Stacey's, if this doesn't work out he plans on medical school to become a prenatal child psychologist) are dull-eyed and speed-sorting and recycling their way to completion, moving at blurred speed as they deconstruct the deluge of Douglas Coupland's literary acumen in glistening promo-material pamphlets strewn about the banquet hall like landfill foreplay.

The interns agree that the boldface blurbs *sound* like the opening pages of the next great Coupland novel (this one attributed to Lorne Michaels, creator of *Saturday Night Live*): "Douglas Coupland is quite possibly the most innovative creative thinker on the planet."

Not to be out-hyped, the publisher has arranged dozens of book synopses for the author's complete works. Take the gold-plated shoe horn with the inscription in tiny font "Winner of the 2019 Giller Prize: *Foot Locker* by Douglas Coupland."

"This novel was good though," says Samantha, going on now, not so hush-hush, a bit loose, having downed the remainder of someone's lipstick-free glass of merlot. She has the urge to dance to the waning music, playing spookily as if the deejay has been murdered.

"In many ways, along with *Life Before God* and *Gen X*, *Foot Locker* is the crown jewel of tonight's celebration," Samantha says.

"You're off the clock now dear," Jackie says with a smirk, swigging back a bit of white.

"I fucking hated Mandy Crosby, the lame seventeen-year-old slacker high school girl. How do THEY describe her again?" Phil says, shuffling for the right glossy piece of paper. "Blah, blah, blah, Mandy . . . who was in the midst of a full 180-degree lifestyle change complete with improved grades, no drugs or alcohol for a year, physically active, part-time job, yearbook committee member as a lead photographer and set to be what her coach referred to somewhat dramatically as 'an equestrian genius,' before she broke her foot and got hooked on laying around playing video games and reading graphic novels. Oh wow! Such a great protagonist. Might as well be a kid in a mayonnaise commercial."

"I thought it was cool how she was limping along a beach in her cast and comes across a severed foot. You can totally see why Sarah Polley likes it so much," Jackie says.

"Yeah, a severed foot is Oscar-bait for sure," says HIM, shaking the glossy page, half crumpling it up. He reads, "Afraid to touch the limb, she takes a photo and posts it to Instagram and then calls the police. Over the course of her rehabilitation, she follows the mysterious 'beach foot' saga with acuity and verve, even combing other beaches in hopes of discovering more clues. When she disappears for seven days her family discovers her secret obsession and fears the worst."

"Booorrr-ing," Samantha snorts. "Severed feet are the new lion's teeth."

Back To the Cineplex (2019)

A science-fictional echo of his classic *Generation X*, Douglas Coupland's latest novel *Back to the Cineplex* imagines a future where fuel is made from garbage and time travel is only a microwave setting away. Also, movie theatres are extinct. Suddenly, seven people wake up in a movie theatre during the opening credits of *Raiders of the Lost Ark*. Is it 1981, or is there something in the drinking water? This time travel to the Cineplex is not a unique voyage; it happens to them seven times a year, usually during the middle of the month.

—Original back-jacket blurb.

"Like all of Coupland's novels, *Back to the Cineplex* is written in immediately engaging, genuinely witty prose. He's the kind of writer who calls a bucket of popcorn in a teenager's lap 'dripping porno suds in a box' and gives one of his characters a hilarious obsession with the show *Family Ties*. Shuttling quickly between the first-person perspectives of his seven Cineplex guests, Coupland quickly sketches a world where everything is just a little slower than it is now. Still the world is recognizably our own, especially once it's made familiar to us via the nerdy, awkward antics of Coupland's characters. Hans survived a 1979 mall shooting at West Edmonton Mall, (but his babysitter didn't) and now he works in a Vancouver call centre for Reebok. In his spare time, he's created a fake basketball-memorabilia website that sells 'ring worn shoelaces.' Jesse creates a hybrid marijuana plantation in his father's decrepit baseball diamond that used to be the family farm; Jenny is obsessed with *Saved By The Bell*; Samantha is obsessed with various trivia games online (creating her dream team The Tens with teammates who are ten years apart in age: John who collects Tonka trucks and Frisbees; Brenda who runs an online cookie store and uses an Easy-Bake Oven for her online podcasts; and Guy and David are twins who are breakout stars hoping to go pro but are ultimately stuck in a Baptist church hockey league.

"Once the moviegoers are released, they discover they can't simply—or at least mentally—return to their old lives. Something about them has changed profoundly, and they need to come together and talk about it.

"The entire second half of the novel is taken up with the stories that these characters tell each other. Some are clearly based on their life experiences; others are parables about storytelling itself and the meaning of human connection. Taken together, these discussions begin to create an organic debate, a system of people obsessed with finding connections, even in isolation, with one another and their secret time-traveling lives.

"When Brenda attempts to bring her children with her one night to 1981 (she sits up with her two daughters in her arms, staring up at the ceiling, explaining to her eldest daughter that they might be going on a special adventure), you can't help but feel like Brenda's desire to share everything in her life demonstrates the compassion she has for the world around her, time-traveler or otherwise.

"Despite the unsettling thought of messing up the universe because of time travel, this is one of the rare science fiction novels that will make you laugh out loud."

—Charles Dentille, the *Montreal Gazette*

✳ ✳ ✳

"'This is a total rip-off of *Back to the Future*," Phil says.

"What's what now?" Jackie asks, pawing at some fluffy cheese.

"You know that movie about the kid who goes back in time and fucks his mom or whatever."

"Oh right," she says, not really listening. "I wonder if that chicken is spicy…"

The Sports Network (2020)

"Forget sports man! This is real life dammit!" At a national sportscasters' conference in Albany, New York, in the year 2059, a hotel room full of redheaded female sportscasters and their male counterparts weather a terrible and unusual tropical storm. It's game seven of the Stanley Cup Final between the Dallas Stars and the New York Islanders. The visiting team could make strange history if they can stave off elimination and win the Stanley Cup for the first time since the last and only time the team won it in 1999. That is of course, if the game actually happens and the world can stop wor-

rying about their beloved sportscasters who have somehow become more important to the strangers they
read the scores to than friends and family.

—Original back-jacket blurb.

"In 2059, transportation has gotten incredibly cheap due to
new-aged fuel alternatives, DIY cars and motorcycles; the court
systems are all backlogged with corporations trying to shut
down grassroots upstarts like Honey Mason who have discovered an incredible way of mimicking bee's greatest export:
honey into a semi-natural fuel.

"All the networks have been advised to dump their guaran-
teed contracts with the big fuel companies because their market research says the economy is headed for a massive change
across the boards, and these small media darling upstarts, all
willing to 'play ball' with larger sports networks wanting to do
business with them, who all qualify for research grants, who
clutch all the environmental brass rings, who are beginning to
become the go-to energy source for the 'smart, young, desirable consumer,' have a huge underground following, are cutting edge and current and, based on extensive research, will
eventually bring in a larger return over time.

"Sports itself has changed drastically. Televised sports (and
this term is expansive based on the continuous tech-boom,
everything from trampolines[1] to portable dishwashers[2] to bike
pumps[3] are used for profit-making dramatics that rely on sports
competition for narrative structure) are shown at school during
recess, in study hall, on buses, trains and on busy city streets, on
university campus lawns with live-event tickets, live-event
streaming and even sweepstakes in which fans can become

colour commentators by a simple click of a button in most major urban centres. Another milestone was the outlawing of any minor league sports sponsorship by individuals or organizations, even at the level of school-aged children. This ruling came from a ten-year study headed by a global collective of economists (anonymously funded and founded) who believe fans of real sport should be siphoning any personal economic excess into professional, not amateur, sports performance.

"As the snowstorm continues to bury the Eastern seaboard, thousands of media centres in North America are in disarray over the fate of their beloved 'sports babes' and 'desk hunks.' Despite lives at stake, despite the NHL's highest rated playoff game in jeopardy, the world tunes in *en masse* and boosts ratings like the networks have never seen. While the NHL brass gets worked into a frenzy trying their best to appease ticket holders, the external, non-sports media scratches its head at the spectacle. While sports itself faces a major change in range and coverage, the mainstay known as sports media continues to be the economic backbone of the Western world. In fact, some studies suggest that sportscasters reduce stress, are drastically loved more than psychiatrists, hairdressers, bartenders, baristas and cousins. While network fat cats are praying their talent make it through the storm unscathed, some executives, knowing the world is watching, hope that the 'storm of the century' lasts just a bit longer."

—*ESPN Review of Books*

1. ESPN's coverage of TBL games (Trampoline Badminton League) drew an average of 461,000 viewers on a summer Saturday evening during regular season play.

2. TSN regularly aired downhill dishwasher racing as part of its Thursday night line-up of Fledgling Sports of the New Millennium series.

3. The Winter Olympics recognized conversion skeet shooting (airsoft guns made from old bike pumps using electrical tape, a pen, bee-bees and some elastic bands) starting in 2041, twenty years after The Sports Network was published.

* * *

"What you up to this long weekend?" Phil asks.

"Fire-skiing with the boyfriend, after that we're relaxing at his parent chalet thing," Jackie says. She's put a few veggies on a napkin and is squirreling away.

"Did you read *The Sports Network*? I did I thought it was all right. It seems hell bent on exploring sexism in the workplace which is admirable but I've seen so many documentaries on it on WeeToob that my mind seems to have already been made up on the subject. It's like ancient history."

Jackie wipes her lips with a tiny napkin, "Not really."

7-Eleven (2021)

The funny and poignant coming of age story of fourteen-year-old stamp collector Dylan Simmons' summer vacation with his mother, Pamela, her over-bearing boyfriend, James, and his daughter, Jane, who has Tourette's. Having a rough time fitting in, the in-troverted Dylan finds an unexpected friend in gregari-ous Trevor, owner and manager of a local water park. Through his funny, clandestine friendship with Trevor, who picks him up every day at 7-Eleven to se-cretly work at the park, Dylan slowly opens up to and begins to finally find his place in the world—all dur-ing a summer he will never forget.

—Original back-jacket blurb.

"…Some sections of dialogue are heartwarming, tender and downright maudlin, especially moments of befriending between Dylan and Trevor who, for the novel's sake, have to make quick work of getting to know one another for the story to move along. When Dylan hides his mom's new boyfriend James' keys, it's a comical back-and-forth that plays with the perils of true adult-male and child roles. What's astounding is the contrast in compatibility between Trevor and Dylan and James and Dylan. You can't help but feel bad for Dylan and wish his mother had better taste in men. Yet it's this conflict, and the additional pressures Jane faces on a daily basis that makes this blended family in progress all the more real. The escapist relief comes in the form of highly planned-out getaways with the siblings running off for a few hours with Trevor, owner of Samson's Family Water Park.

"The two chapters devoted to Dylan sneaking his sister Jane into the park with Trevor's help 'so she can scream all she wants, down The Giraffe, the park's legendary sixteen-storey-high waterslide with a three-second free fall up to forty miles an hour, is heartwarming. Trevor comes off as a summer alternative fun-loving father, even taking the siblings to the park in off-hours so Jane can enjoy the park without any judgment from the public. *7-Eleven* is a post-family novel that plays with our emotions but also offers readers levity when it's needed most, during that tumultuous pre-adult decade, some of us never fully recover from."

—*This Magazine*

Jean Coutu (2022)

It's 2010. Blockbuster Video is no more. Stuck with limited selection, those not streaming or downloading films online are buying Blu-ray and DVDs from gas stations, drugstores and shady convenience shops. Barbara is a twenty-four-year-old teenage-cosmetics counter girl at a Jean Coutu in Old Montreal. On a cold night in February, when fragrance heiress Emily Printemps arrives at the store to promote her latest perfume, Barbara's life is turned upside down when the store is robbed by two out-of-town newbie robbers, posing as fans who wind up panicking and taking the heiress and Barbara hostage.

—Original back-jacket blurb.

"For those who haven't spent any time in Montreal, you might not know the name Jean Coutu as well as others. It's essentially the go-to pharmacy chain in Montreal and sports an iconic, almost taxi-like logo that calls out to you during a minus-seventy blizzard or a desert-island-like heat wave, taunting a cool drink or pack of gum or Band-Aid just up ahead. It also happens to be the setting for the entire first half of Douglas Coupland's latest offering which plays with the heist formula, minus the usual 'one last heist before I go straight' mentality of most Hollywood crime thrillers. Coupland makes it his own of course by forcing complete strangers from different classes, power structures (a fragrance heiress and a common counter clerk? Pa-lease!

"The ubiquitous drugstore is the stage, which is so hyper-coloured and vivacious in its description, you almost get the sense the characters are constantly rubbing their eyes from all the bright lighting and general brightness you'd find in your neighbourhood drugstore. Elements of Arthur Miller's *Death of a Salesman* creep into the narrative oddly enough, despite the fact that there are no elements of family in this novel and all the characters are complete strangers. Several symbols, and even riffs off key lines, from Miller's iconic play make their way into this odorous (in the commercially fragrant sense of the term) novel. Stock boy who gets shot, for example, is named Biff, Willy is the security guard and there is a scene in which the sample clerk/hostage thinks of using a rubber hose to strangle her captors, similar to the hose Willy almost kills himself with in *Death of a Salesman*.

"Though *Jean Coutu* has a great ending, the women hostages appear to simply get derailed in terms of victims turned heroes, or so it seems when the characters tell stories in hopes of connecting them to each other through this crime instead of finding a way out of their particular predicament.

"Arguably, storytelling is what connects them, gets the women inspired and leads to their ability to foil their captors and bring these rural thugs to justice in one quick wave of a perfume sampler strip. In true Coupland fashion he tries to throw us off the scent, so to speak, with the upcoming heist gone wrong, when readers get hints that an unnamed company is perfecting a perfume drug called 'Wafto' that is released into the bloodstream through the skin that makes its wearer tell the truth and also become overtly empathetic."

—*The Toronto Star*

❋   ❋   ❋

"I've been to a Jean Coutu in Montreal. Every time I go I get the willies that I'm going to be held hostage," Samantha says, popping an olive in her mouth.

"But then if you did you could learn about yourself through intense conversations with your prison mates, right?" Phil says, his face holding its wry pose.

"Totally," Samantha says. "Instead of a good hair day, you wind up with a great life day."

Star Wars (2023)

Tommy is a paperboy, with a secret disco farm-boy fetish, living in Calgary. Obsessed with both the arms race headlines, comics, cutting yogurt coupons he finds in the daily newspapers, he busies himself with hobbies (both secret and for all to identify him with) as the popularity of disco begins its final descent into extinction. Tommy is constantly dreaming of far-off places, miles from the comforts of his own familial system. But when he reads about America's new Strategic Defense Initiative, he starts researching as best he can using his older brother Larry's new computer. After he accidentally hacks into a US Defense database and engages in a heated war of hangman with a giant nuclear arms computer, he realizes that his headline daydreaming has become an all-too-real reality.

—Original back-jacket blurb.

"The setup for the novel is simply terrific, and the subtext is intriguing from the start. Flowing beneath the surface of this quirky homeland-thriller is a meditation on the way personal media consumption has become a form of therapy for our characters—and, by default, the whole living planet. What's par-

ticularly smart is the way Coupland makes no distinction between the addictive allure of secrets and the distractions of
global disasters. All are, ultimately, ways of feeding our sense
of purpose with a combination of obsession and curiosity.

"With the whirl of audiotapes churning out the Bee Gees
and Donna Summers, Tommy compiles and investigates all that
his low-watt computer curiosity can manage. What comes
across most authentically is the author's verve for (now) anti-
quated technology. The floppy disks and modems and Beta
tapes (the family was one of those few selected for consumer
purgatory to actually live out the mid-eighties with Beta as their
video entertainment's fate) all act naturally as themselves and
you can't help but go to YouTube to watch old ads for these
relics of convenience. When Tommy tries to outrun RCMP of-
ficers on his BMX (while they gallop on horseback and motorcycles), you can't help but imagine the iconic moments in
Spielberg's 1982 blockbuster *ET*. The Cold War may be over,
but this book hinges on the concept that it was a golden era to
come of age."

—*The Province*

Bye, Bye Mon Cowboy (2024)

In *Bye, Bye Mon Cowboy*, Laura, a famous Montreal
pop chanteuse who peaked in 1991 has settled into middle age with grace, a divorce from a country and western music producer and a bit of infamy that appears to
remain permanent. When Laura finds herself at an *Elle
Magazine* fundraiser co-hosted by Celine Dion's sister,
she meets Tyler, a retired tennis coach, and quickly realizes her real love song has yet to be written. What hap-

pens when two people from the same city who have never met meet and find there is one more spark and chapter left in their otherwise quiet lives?

—Original back-jacket blurb.

"Laura's act in its prime was not without its fair share of controversy, with comparisons to Madonna, threats from the Catholic Church, school board trustees and parent's groups throughout Quebec. One of the most difficult elements Coupland had to face, according to the author himself, was writing flashbacks to Laura making suggestive music videos, her press conferences, using bad English in interviews and of course writing the singing portion of Laura's live acts, all of course done in flashbacks. Present day Laura, who is nearly fifty years old, lives a demure life similar to that of any number of blond bombshell actresses from the mid-twentieth century."

—*The Regina Spectator*

Zine (2025)

In *Zine*, fifteen-year-old Catherine Horton has a dream of selling out her first copy of *Pink Football Fan* zine. The only trouble is her conniving and monstrous stepfather Jack is obsessed with taking pictures of Catherine's boyfriend Charles whenever he comes over for Sunday dinner because of Charles' resemblance to Jesus Christ. Catherine can't stand her stepfather's obsession, but doesn't want to ruin the lives of her family by writing about her father's strange obsessions in her fledgling zine. What will the featured story of her next bound-for-the-consign-

ment-rack issue be? And will she confront her stepfather before her deadline?

—Original back-jacket blurb.

"'My dad is being a jerk for realz,' Catherine writes in her Live-
journal entry for May 5, 2004. She is fully realizing her father's
form of protecting her from boys and their filthy minds is not
by talking to her about the birds and the bees but by spending
every waking second Charles is over pestering the both of them
and asking Charles if he is 'the comeback Christ kid' returning
to the earth to save mankind. Catherine continues the entry, trying to present her side of things without totally losing composure. 'He keeps taking pictures of Chuck whenever he comes
over, just because he has a bit of stubble and long brown hair.
He calls him MY LORD and other shit like that, asks him to tell
grace and makes jokes about lepers. Charles is shy as it is and it's
making it superhard for him to even come over for like, um an
hour or whatever. Last week we tried to watch a movie and my
dad kept coming in saying he was going to sell tickets to meet
OUR LORD AND SAVIOUR. He's taking what he thinks is a
joke like WAY TOO FAR! I can't put any of this in my zine or
else the world would know what a fucking weirdo my dad is but
it's so distracting I don't even know what the FFF I'm gonna
write about for my debut zine!'

"To me this novel reminded me of *The Gum Thief* in terms
of how one character is documenting another character in a
really obsessive way and also allowing them to fully, to a
degree, participate in the tribute. While Catherine's father isn't
writing about Charles' possible lineage to our lord and savior,
he is documenting this likeness storyline through photogra-

phy and verbal confrontations. A strange twist on the complicated world of father-daughter relations to say the least."

—*Broken Pencil*

2 ½ (2026)

In *2½*, Malcolm Brewer is nearly forty-one years
old, living as a freelance carpenter in Montreal. In
between apartments, he house-sits for his award-winning choreographer friend Chin Yam when things get
too crowded at his girlfriend's pad. A decade and a
half of The Magnetic Fields, Arcade Fire, Belle &
Sebastian, Destroyer, Frank Zappa, The Rolling
Stones and The Band has taken its toll on his periph-
eral discourse. Depressed at routine, tight jeans,
chain-smoking and other urban rituals, Malcolm
vows for drastic change.

—Original back-jacket blurb.

"In one of many inner monologues, Malcolm pines for
emancipation, dreaming of a new life that always seems just
out of reach: 'My house is full of used books I never meant to
buy, to read or own. My clothes are the clothes of dead men,
bought from girls in boutiques born during the Gulf War. My
girlfriend has had the same job as a vet receptionist for thirteen
years, hasn't digested a decent meal since preschool and her
stinky cats are plotting my death. When he visits, my asshole
of a cousin's idea of taking me out to lunch is a half a club
sandwich at a lame sports bar while he makes notes for his
humour blog about sports bimbos and jocks who kill people.
I'm trapped in a life that has tattooed itself onto my balls in

my sleep. A tattoo I can't see, and no matter how many times I wash, is still there and fucking annoying as hell. I just know it's there, you know you know… I don't want to kill anyone, including myself but I feel homicidal. My father is a doctor; my mother is a retired teacher. My sister has three children. At Christmas I feel like that monster from *Goonies* who got dropped on his head and fed in chains.'

"If he attends one more yard sale, bagel-infused brunch, concert in a Laundromat, hipster badminton tournament, indie wedding or Mile End zine fair, he's going to go on a murderous rampage (if only in his own repressed fantasies), starting with his pet store manager of a girlfriend Sherri, whose pants get tighter every week, and whose biological clock won't stop its incessant ticking. It doesn't help that she hates almost everything she eats, feels sick after every meal and cries uncontrollably when the weather is cold, which is, let's face it, in Montreal, always.

"With matching shoes, jackets and cigarettes, the fledgling couple is heading into an adorable state of denial that teeters on the cusp of right-on-time double-suicide. Things get more abject when Malcolm's treacherous cousin Nelson Radcliffe – an aspiring lifestyle blogger shows up and won't stop listening to Katy Perry and Lady Gaga and wanting to order in from several local restaurants. Faced with another night at home with his maniac cousin or an impromptu night on the town with people a decade younger than him, the ever-aging Malcolm must sort through a personal inventory of self-deceit and lose the ones he could care less about. When Malcolm winds up in the emergency room with an ear infection, he begins having auditory hallucinations of his father, a dick doctor who lives on the East Coast, giving advice to aging men battling prostate cancer and impotence. Unable to comprehend the meaning behind the paternal podcast, Malcolm's life becomes a chaotic, malnourished telethon without the television. Attempting to clear his mind he packs a lunch and heads to the mountain where he's gobbled up by his retinue of hangers-on and podcast chugging contemporaries. In the midst of an impromptu badminton tournament, he notices (through the grid of his racket) debris falling from an overhead airplane. 'I'm totally falling apart. Badminton is not the fucking answer!'

"Coupland's comic prose is simply terrific, but never in a way that feels wicked or mean. He's completely in love with his characters, and their weird observations and sense of what is important. Regardless of whether you despise the hipster storytelling half of the novel, you'll be amused by its references to classical mythology and vintage advertising slogans. Especially if you've liked Coupland's other novels, you won't want to miss this one."

—Jason McBride, *Maclean's*

※　※　※

"I'm beat, man. It's clean enough. Janitors can do the rest. You wanna split a Skycab?"

"Where you headed?" Jackie asks.

"Lower Tinga Square, near the Dove Towers," Phil responds.

"You live there?"

"No, but I'm staying with my Aunt tonight because my place is being fumigated for bees or some shit."

"I'm taking this bottle of wine," Samantha says, sidling up to Jackie, adding to the pasticcio of surprised burps.

"I have like two in my purse," Jackie snaps back, checking her makeup in an exiguous finger mirror. "So … drop me off at Bates and Commercial? We're sky-cabbing it right?"

"There's a frantic swirling energy from the get-go in
'Jaws' that'll knock you on your ass and keep you deliciously off-balance right up to the moment you wake
up from this hallucination to find you are at the end.
A fierce eroticism simmers below the surface of this
skittering, skittish story, pushing at the surface of
the narrative like a hard on pushing on a pair of zip-
pered jeans. The smallest of moments accumulate, gathering together into festering hairballs of hunger and
longing. I never once continued to read because I
wanted to know what was going to happen next. I read
because I wanted more, losing myself in the moment,
moving forward only to experience the deliciously
erotic moment of feeling lost again and again.

At one point in 'Jaws,' the couple at the centre of
the story are watching grainy black and white horror
films. And that's what 'Jaws' is or at any rate that's
what it seems to devolve into at times, the characters
dropping out of a world of colour that they seem
barely able to keep their heads above the surface of,
sinking into a sometimes hilarious, sometimes painful,
but always beautiful world of black and white that
tumbles boisterously into and out of the maudlin and
the clichéd, but in a way where what begins as a
threat of cliché finds its way always into poetry.

At bottom, Nathaniel infuses his writing and his

characters with a sense of earnestness that seems almost impossible, not because it's so hard to be earnest, but because so few writers seem willing to brave the risks involved in revealing themselves so thoroughly.

If, at any point while reading 'Jaws,' you feel you've got this thing figured out, Nathaniel will set you straight and in the process reveal that you don't really need, or probably even want to understand — you'll find yourself wanting instead to ride along the foamy mystery of Nathaniel's twisted mind made manifest in a narrative that winds crookedly through a forest of prose where you lose the narrative path and wander aimlessly till you stumble again across what might be the remnants of another path, but is in fact probably another exuberant side trip that leads nowhere, except maybe straight into your heart, the way music is able to do, arriving complete and altogether unencumbered by meaning."

—Ken Sparling, author of *Dad Says He Saw You At The Mall*

Jaws

Your Aunt Louise was far off in the distance, flush with the counter tops, the lunch board glaring in its list of options, her infamous dirty light-brown hair was cut into a short fuzzy and sweaty bob, yet bits of it were abstracted in screaming pigtails, not the long "tentacles" you were used to when she'd hit the gym I'd built for her in our garage. You used to call them tentacles but she would laugh and say, "No, pigtails, like this," and then she'd show you on your own head with an elastic or two.

She approached me through a slow wave of egg-salad-scented air. With one hand over my gash I acquired at the plate-glass factory where I'd been working for the better part of two years, I felt like a stud, hazily wondering if I had to go to the counter or if someone would come to me. My fingers reddened as they crushed against the windowpane.

Standing at my side, Louise it seemed hadn't showered in two days. Her navy-blue cords faded in the seat and knees could have walked on their own if called upon, while her flour-pale skin seemed to flicker in the sunlight. She wore an ergot vest, handcrafted in wool, which was outlined in sunlight.

Beneath it she wore a navy-blue T-shirt which jokingly hid her large breasts under the threadbare, wimpy cotton.

She cleared her throat in three slow installments. I looked up from my creased phone bill.

"You need me my pet?"

Without looking away from the window I placed portions of my discarded mail on a table behind me, and tried to shake snow off a tree branch that insinuated itself in through the window. In a bloody daze, I didn't notice her speaking and continued playing with the tree.

"Dude?"

In a strange trance I sat there: one hand playing with the branch, the other squeezing out my ice pack. I continued to ignore her until the adrenaline was too rich. I could smell the moment, mainly her. I was hard at the thought of it all. The corduroy realism, the toxic pain she'd put her hair through perhaps, her buoyant breasts mugging for attention from her wimpy vintage Tshirt, the wild thoughts of turning around and biting her stomach all raced momentarily through my stinging mind.

"Are you gardening?" Louise asked.

I turned from the branch and gazed at her, half-hidden in the wall of light that seemed to capture her. Now locking eyes with her, realizing the earnest delivery in her voice I acted with acuity, smiling in recognition of her efforts. I wasn't nervous but twittered in the sunlight like a cheap bird. It was obscenely bright.

Louise made a series of small fish-mouth movements with her lips. She sniffed the air, looked at the dead ice pack shriveling in my hands, the dribbles of blood pooling on the table. "Have you ever bled a lot?"

"Once in a while."

"Do you want some more ice?" she asked, noticing my impotent pack was now a mere puddle.

"Yes," I said, locked into her eerie green eyes. She fetched my ice and returned.

"What happened to you? You look like you were jumped."

"A large shark attacked me."

"Are there sharks in this city?"

"No. Not in the city, in the ocean. But earlier today I was at this aquatics conference. I fell in the shark tank."

Louise was standing directly in front of me and I moved my gaze from her tiny cotton prison to her nose. All erotic baristas are, at some time or another, obsessed with vintage clothing. No formulaic costume exists to hide their delightful curves and expressive eyelashes.

"Coffee?"

"Yes."

✳   ✳   ✳

When asked about it, Louise spoke about her life in a general way: she was a bright award-winning Theatre, Gym Class and Literature and Anthropology of Books and Brains major, on her way to a Master's and other pedagogical acumen when she got sidetracked into pot and minimum wage. It happens I guess.

Bloody and wounded, pawing at my mail—that's how she discovered me one day; a young woman with the palest face I'd ever seen—translucent even—who served me blueberry tea. I looked up at her again, taking the kind, fresh ice pack from her hands, noticing a waft of body odour accompanying the ice, her scent; from her armpits or something or the frail café vest and weak T-shirt combination, the pink cotton looked like a fake skin, as if spit or wind would dissolve the fibres.

"Have you worked here long?"

"Not especially." Louise said, staring at the ceiling for effect. "You're totally fibbing about the shark aren't you?"

I felt so alive, so alive, intense and present.

"I'm afraid I don't believe the shark anecdote to be in fact at all true," Louise said.

"Why would I make it up?" I said, looking up at her oatmeal-toned face, sparse freckles, and pale ghoulish, alien-green eyes. I felt dizzy. Still, I couldn't look away and she caught me scanning her from neck to crotch, from blouse to mouth, from eyes to nostrils. Yes I know it's your Aunt but I want to capture the mood OK?

"Want a menu?" Louise scanned the café to see if she was being summoned.

"Yeah, a menu would be fine," I said. "Do you eat here?"

"One menu for the liar," she said, walking away. "And yes, I eat here."

Your aunt vanished into the brightness and returned shortly with a cup of fresh coffee.

"So where's your shark now?" Louise asked with a smudgy smirk.

"In his hotel room, resting," I said, laughing, a laugh that invited anything. I eyed the sugar in her hand.

"Yes?"

"Sure," I said, taking a packet.

"Wait, let me get you some brown sugar."

"Yes, brown is great. A great way to enjoy sugar."

"Oh my," she burst into laughter.

"I'll be back in a moment," she said, and the view of her squirming off in the dusty light, the smell of blood in the air rippled over my face or something like a red wave. After my hot drink I left a generous tip and headed home.

One morning on my way back to work for the first time since the glass accident, I thought of Louise naked, what she would look like, how she would behave, what her kitchen looked like what time it was and how long it would be before I could realistically return to the café and ask her out. I contemplated her availability throughout the day, if she was working, walking somewhere, going grocery shopping, pawing through racks of barely-there t-shirts at a second-hand shop.

I catapulted myself into an after-work drinking session at a local bar; Louise just happened to be trickling through its substandard atmosphere with her spaced out, freshly drugged roommates Jen and Christian.

"This is Jen and Christian," Louise said. "How is your shark bite doing?"

"Great." I said. "Want a drink? Some cranberry and gin, it's called the Shark's period in some parts."

"You're fibbing." Louise said. "I'll have a Caesar."

❋   ❋   ❋

The hot summer night filled with celery-salt-rimmed repetition, celery stalks themselves, red wine and an outdoor patio replete with geranium petals and beer bottle labels flapping in the meek wind. An entire cutlery set of lightning filled the sky in jagged mood swings.

By three in the morning, Louise and I were under a pink sheet in her attic bedroom. A streetcar's thoughtless clatter billowed up through the bricks of her house and seeped into our little hot jungle.

Yet, children, despite this spicy union of love and aliens that was presenting itself in Toronto's west end, the natural world was in a state of unrest thousands of miles away. A mid-sized boat with four divers with underwater media equipment was on the prowl to document nighttime underwater behaviour in the Sea of Cortez. They were not alone. On a small dock, one hundred metres from their boat, a local fisherman battled to land a fourteen-foot thresher shark on rod-and-reel. It was nearly midnight.

The four divers had settled near the dim fringes of the boat's lights. The men could see the tiring shark being pulled towards the dock. Below, dozens of squid began flashing iridescently, red-white-red.

"A good chance they're communicating with a colour-coded flashing routine," one of the divers told his crew. "Studies have shown this to be the case most times."

A five-foot squid flung itself onto the shark and tore a grapefruit-sized chunk from its head. Another squid zoomed forth, tentacles clasped before its beak, and snatched a long needlefish, leaving in its wake a trail of blood and scales.

The frenzy built to a swell as the four divers started to retreat to the boat. One squid grabbed someone's left swim fin and pulled down. The diver kicked it away but another grabbed his head. The cactus-like tentacles found his jugulars, the only part of his body not covered with neoprene. He bashed the squid with his dive light, far less bright than the movie lights, and it let go, but it swiped both the light and the gold chain he'd been wearing. Another squid wrapped its tentacles around his face and chest and the diver manically dug his fingers into its clammy body.

The squid slid down and around his waist and pulled him downward in pulsing thrusts. Then it suddenly let go, leaving with his compression metre. The shark floated dead in the water while the other divers, holding their wounds, climbed slowly to the boats. On their backs they bathed in the healing moonlight.

"They'll be back," one of the divers, said. "They're just warming up."

The next morning I awoke to the sound of Louise splashing and chopping, bouncing and smoking, sipping and twitching. She blew her hair from her face, never taking the time to tie it up or anything.

"Earth's temperature is a wonderful forty degrees on the surface!" I said, running downstairs from the bedroom with the delicacy of a dieting bull.

Louise cut through the juicy vegetables and she cut through the juicy fresh fruit. The next morning, she explained something to me. "I had a shark dream last night. We drove out to the beach. The headlights stayed on and we walked out into the water. I was dressed like a Bond girl. You were in a tuxedo. We were drinking martinis."

"Did we go underwater?"

"Yes. And then it came at us, and bit into us. The screen went all red as we kissed."

"That's romantic," I said to Louise.

"Maybe I'm a masochist."

She paused then turned around, making a fish-face before speaking, "I would be the Bond girl who died in the first thirty minutes of the movie. I know it." This epiphany both disturbed and turned me on. She also liked to play original games like Smoking Cold War Jewel Thieves, Re-Murder The Already Dead Clown In Interesting Ways and, her personal favourite, Vibrating Egg Brunch Catastrophe Set in the 1970s.

"I had this other dream too," she said, pivoting slightly on the kitchen tiles. "About a guy, who I assume was you, and you wanted to kill a shark by cutting its belly with a dagger," Louise said, not looking up from her warpath of incisions.

"My own belly?" I said in staccato.

"No Ben," Louise said. "I said its belly, the belly of the –"

"Right. Sorry, I misspoke."

"He, or you rather, had a bunch of people holding the shark upside down by the tail from the edge of a boat."

"The shark would be dead then. Tummy tuck or not."

※　※　※

From time to time, Louise would start acting like she was in a dystopian battle with reality: eyes drained of life, face growing pale. "I must leave now. I am afraid I do not feel safe," she said in a slow dry voice. She ran into the bathroom and shut the door behind her. This was how she played. This was her monster game, afraid of being bitten by creatures. The water poured. The bath was her coffin—crazy.

Often Louise would cry uncontrollably, turn her back to me

while sitting on the edge of the bed talking to herself: "Yes . . . Yes . . . All right, I will."

"Who are you talking to?" I would ask, sometimes through a closed door.

"Ghosts." Louise would say. "I'm saying alien prayers to my friends. They visit me."

It could be argued that the Louise algorithm of love was, in fact, a dirty fluke: we were from different science experiments all together—different kits, different department stores. She was getting under my skin in a good way. The kind of way restriction can be good for you; the kind of way being slow is healthy.

The next night, over a large salad-based feast, we watched two grainy black-and-white horror movies that had castles and monsters throwing children into rivers, strange lightning bolts that cut open the night and grave robbing maniacs with twitchy eyes carrying bags of brains and scraping shovels as they limped home.

In bed we both read a newspaper article with the same sad, silent reaction. On page A17, a gruesome trend was revealed: "For the second weekend in a row, several swans were found on Toronto Island, apparently choked out, their necks broken. No leads or witnesses to what local residents are calling 'a sick and disturbing act of cruelty.'"

Louise turned off her lamp and lit a small candle. She then slid her pale arms under the pink sheets and exhaled and turned her face towards me. My eyes were closed. I felt a breeze trickle across my forehead. From the darkness, Louise reached out in voice and touch, sharply interjecting to her new companion, "You sound like two people breathing."

I was startled; the bedroom's energy and all its invisible teeth were vibrant, grazing us with shadows and tickles. The room now seemed larger and I dreamed of placing a bag over my head to mellow out in and to pretend die. I was nervous.

"Ben stop it! I hear one breath in addition to yours, all coming from your mouth," she hissed and my heart thumped, interrupted by the familiar bouquet of Louise's voice.

I could hear her head turning across the pillow's surface. I held my breath, still as death. "Ben…"

"Ben," Louise repeated, squeezing my arm. She lifted my hand from the side of my resting body and put my fingers in her mouth and startled sucking hard. She then bit down. I had taken the dark for granted. She released the digit from her mouth and said softly, "Just calm down." I was exhausted.

Every inch of her bedroom pulsed in pink. In the morning we'd be consumed by a soft tidal wave of pink heat, a pink phoenix flapping and gushing animated rays that softly enveloped our rising corpses.

"Your room is insane, so pink and crazy. Like I'm inside a giant vagina."

I tried not to breathe. Louise grabbed my face. "Just relax, quit your Damnation Street routine. I can feel your energy, it's so intense."

Sometimes kids, when I was with your Aunt Louise, it felt as though the entire world coursed through my circulatory system, that I was simultaneously processing entire buildings, transit angst and fiberglass shipments inside my bloodstream.

She was restless and kicked at the sheets. "Why did you use so much?" Louise asked.

I had put baby powder over our legs, a trick that I heard divers used to get their wet suits on. I had used more than a normal person would have used.

"I loved that cute note you left on my dresser this morning: about your dream and you putting my head under the water, at the pool, me trying to get up the ladder and you pushing my head back under water."

"I'm glad." I said. "I didn't think you got it."

"Oh I did. I masturbated three times this morning thinking about you trying to drown me."

It was so hot kids, I swear, I never felt so drugged out. I looked out the window into the wild funk of night and saw the trickling beginnings of soft rain. I played with the tiny radio beside the bed. "I want to check the reports, we might be in trouble Louise," I said, staring into her bottle-green eyes.

"It's worse than I thought Louise, worse than this heat, but accompanying the rain tonight is a ghoulish pack of wild Humboldt squid, flying in a V pattern, straight from Lake Ontario."

"What are?" Louise asked, noticing my stoic mood.

"Something is circling the house, in the rain, I can hear the wet fluttering. Can't you?" I said. "I saw it just sweep past the window, heading upwards."

"What is it?" Louise asked, now sitting up in the bed. "Is it a manta ray or jellyfish?"

"Maybe. Maybe a jellyfish." I said, patting the top of her head.

I held her still. This could go on for hours, I thought.

"I'm scared," Louise said. "What will we do?"

I reached under the bed, pulled something out in the darkness, and then straddled her. It was a life preserver.

"Lift your arms." I put the life jacket over her upper torso, fastened, squeezed.

The rain was senseless. I could hear no cars. The rain was

harsh and her windows were open. I saw the tiny pulse in her jugular had stopped but only because I was on her neck, swallowing her little treble. I sucked, released. I tampered with her neck and daubed at it. Louise took off the life jacket and ran to the bathroom. I chased after her.

So what was outside for real? you might be asking. This impromptu night apparition was like dark microscopic orgasm samples, malevolent nightmares that dreamed of teething on your Aunt Louise and I, an otherwise sweet couple.

"Are you ready?" Louise asked. "Are you ready to save me, and be my warrior?"

I tightened the life jacket. "Why do you keep putting this on me?" Louise asked.

I looked at the open window, then back at Louise's green eyes. She squirmed in the life jacket. "Just a minute. Be very quiet."

❋   ❋   ❋

That year the rain had been biblical and thorough. I praised her for cooperating, noticing how her breasts were garrisoned in the floatation device, crushed together, and how the lightning illuminated her pale face, revealing silver and gold veins along her temples and flashes of red and purple blood droplets in her green-lake eyes. It was all very beautiful and dirty.

The lightning continued its hallmark; the rain was sleek and consistent, cresting the night sky with yellows and hot, electric whites. "I just checked with a friend of mine who works with this alternative coast guard outfit, and he says that about an hour ago, he spotted a large, aggressive group of predatory squid just skimming along the lake's surface, about three hundred miles south of the city."

"What!"

"These rebel squid are found in the waters of the Humboldt Current in the Eastern Pacific Ocean. They are attracted to getting involved in dangerous nautical missions. Scientists believe they are highly communicative with one another while they 'fly in the wet' as they call it."

"Fly in the wet?"

"It's good you're not wearing anything but this vest," I said, and breathed into her neck. "Close your eyes. Just relax. You'll be free soon."

The lightning. The eyes. The life jacket. The swelling summer breasts of Aunt Louise …

"They're coming for us!" I shouted, pacing by the window. The rain squirted in. The pink curtains whimpered wet.

"Before you say who, I'll tell you: The Humboldt Squid (*Dosidicus gigas*), also known as Jumbo Squid, Jumbo Flying Squid, or Diablo Rojo (Red Devil)."

"Why are they after us? Louise asked.

"These wimpy pink curtains, they're no protection for us."

I pushed her dresser so it would block the window. All I could smell was the stale tea, cold rain, tartar sauce and the perfume of electricity that seemed to charge through the night. I glanced at the damp pink walls, and listened to the thunder orchestrating the rain and encouraging droplets inside her bedroom. The floor was trickling wet. Our bodies engaged in sweat. Rain was everywhere in little drizzly bits. Bits of it along the wooden floor under the window.

"This is what I was afraid of Louise, you see, I know we joke about sharks and stuff in our sleep, but you see that weather out there, it's a lubricant for a menace so dangerous I tremble at just the explanation."

The rain and lightning bolted into our lives, through her window. A giant gust of concern washed over Louise's horrified face. Her eyes the size of plates, tiny nostrils stretched as far as they could, as if to scream better with a whimper of effort.

"I think it's best that we lay as still as possible."

I tied her legs to the bed. The lightning. Her whimpering. I took out a small walkie-talkie. "Hold on Louise, I have to listen, I think there's an update."

"Ben, I'm scared."

"The first Humboldt Squid is well ahead of the formation."

I touched her bound legs. "I'm so scared," she said in whisper. A crack of thunder followed.

"You wouldn't believe the formation—a violent constellation—each one up to six feet, weighing as much as one hundred pounds."

I looked out her window with a set of binoculars. "The first Humboldt Squid is well ahead of the formation."

"Oh no. What will we do?"

The monsters moved through the rain in vitriolic thrusts; their beaks jutted out like tight spikes of polluted industry in an evil-beaked choir of poison-spirited nature.

"What's going to happen, Ben?" Louise asked.

"These Humboldt are reckless. I didn't want to have to tell you about them because I was convinced they weren't coming. But this rain is just too tempting for them you see. I thought it was just in the States, I didn't think it would get so hot and tempting for them up here. When they get here, they're going to kill us. They'll use these sharp, barbed suckers to stab our flesh, like a fork right, they'll break right through the window."

"Oh no. Is it true?"

"Yes, I'm afraid. They use the rain to push themselves further, towards us. Once they smell hot flesh they'll send for more of their species; if the rain keeps up, the whole sky could be filled with them, hundreds of them, really."

"Yes," Louise said. "I understand. I am prepared. I'm glad you are with me."

"They bring the flesh to their mouths where a malicious, shot-put ball-sized beak tears the meat clump to pieces."

"I hate them."

I wiped the hot tears from Louise's eyes. I told her with delicacy how the sea-to-air beasts could tear through the weak umbrellas of night, the sky itself would become part of our blood course, how these beasts pushed themselves through the hot orgy of rain; they sharpen their beaks along the telephone wires, like they're daring themselves to colour outside the line, to do whatever they want to the world they are engaging with. There have been reports of thousands of squid bodies suiciding on beaches in Mexico, that it is impossible to determine a pattern.

"Fuck."

"We are so fucked."

I checked on Louise's straps. "You seem secure."

"Are you sacrificing me?"

"They'll have to get through me first," I said, turning on the radio, the station, half in, half out, affected by the storm.

"It's so loud."

"It'll work to our advantage; the radio signal might throw them off, you know, their flight pattern."

In addition to the sound of thunder, the room was now full of swathes of headlights from the street. Louise began to scream.

"No!" I shouted, close to her nose, "Don't make a sound."

I covered her mouth with my hand. "Not a peep."

The rain continued to tease through the hot night. I lay beside her, stroking her hair and feeding her from a wet face cloth. Soon we slept and it seemed like we had been spared.

❋   ❋   ❋

On Cherry Beach, the burnt cologne of strong wood and coal was fragrant on your Aunt Louise's lips and tongue and under her nails. Of course by now children, as you may have always suspected, your Aunt Louise was anything but—she was my girlfriend before your mother and I met, and then after your mother and I fell apart one terrible Christmas eve so long ago.

She had these hippie friends, you see, and the party just unfolded into a communal banquet with food strewn across various blankets right there on the beach. The evening's eerie synergy was raw and full.

We stayed for hours wedging our sandy butts beside the big brimming fire and cauldron that shepherded the lobsters to their death and lured the swans from the sleep of the lake. The remote city skyline vanished and we were all mesmerized by the flames.

"And that swan just showed up out of nowhere."

"It was magical."

The impromptu lakeside picnic of lobster and shrimp and

more was a delicious memory that hummed with us the whole way home.

"Did you see the water? You know what is out there?"

"No. Don't scare me."

Back at home, Louise slipped into the bathtub and began to moan softly. When the moaning turned into screaming I ran in, bursting the bathroom door open heroically. The lights were off. Louise was in a hot bath and began to curl her toenails around a rubber toy shark, its mouth molded open forever. She went underwater then surfaced, exhaling and spewing cranberry juice down her chin, between her breasts and down her stomach.

"It bit me, help me!"

"I thought you were really hurt. Don't scare me like that!"

"Kiss me, Benjamin," Louise said, and grabbed the glass of juice with a laugh. The bath had turned red. She lunged forward at me, arms flailing. She screamed and started spewing the juice along the wall of tiles. We kissed, her toes scratched at the walls. She slapped my face.

"I'm cold," she said, violently gulping the rest of her juice. Nestled in my difficult chest hair was the alarming scent of lobster brine and campfire: to the both of us, a reminder of the night's playful mystery. She ran to the bed, swallowed by a blanket, head cradled in the thick pillow. I watched her tiny feet dangle. We quarreled and made up erotically. After a tearful argument that went on for what seemed like days, I sent Tiger lilies to her art house attic asylum and Louise later told me she bled on them, ceremoniously, with her period. She kicked me out and then, two minutes later, waved me back from her front porch. We evaporated by Labour Day.

Children, after that summer we went our separate ways until
the following spring, when Louise managed to lure me into visiting her in Thailand. She met some hotshot scientist and I guess
wanted to rub it in my face. I didn't know the exact nature of
their relationship prior to my arrival you should know.

In the plane I drank ice water and munched on a small bag
of Bangkok almonds. The rain was slick as three baggage han-
dlers in black rain slickers, resembling beetles, moved with
agitation along the wet tarmac as they loaded up a real feast
for the airplane's ample gut. The sky filled with heavy jellyfish
silver clouds and lightning tore up the tarmac.

After getting off the plane I took a wooden taxi and found
the river-side chalet Louise described in infinite detail with its
indoor fire pit, four sunrooms, a sauna, large event-friendly
kitchen suitable for wine and fruit stand-around-chatting gath-
erings overlooking a sloping hill that led to the giant river and
the overwhelming scent of pine and daffodils. Your Aunt Louise
was prancing all around in a swimsuit cutting up fruit and vegetable matter as usual, and there was a rather large scientist
dude on the balcony testing lasers.

"Oh, Ben, it's so refreshing to get away from petty city life
crapola, even just for a weekend. Would you look at the size of
these avocados!"

"Yeah," I said, not looking at her but out on the balcony
where the activities were beyond the cutting board norm.

"What are you looking at?" Louise asked, noticing my odd
positioning and squinting face.

"The scientist."

"Oh, Sam is just testing some equipment or something outside."

I moved around aimlessly, not sure where to stand.

"You know what is most impressive is they are keeping the finds, for the most part anyway," Louise explained. "Sam is getting into breeding fields, saving the species, so to speak, but he also interacts with them in their places of discovery. Sure, they've had to gate some parts of the river, to a degree, but it's far more progressive than the prehistoric measures of years gone by when biologists were more ah—"

"Vampires of the sea?" I said.

Louise described her previous weekend in gorgeous detail. She was sweating away hash-stoned, vintage bikini-clad, squatting over a long banquet table at some art gallery drug party giving birth to a school of seahorses. One, two, three, four and five—PLOPPED out while people did lines of cocaine and laughed and screamed along.

"It turned into a big drug orgy for a while," Louise said, as she mimicked her motherhood process. I shivered as I visualized her clenched thigh muscles flexing and releasing, her hands on her knees as each new born seahorse fell into an awaiting aquarium to a smattering of oozy, topless applause.

Children, I know now, living the way I do in a modest derelict of a condo, a fancy pre-coffin if you will, with most of my memories in storage, personal stories such as these are all I have. Perhaps your memories of Louise and I and the times we shared are vague or repressed. I wish I could have offered you a better family structure, a better history. But I'm glad I could at least share myself with you and watch you grow at an early age when I was the happiest.

It could be something as simple as a night of old cassettes and Louise standing over the stove, neck clams boiled to death, her overalls balled in a corner, hips moving side to side as she stirred the pot. Or the four of us watching a movie and Louise adding cumin to the popcorn, then lemon juice and always experimenting with alternative snacks like roasted pumpkin seeds on Greek yogurt fruit salad, or those homemade Cheetos she once tried to make because you both loved them so much.

When the sun rises or it rains hard, the sensation of being in her midst is as raw and real as I could imagine. OK, so back to Thailand:

"The wind is terrific today Louise," Sam the scientist said, now noticing me. Sam put on a beige vest, which had several pockets, all loaded with wizardry and electronic triumphs.

I was looking at a photo of a giant fish when Sam touched my shoulder, offering his hand to shake. "It would kill your back to pull that son of a bitch out of the water." Sam said. "I trust your flight was enjoyable."

"Yes."

"Last month," Sam said, staring at the photo in my hand, "a team of fishermen struggled for more than an hour to haul one onto their boat. Just a mile from here."

"It fed the village for days," Louise said, bringing Sam a cup of tea.

"I've fed on my city for years," I said.

"Mekong giant catfish, or *Pangasianodon Gigas*," Louise said. "I'm learning so much from Sam."

As Louise moved erratically through the kitchen, her brutal green eyes bore past my balmy skull; down towards the frothing river, so dark green and thick and raging. "Sam wants to see if the fish he tagged has returned, or possibly spawned, or what was the other—"

"I'm interested in measuring it as well. If it's in fact the one I tagged, it'd be almost two months since I last measured it," Sam the scientist said masterfully.

A large aquarium tank roughly fifteen feet in length and three feet high sat in an otherwise empty living room.

"More children?"

"No, that's Sam's. It's for his finds," she said, taking a seat on the couch. "He wants to show you the spot where they last reported seeing—"

"The monster catfish?"

We came up to the jacked-up river after a terrifyingly steep hill and Louise motioned to me and sunk into the water with a rapid, impulsive stab. The river was freezing, giving off a gust of frigid angst.

"This is where I saw them last, weeks ago," Sam said. "You never know what is in this river—a school of bass could be cruising by, or tuna, salmon … even piranha."

From the shore, we all sorted through the pack: blankets, food, chains and electronic equipment I had no clue how to use. Sam waded out, a rope attached to a rock on the shore.

I remained on land (a small beach with just enough shade was comforting) watching both Sam the scientist waist-deep in the chop and Louise splashing about. "For God's sake Louise, you'll disturb the expedition!" he shouted.

Louise looked at me with her heavy-lidded eyes as the sun ate up her face. "Relax Sam, I'll be good," Louise snapped back coyly, spouting water playfully from her wet mouth.

I sat there for quite a while watching the both of them go

about their different business, pulling at dry weeds and rocks and sticks I found on the beach without looking down, my hands never stopping for any reason.

She nuzzled the water with the crook of her neck and Sam held an electronic device over the water. Louise swam into the current with strong strokes, turned around to face us and began to tread. Sam faced the setting sun. I watched from the shore, poking around in Sam's gear. "I may need your help in a moment," Sam said, watching me do nothing on the shore.

Louise moved through the afternoon stream; she sprouted *mako*-style fangs with rows of horrific razor-sharp terror teeth, catfish whiskers, and eight elongated tentacles emerged from her ribcage and hips as she dropped deeper into the river. She was thirty feet away from Sam when she began swimming rapidly towards the shore, lured perhaps by his scent, his familiar appearance underwater up to his hips, wading out patiently, careful not to extend the splash sound, which disturbed more than just the natural habitat.

❋   ❋   ❋

Without warning, a horror consumed the late afternoon: Louise bit into Sam's ankles, snapping the veins I believe because he said he was bleeding "from my ankles, I can't feel my feet anymore!" and that Louise was biting him hard all over. Like an electrician goes at a vulnerable cable, she was chewing and wriggling Sam's arteries and wiring and not letting go. I watched as Sam sank underwater. Silence took over the world around me.

Ripping flesh from the bone, and the terrible hissing noise

was too much to handle all at once so I hid my face in the sand. What was left of Sam's throat and mouth let out a halftone scream that deflated into a bubbling whimper.

Louise's serrated, triangular teeth were drenched in blood and teetered on the water's edge until she disappeared below the surface for a moment. My foot touched the water. I looked intently at the river's disturbed texture. Louise swimming at full speed towards me.

Louise broke through the water, mouth full of fresh meat, she stretched herself wide, bits of red and blue wiring dripping red with blood in a frenzy of colour and chaos from her jaw. Blood coloured the cool water all around her. A whirling sound from tentacle and gill activity came out in a series of thrashing blasts. In her classic orange bikini, now softly stained with a rinse of red blood, her tight back muscles flinched wet; she looked prehistoric.

Shaking Sam's severed head from side to side, she tossed it onto the shore. I moved quickly, not thinking, throwing wrenches and batteries at her, hitting her in the chest with a flashlight until things made sense.

Above us, the now overcast sky was mad with rain, and the sound of jumbo flying squid sharpening their razor beaks against one another filled the air with a calculated cruelty.

I dodged Louise, who leapt at me, landing on the small beach. With both hands on her wriggling rear, I forced her into a sleeping bag we had dragged down with the other equipment.

Overhead, the squadron of jumbo flying squid circled the river, eyeing bits of blood and cartilage that floated like soupy noodles.

I stuffed her deep and wet into the bag. I tried as best I could to zip it up and with long and graceful strides, ran with her up the path from the beach to the chalet.

Once inside, I emptied the sleeping bag into the large tank. She tore around inside like a sick Houdini trick and I just stood there, watching her banging her head over and over again against the tank glass, her rather delicate gills flipping angrily for more oxygen.

I stood in front of the tank aghast: Louise wriggled and contorted in the tank, her teeth morphing from sporadic, uneven cave girl sweet to predator and razor layered, jagged as alien rock. She began to hiss bubbles rapidly, her nostrils snarling and lighting up the surroundings with her now eerie incandescent yellow eyes. From her nostrils ribbons of blood began to float.

❋　❋　❋

As I rifled through Sam's paperwork looking for emergency contacts, agencies, marine experts, your Aunt Louise bit at the glass. I began a crude list, continually throwing an eye over at the tank. I found this address, which I can't recall verbatim, but it was in Thailand, a National Park Department near the Andaman Sea, some branch of the World Wildlife Fund in Greater Mekong, and I began a draft of a fax to those guys and to Mr. Chalermsak Wanichsombat, Director General of the National Park, Wildlife and Plant Conservation Department.

I filled out the basics: Age: 28; Sex: female; Name: Louise Connor; Species type: catfish, manta ray, octopus, oceanic white tip shark, *Carcharhinus longimanus*; Injuries: emotional, exhaustion, bruised ~~knee~~ ribcage (left), sty in left eye, gash on right cheek.

※　※　※

I didn't hear from Louise for several years. An audio cassette came in the mail to me, dated shortly after I last saw Louise in Thailand. I've enclosed the cassette for you to listen to at your leisure, giving you a sense of the pressure I felt from her to leave your mother, or, how I liken it at least, to solidify the union of love your Aunt Louise and I were destined to play out.

PLAY> "I know you know where I am, Benny. You pretend friend to animals. I know that you can find me and set me free—in more ways that you think. You are the one feeding me synthetic pellets and feeding me both food and lies. Ben, can you hear me? Your skin is cartoon blue bubbles, and with underwater Speedo kisses, your dick hard veined so strong, my legs held open by your hands until I'm opened wider. I try to wiggle free rubbing my pussy shimmering with pink scales against that mound. You may kiss my soft cream tits and I will weep cow tears over your spirit and heal you. As long as I breathe, I will love you and watch over you. Your pain and suffering is mine as well and all suffering eventually leads to deeper love and stronger security. You can ignore me if you like and pretend I am nothing. But I do crave you. But at home, our home, if we had one, Ben, I can be very sweet. I love to bake berry pies topped with cream out of our love. I will smile submissively in a gossamer nightie in front of the fire. I am very good with crafts and sew pillows. Oh, Ben, please, it hurts so much. My heart's a wrangled, tangled mess; it toughens as it cooks. I think you have this de-personalized awareness outside of your own shell. I want a mystical dimension, a love so strong it annihilates me almost physically, puts me into a trance. This is basically the whole story. If you know this about me, you know everything. Also, don't think that I need someone to say, "Wow, thank you for making me think. You're really good for me." Because what I really want is for you to fucking wake yourself up and give some real communication or go and find the simple infantile life where your wife is your mother and you can live in neutered domesticity and self-denial while internally you are self-absorbed in your own fantasies, which you never shared. I can forgive the ego, baby, if it's incorporated into the whole you, not fragmented and denied. You know, I am the ocean, the mother of mothers. I can allow anything, complex and full to flow whole into me. I give myself to everything, even if that means I am also vulnerable to unconscious unreceptivity. I love you. I love you. I love you. Please tell me about sand dunes joining our skins in whirling particles, sliding down long spiky grass into the jelly sea. Tell me about abusing my secretary petulant mouth, smudged with birthday cake cream. I'm so hungry! Tell me about orbiting my donut centre with your Apollo 11 trinity rocket blast like a rock 'n' roll diner devours the moon in cheeseburgers and Johnny's Catholic school date sucks strawberry swirls to Dean Martin. Tell me our next date, so I can write it in my bad-girl panties, making little stains, excitedly thinking of you. Tell me anything mundane or temporary, about what you're doing and thinking. I love you. Don't doubt it ever. Even if I had to watch my whole family have their mouths bit by sharks as they cradled them upside down and tried to kiss them for some home video campiness on a nightmare vacation without you, I would, just to know you would comfort me in the end. If I were a broken deer on a country road, would you eat me?" STOP >

Louise came back to me when you were still very young. One Christmas Eve, I scooped you up, my beautiful children, and took you home from daycare where your Aunt Louise was waiting in a magician's box, wrapped in silver decorative tissue paper. I still have no idea how she wrapped herself up for us, but that's your Aunt Louise for you. You both opened up the giant present and she gave you each a big hug and kiss and promised you both pancakes for breakfast for an eternity. Your mother had left earlier that morning saying she couldn't continue in this charade of a marriage.

Later in life, probably because I felt so strongly about your Aunt Louise, I realized and accepted the fact that your mother didn't really love me, and that I never fought for her. But to be fair, she never once called us, followed up on your schooling, or haircuts, or sense of self. Aunt Louise did, and she should be given fair credit for the way you turned out.

❋   ❋   ❋

All I can leave my children is, perhaps, something that, quite honestly, they don't even need or more than likely won't even want. I'll been sitting here now until time permits, sitting here recording my life story on some T-90 audiotapes (1 BASF brand cassette and 1 TDK, respectively). Just a few more spools of thin metallic tape remain, so I will end with this: To hold my children and to see your eyes and blind them from our civic fate; that would be something now wouldn't it? To climb once again proudly from this negated after-earth program and save the day. Salvage a remainder of hope and prestige. To honour the concept of family for my strange murderous father and the grandparents that raised me. To even let them know I care about you and have warm embers as memories for you both, as well. To cook a casserole one more time. To provide bounty of both the superficial and the emotional—to be that person, for you both. For my people and our grandness. I hope for a grandness of human reconnection even if it's macaroni and cheese and a coat hanger and a mobile made of dental floss and chicken bones. There is hope in the simplest dreams: when Jesus sang his song, when he was chased down, mouse trapped and bounced back. When Hercules bit into the woman's breast by mistake and created the Milky Way, he made those stars for us to see. I want to see those stars again. I want to hold the hands of my children, while they are still attached to their arms, light a firecracker and watch our skeleton shadows skip through the sprinkler of wild powder as it spooks through the night air, as our running laughter syncs up for one final belly roar; be it Victoria Day, Christmas, Thanksgiving, Halloween or Remembrance Day.

So children, the yawning blankness of my own perspective sickens me, and I'm tired of pining away and this dejected jealous wanton torture seems to have no end. I feel robbed of the greatest thing on earth: never seeing you both again, ever. I endure this obligatory regret. I will look for my stupid place in the Paranoia Ohio Home for the Elderly and Neglected. Good night my darlings.

"'The Amazing Spiderman' is a late 90s anti romp. Moore gives us Peter, eighteen, and Mulysa, her gothic panties, Panda Express, overdue VHS tapes for pages. Dark humour and wet lust Moore takes us from the height of human feeling with a flashbulb love story and cold-cocks us with a festering Floridian bug bite and the Ontario cold. 'The Amazing Spiderman' is a story about you, walking alone, looking back for those glimpses of white hot life, and looking for an after- hours clinic to treat the unpreventable, 'the night is a boy with arm in self-sling' after all."

—Evie Christie, author of *The Bourgeois Empire*

The Amazing Spiderman

I t never occurred to high school senior Peter Parks that one day, 1,572.71 kilometres away he would be so greedy for Mulysa. That his telescopic pupil and his sentimental lens would never capture her in real time ever again. His summer holiday was now over and the cold weather moved in with a sadness visible from tree line to sidewalk. This tornado feeling in his stomach was only exacerbated by the gray wash outside—though snow had been forecasted for later in the afternoon—it was still one bleak November morning. Mulysa's likeness would wash away like a name in the sand, fashioned with a branch's finger, forever.

Moving from the couch to the bathroom, Peter Parks looks at his arm in the mirror. Three o'clock, he thinks. If I last that long. He paws at the newsprint with his ear to phone.

"So he is seeing patients today? Good. Until four?"

The newsprint makes a sinking sound as he lays it back on the classifieds. The clinic usually has a forty-minute wait upon arrival regardless of when your appointment...

The sound of everything disturbs him immensely: the sliding of his skin on his mom's rubbery couch, the crinkling of newsprint, the shuffling of feet across hallway runners, taps being turned on and off are all so very loud and clamour against his ears. He becomes still and now hears a buzzing. His eyes graze the travel section. In a bubble graphic are prices for trips. The pain from his tropical bite forces him to trace its source. "It's for Peter Parks. P-A-R-K S. Like the place you go on a swing, yes, but more than one of them, plural. Three o'clock is fine."

Months after the bug bite fiasco, AKA the cousin vacation from hell, Peter would try to recollect his Mulysa moments with accuracy, but always fail. Coupled with the pain in his arm, which no walk-in clinic had been able to alleviate, the memory of Florida was a bitter one. The desire for preservation is a heartbreaking mindfuck, Peter might be thinking at this time, perhaps not in those exact words as he sips his orange juice. Further, no mental thought can hold Mulysa's simplicity; by that I mean, perhaps Peter now genuinely accepts in his heart how easy and light it all was with her. And it should be noted, in my opinion, the fact he didn't have sex with her has made Mulysa all the more memorable. His Florida Girl. Her Canada Boy.

And his goofy indie cousin making sweet mouth love to a porcelain mug of hot chocolate each night. In Florida for Christ's sake. That cocoa-slurping, taco-making straight-A student who will move to England next year for more education, with all her quirks—ones which occasionally override the straight and narrow edges of all things Mulysa, the mime-like Goth doll who could never pay her phone bill, return a video cassette, or make rent. Peter only knew her for a short while you see.

* * *

Now, about his cousin Cindy moving to England: Peter will soon receive this information from his mother whom he will continue to live with alone until his twenty-second year of life—four years from now. After the Florida trip, Peter has had no desire to be Cindy's cousin, no desire to write her or have any understanding of her life's "exciting trajectory."

"I don't care," he will say.

That first night in Florida, sixteen long weeks ago now, Peter met Mulysa, fresh from the airport. His cousin Cindy picked him up and they drove straight to her rather dull apartment where he was introduced to Mulysa by way of speaking and pointing: "That's Mulysa." She had popped by to say hello and wore a purple boa and a black poodle skirt with a white tank top. She had just returned from a neighbourhood bar where a friend had been deejaying. She walked around Cindy's living room, in and out of darkened pockets, her bony fishnet legs scissoring across the room's uneven light. She had what appeared to be colourful yarn (orange and purple) woven into her black hair.

"You guys should come out some time," Mulysa said, flapping invisible wings momentarily, simultaneously rattling a videotape in her left hand. His cousin might have nodded; Peter can't remember. He just saw Mulysa standing like an alternative-lifestyle Barbie doll with the bony legs, facial piercings, tons of vampire makeup hiding what he'd eventually noticed to be sparse freckles.

"OK, I gotta return this to Blockbuster!"

MOORE » *193*

"We'll call you later Moo-liss-ahhh," Cindy said in a Count Dracula accent.

For Peter the final dregs of high school were a waning bruise of circumstance with little pomp and so he had taken his first plane ride ever to the muggy tropics of Florida.

Watching Mulysa leave, he returned to Cindy who was talking about the people she knew. Many names were coming up. He stayed quiet, not jet lagged, not shy, simply in a state of newness. She wrote out the name M-u-l-y-s-a.

"That's how she spells her name Pete, like I think she's trying to differentiate herself from other rival Melissas in the area.

"So she's a Goth."

Out on the porch, the Florida air hung heavy; the night itself was stark with tones of black and an earthy orange, almost rust. Peter inhaled the warm air, fragrant with flowers and salt water, he thought. It smelled a lot different from the smell of summer in Ontario.

The trip would be two weeks devoid of his parents and their insidious meatloaf fetish. Two weeks with his cousin whom he barely knew. Two weeks to check out the local colleges and think about whatever it was he was supposed to be thinking about. Or to paraphrase his father, "Get your cousin to show you around the campuses and check out the library and talk to some students."

❈   ❈   ❈

What would eventually become the most pronounced pain he'd ever felt in his entire life all started on the fourth day of his visit. Like the three before it, this day began as they all did: a bright morning sky, a crop of palm trees, thick air and Peter touring around the familiar twelve-block radius near the University of Florida. A spectral force pulled him towards a bucolic, insect-filled ravine, a natural and local tourist attraction. A spectral force called Cindy.

"Here we are: Devil's Millhopper Geological State Park," his cousin said as they drove through the gate. She thought he'd enjoy it. "They've found shark teeth fossils here, and other weirder animals that are now extinct."

During the day, Gainesville was clogged in what Peter perceived to be constant smog with hints of noisy bugs and dust, gravel and the odd Goth couple making out under a palm tree. On the morning after he visited Devil's Millhopper Geological State Park he felt a lump on his arm. Maybe it's nothing, he thought. He ran his finger over the raised area along his right tricep, which throbbed unevenly, never completely disappearing, always stirring up worry and dread. Maybe it's nothing.

The smell of his cousin's hot chocolate rotting in a mug disgusted him. His cousin Cindy, who he now felt was mostly gross—mainly because not only did she slurp her hot chocolate while staring at him without blinking, but she had a distinct smell, some type of herbal cleanser, and she also left the hot chocolate to harden and rot in the hot, lizard-filled air every night—and was nothing like him. How they were related was obviously no mystery, but he felt sadly stoical about the possibility of turning cousinship into friendship. She barely drinks the stuff, just makes it and lets it sit there to rot and harden. Fuck!

All of this, plus general-level boredom, made Peter plot

hard and devise an excuse—anything, really—to stay out late the following evening.

Besides the bright streets, the only other place Peter could tolerate was his cousin's kitchen. It was a sort of comfortable version of house arrest and, like a prisoner, he would often sit alone and look out onto the sunny road and daydream.

Cindy was a year and a half older (twenty), but was far more bookish and quiet with short red hair, a nose ring, and she was vegetarian. She wrote him for two months, so excited to hang out and show him around.

"I've been taking two summer classes before I start full-time again in the fall, but we'll still have time to do stuff. We can go over to Mulysa's on the way to the university; you want to check it out, right? I have to drop off a book I borrowed from her anyway."

Peter was disappointed when they arrived at Mulysa's house to find she was not there but at work.

"She'll be home at seven," a roommate mumbled.

"It's OK," Cindy said, heading back down the stairs. "We'll stop by her work."

And that's how Peter found himself at the second sighting of Mulysa, the bony and pale, short-skirt wearing creature of the night.

"She works at a beauty supply shop, mostly for salons and things. All her friends are either hairdressers or deejays," Cindy said. "We lived together for a year but were too different so she moved out and Melanie moved in. Melanie is never home though these days; she's got a man."

At the beauty supply shop, Peter gazed at Mulysa who was dancing beside a mannequin. After returning the book, Cindy suggested Mulysa call them if she was doing anything fun later. Peter couldn't wipe the smile off his face at the sight of Mulysa.

Again, Peter said nothing, but blankly stared into the stranger's face. Getting back into the car, Peter was hit with a perverse cupid arrow, one he would wear like a badge of honour for the rest of his trip.

"Vampire Barbie comes with Gothic panties," Peter mumbled.

"What?"

"Nothing."

❋　　❋　　❋

The next morning Peter awoke to a sharp pain in his arm. His other hand clung fiercely to the bite area.

"What's wrong?" Cindy said, noticing Peter's preoccupation with his arm.

"I got bit, you see this?" He lifted his shirtsleeve. "Must have been at that ravine we went to with all the bugs."

"It doesn't look that bad."

"Lots of little lizards around. Any of them poisonous?"

"No. Why?"

"Just paranoid, I guess."

"So are you coming with me to class? We have to leave soon."

"No I think I'm going to stay here and write some postcards. Plus, I want to go to the pharmacy for some bug bite stuff."

"OK SpiderMan, see you later, I should be home by four," Cindy said, nervously chewing on her nails. "We can do something tonight if you want."

Look out, here comes the spider-man. Great. Now that stupid cartoon song was in Peter's troubled head. Bouts of dizziness pervaded his morning and as he moved around and the animated jingle moved with him, he thought, *I have none of the abilities the theme song's lyrics boast.* He could not fool criminals; in fact, he didn't even know what they looked like. *I've never even seen a jewellery thief in person.* He could not crawl up a wall and insisted on always using elevators. He was not special in that radioactive sense. He rubbed his arm gently. Cindy's behind this. She probably harvests cousin-killing arachnoids in her closet. Maybe under the bed? A giant nest with spiders oozing from eggs. He looked for a nest under her bed.

❋   ❋   ❋

Peter thinks, things might have been different if they'd grown up together, but they didn't. Cindy and Peter finally connected over Easter weekend at a mutual Aunt's birthday in Buffalo and that's when both their parents put this travel brochure together and kept saying the word wonderful as if the word had suddenly become the must-have adjective of the late nineties for fifty-somethings. The gulf in time between reasonable connectivity was their problem. One slice of chocolate cake buffering this trip and random childhood encounters does not a friendship make. Oh God, I wish I was in a hospital. I wish my arm could be drained of whatever vampire bat lice have sunk their dirty hobo bug venom into me.

His arm was burning now, waves of boisterous pain coming in every ten seconds just beneath his skin.

During those Gainesville days the underbelly of autumn resembled the pink tones found in the lining of Mulysa's micro-skirt. The one she wore that first day at least. Peter busied himself with a local newspaper (Fire Hall Open House unites community ... the rules for your dog this summer at the beach ...a profile on the new hair salon for teens), absorbed only as a means to distract himself from the burbling pain that sharpened itself inside his biochemistry. While his cousin was at class he took cold showers and short walks, trying to hide from time itself.

On more than one occasion, Peter wandered bashfully along the university campuses. They weren't that far from Cindy's place and all you really had to do was follow anyone under thirty wearing a backpack. Done and Done. Libraries, muscle-bound freaks, girls carrying books, fire extinguisher, people walking beside bicycles. He went to the US Post Office, bought a Frankenstein stamp and sent his mother a postcard. *Dear Mom, I hope this finds you well. I'm learning a lot about the southern states' urban culture and possibly my academic fate. Don't run to catch buses. You are brittle. Cindy has been great though and I bought you a souvenir t-shirt from a school I'll never get good marks at. This is what I look like now* (An arrow was pointing to Frankenstein) *XO Peter*

Under the sun, his face was a distant highway; rippling concrete and sand and traffic all wanted to melt into the hot tar being laid out. He was dehydrated.

Sending the postcard reminded Peter of his actual life: upon returning home he'd be starting summer school to upgrade, taking the bus for forty minutes each way and packing his lunch to save money. He'd be mowing lawns and looking for a job at a video store or music store or a pet store or a beauty-supply store. He'd be doing this, Peter thought, with one arm.

※　※　※

Later that afternoon, after awaking from a heated nap he discovered a voice message on Cindy's machine indicating she would be going straight to work from class and to fend for himself food-wise. The early night air was soft but smelled rotten, a mischievous rotten that dissolved the sequined stars and blurred the moon and the whole simplicity that went with that predictable image. He left a note for her saying he had gone to help Mulysa try on her Gothic panties.

The night is a boy with arm in self-sling; the night is a boy walking with purpose to Mulysa's house. He paced himself, fervent, sweat gushing in each stride, walking manic, as fast as he could, living inside the cagey confines of what felt like a shortness of breath. Taking a break near a palm tree—its insincere physicality presenting itself like a prop in some terribly deranged movie set—he closed his eyes and focused.

Mulysa's place: he only needed to walk a few more blocks and he could collapse and the sawing pain throughout his upper body could do its worse. The jutting pain, however, was becoming more than a temporary soundtrack.

Her roommate let him in, returned to the TV, her tired eyes sprouting like bulbs unearthed. She told him Mulysa would be right out, that she was getting dressed.

"Hey you." Mulysa draped an arm around the back of his neck.

The dark bite took its next symptom in the form of paranoia. Nausea was around the corner. He didn't know Mulysa
that well but they played out a flirting session on her couch: a
game of hypnotic insomnia with staring and soft kissing. You
smell like baby powder and vegetable soup, he mumbled in-
audibly, their lips like bumper cars, melting into each other
slowly on horizontal cushions.

✳   ✳   ✳

They played with Lite-Brite. She made two fishes kissing. They
read from Georges Bataille's *Story of the Eye*. These were the
dumb things they did, which Peter would cherish—with or
without both his arms.

"So do you sit on saucers of milk?"

"No," she half-growled, clamped down on his top lip, and the
new feeling rapidly looped in his silly Cineplex mind now being corrupted by erotic twentieth-century literature.

"I like the part where the milk drips down her stockings."

"I bet you do." She moved his hands under her shirt. He felt
her edging her legs and bum into position over his lap.

Her roommate popped her sweaty head into Mulysa's box
bedroom, "Hey, sorry, um, Mulysa, the video store called, you
have a late fee or something?"

Mulysa nodded and after her roommate's head vanished, began to weep uncontrollably. "I'm so poor," she said in a sobbing
bog of beauty and vulnerability, a confluence Peter found both
anxious and attractive.

"Your cousin will wonder where you are."

"Yeah," he said, swallowing a nervous chunk of air and spit.

* * *

Peter walked back to Cindy's place. The range of colours at eight o'clock in the evening startled him. Giant muscular jocks on top of their frat houses posing. Town girls pointing in their direction, saying, "That place is a fucking brothel!" He held his arm while a striding pain now galloped through his legs. Mulysa told him this is where he keeps his stress. On his way up the stairs he checked his cousin's mailbox for plane tickets, imagined the Canadian Embassy had sent him an inflatable raft. Saw Cindy puncturing it, with a fork, stirring her hot chocolate. Arm really impossible to ignore now ...

In the morning Peter awoke to Cindy's hot chocolate slurps and other deplorable seven-in-the-morning routines.

"I called Mulysa last night, thought you went over there," Cindy said, putting her school bag together.

"Why? 'Cause of the note?"

"Yeah, the one about helping her try on her Gothic panties."

"Yes, it was a joke. I was at the library."

He waited for Cindy to insist he was lying, that he in fact had gone over to Mulysa's because she confirmed he was there.

"She said she hadn't seen you but says hi."

"Oh, OK."

"So we have to do something tonight, we can go for a drive to the ocean, you can drive right on the beach sometimes; when it's dark it's great. Also, my friends from work want to go mini-golfing.

* * *

Peter watched Mulysa's Asian-infused dress crinkle, getting up and down for more food, the red silk framing her ass; he felt compelled to stare at it; she didn't seem to mind and knew what was going on. With oil on her lips she moved forward and pulled him in for a long, hard kiss.

"Yum," she said softly.

They were at a Chinese restaurant, ™Panda Express. He couldn't find his way through the squid. Mulysa's lips destroyed a spring roll and Peter watched the tight oily carrot strand slap against her tight, rose-shaped lips. The squid on his plate was lifeless, and despite his comic imagination, Peter imagined his arm swelling like Popeye's.

"You want some Jell-O?" She rubbed his leg under the table with the tip of her boot.

"I want a pop."

"We don't call it pop we call it soda, OK Canada?"

"I was wondering if after dinner you wanted to help me try on my Gothic panties," Mulysa said, quoting his note, which Cindy had invariably shared over the phone. He blushed and found his lips aching for another biting session.

A thin, pointy face, ignited with powder and rouge and whatever else he imagined she put on her face. She plucked an ice cube from her glass and slid it into her mouth, juggling the act of laughing while ignoring the single cookie on her napkin.

"I still can't figure out what bit me." He held his breath, full of American food, air, and...

Outside, new air wrapped around his limbs.

"So where's your broomstick?"

"Yeah, ha. You're so clever."

The doors opened to her black car. He counted the Hello Kitty stickers all over the dashboard. He looked at her knee socks as she parked the car in a vacant lot. They began to kiss. Tongue deep in his mouth, biting lips. He moaned, a soft painful moan which aroused her, she seemed to be crawling up over top of him now.

A police cruiser swished into the lot. Palm trees pointed towards the black car.

"What are you guys up to?"

"Just talking."

"Can I see some ID?"

He handed the officer his Ontario health card. She passed it to the officer.

"I don't know what they're gonna do with that here."

"One time I was taken into the station here," Mulysa said. She was sitting completely still. She looked towards the police car through the rear-view.

"What for?"

"Just for mischief, it was four years ago, I was like seventeen and I didn't have my ID and I was kind of rude."

"What happened?"

"They let me go. My dad came and got me. But I had no belt for my pants, I was just out driving for cigarettes, so the police officer was like telling me to walk faster and I was trying to explain to her that my pants would fall off."

"What did she say?"

"She didn't care. And I wasn't wearing underwear."

The police officer returned their cards.

"All right you two; I want you guys to go get a Coke at a restaurant or something. You can't stay here."

Mulysa drove slowly from the parking lot.

"You want to get some fries or something?"

Peter nodded and touched her bare leg. His body parts took turn churning the venom. His legs felt stiff and sore. They got mashed potatoes and Coke. It wasn't Denny's. It was somewhere else. He didn't catch the name. The glossy menus reflected on solid lips and cheekbones and whites of eyes.

"Potatoes are squishy," Mulysa mewed, taking a fingerful off his plate and gently sliding it into her small mouth.

She dropped him off at Cindy's. In the splashing macabre of cutsie, black-cat night, Mulysa's brown eyes were unavoidable and constant.

"I don't want to go, it's so boring at her place." The waning college noise, the crickets humping, frogs making noises, planning out their killing sprees; all these echoes collided, as if they themselves were an audience, enjoying his frustration.

Mulysa calmed his night, not with reason, not with any words like *relax*, but with a small series of movements. He asked Mulysa for an aspirin. He concentrated on the first time they kissed. Trying to move the blood away from the bite on his arm with his thoughts. A fashion runway on TV spat out of a curtain in a tight Gothic ensemble.

He looked at Mulysa, moving his eyes from face to clothing.

"What? I'm not Goth," she said, slightly annoyed. Then she came close to his face and took his finger into her mouth. Bit down. Followed by a long unspoken hug. Then the big make out session for hours, those lost midnight minutes he would replay in his mind until he'd see her again.

"My lips hurt."

"Good."

＊　＊　＊

Back home, with the aid of the photos he'd developed, Peter recalls the strange gorge, a ravine full of noisy bugs where he still believes something attacked him, stuck him with its toxins, a predator, threatened by his proximity. He shuffled items together and stuffed his pockets with his health card, bus tickets and house keys.

He crosses the street towards the doctor's office. Deep inside his backpack, a piece of Mulysa's boa lay in his brown notebook along with one photo of her eating at Taco John's, her lips around the soft shell, about to smirk. The electronic flashbulb burned that entire day, from that pink morning to the black, crisp eclipse that consumed the tropical city surrounding her tiny bedroom.

"You didn't get this checked out while you were abroad?"

"No. I had no insurance, and it didn't look this bad at the time."

"When did it occur?"

"About ten days ago, maybe less."

"You should keep it elevated," the doctor offered. "I can give you some cream for it as well."

＊　＊　＊

The last morning of his trip Peter awoke beside Mulysa, his arms wrapped around her upper torso. She moved his hand down to her naked body, where it remained, just grazing the surface of that entirely unknown space, perhaps showing him in the dark what was so close, so very near. He was then as he is now, a complete and utter virgin.

"Once when I was thirteen, I stuck my friend Amy's homework pen into my pussy. She used to hump-rape me when no one was around, but we never spoke about it. I wanted her inside me so bad so I used her pen. I didn't know how to come then, I would carefully push the pen up inside and feel the sticky wet stuff and ridges in my pussy. When it got far up, I would almost black out and get scared but kind of swoon with ecstasy at the same time. It felt steamy hot and dangerous, like I was opening a door, daring myself to feel inside the darkness. I was scared it would go so deep I'd never be able to get it out again."

Now she was getting dressed. Rinsed by the soft strokes along his back and the cool repetitive tides the air conditioner brought in, the morning was relaxing.

"I can't believe I'm going back in two hours," Peter said. The giant tropical sun yawned loudly through her venetian blinds, hidden by a gauze of black silk, which draped from her ceiling over the window.

"Just putting on my Gothic panties," Mulysa said, sliding the black lace garment up her sunless legs. The closest he'd ever been to a girl, a suggestive space, a space of opportunity, a girl's bedroom—the door with its unique décor of stickers and photos, the strange lamp, weird silent black cat. He'd never been this close in all his eighteen years. The whole of it, the whole time this was the closest he'd come and his arm was now stinging with stiff, shooting pain.

Mulysa came back with some water and a pill. Would she grow up to be a Goth mom, Caucasoid, capricious, on a doomed Maybelline-sponsored reality tv show. Impossible to say.

He lifted up a can of soup next to her bed. "Soup?"

"Soup is good," she said.

* * *

Even walking now, mid-November, back from the doctor's office, deep within the hurt of Ontario's unrelenting cold, this stomach of snow with its lineups of sore throats and running noses, Mulysa stood in a pile of snow before him in a blustering mirage-defying logic. And then, with the changing of a traffic light, the passing of a streetcar, her likeness dissolved into the powder. Despite his arm and all its realism, he still felt the beach at night, black sand on his sneakers in the closet, his skin embalmed in the grit of hot sand and her hard kiss—hot and sincere. He recalls their pared down dialogue, how her smile would grow whenever she caught him staring.

Back home on the large family couch, his whole body ached; the bite's swell peaked towards an unmitigated intensity as if bees were inside, carving the interior of his flesh with broken pieces of glass for good measure, stinging at intervals and making terrible unified noises.

Brushing past a Mulysa letter, he wishes the airport goodbye was Superglued on repeat in real time instead of the dreadful treble of his bite.

"Thanks for the drive. I'll miss you ya know."

"You'll forget about me once you get on the plane."

Even at twenty—just two years older than Peter—Mulysa seemed to be decades ahead of him. And light years from this bug bite wallow; Peter would remember points from his Gainesville trip like a constellation forming a jagged line or side-ways "T."

Her arm around his arm. His bug bite full of colours and salivating black blood, drying to a nasty scab, then picked and foaming mad on the inside, green, yellow, black, all because of some stupid trip to a ravine in the tropical climate without medical insurance. Peter drags himself through each symptom: the insomnia, the sweats, the fever, the nausea.

Mulysa was like a blank headstone now without dates or attributes, without a symbol at the centrepiece evoking her true essence. He eulogized her and those soft freckles that crawled, sand-like on her pale face. All of this was a part of a conglomeration to idealize the way she had been.

Sometimes he heard her voice: the way she said "soup" and the way her lips made an "o" shape for a nanosecond when she did so. He thought of her later in life when the rent was due, how she cried when her roommate told her the video store had called about a late fee. In between pay cheques he thought of her, how despite working almost every day at the hairspray factory, it wasn't enough to cover her ghastly expenses of food, gas, Gothic makeup, soup and underpants.

The bug bite was one point, the awful sound of hot chocolate another, perhaps the handle of a mug, a few stars there and then Mulysa's naked body lying beside him like a broomstick and a cat's tail. Points of memory bright and alit for only him to see. Some fitting shape like that day on the couch with the crinkle of newspaper and that travel section's bubbled prices negotiating geographic fate and his subsequent visit to the useless town doctor as he called him, the unenthused food-court-type treatment, zero quality and all the hassle; he turned over and over in his mind (not with the restrictions of a coded reality, nor the juvenile sentimentalities of a music video or even a tearful teen postcard) the subjective evolutionary chain of spider into human into nothing.

The bite was part of his negotiation with mortality and as Peter evolved he met Mulysa who showed him he was beautiful and showed him briefly about life, i.e. that he himself was desirable, that she was mesmerized and mesmerizing and that together they made something brief and exciting. He could now see the potential delight in being someone and to eat soup and kiss in the hot tropical night air as her bony legs swished against her car seat and that like the bite itself, now so very present, she would not be forgotten, her visibility outrunning the charging speed the bug bite continued to administer.

When her lips were moist, red and rose-shaped and reached out for him in the muck of fever that invisibly crowned his head, a delirium took hold. As he tossed, strange uneven fevers minced with sensory flashbacks, jolting him with cruel sound engineering, i.e., her voice, her laughter, the sound her mouth made when she ate.

In his moist sheets, the incessant pain in his arm had finally replaced the cinematic airport kiss for good. The bite would settle down, leaving no trace along his bicep, as if it never occurred in the first place.

"'Professor Buggles' is an anti-cerebral stink bomb (and I mean that in the nicest possible way) designed to flush literary pretension out of its fetid hole. And yet there is love here too for the millions of over-looked poets who toil away in the dark despite their lives of quiet, crushing despair. Also, it's strange and sly and hilarious, AKA classic NGM."

—Jessica Westhead, author
of *And Also Sharks*

Professor Buggles

When Leigh received Professor Buggles one Christmas morning she was as astonished as most eighteen-year-old girls would be at receiving a twenty-inch action figure.

"What the hell, Dad!"

"There's a great story to this gift, Leigh," her father said, taking the toy from his daughter's bored hands and running his fingers over the doll's jutting white hair and adjusting its tiny glasses. "It was made by Coward Hash in the late eighties; he was having a nervous breakdown you see, working in the toy industry after the fall of Atari when he came up with an idea for an English teacher action figure for teenagers thinking of not going to university."

"Yeah right," Leigh said. "Coward Hash? Sounds like your name but, like, a super villain from a Superman comic."

"No, I'm serious, the action figure's original creator ended up hospitalized after Professor Buggles failed to capture the imagination of the Cabbage Patch generation, but thousands were produced and stored in warehouses."

"I hope you didn't buy a whole warehouse full."

"No."

"What does it do?"

"It has tapes."

"Tapes?"

As Christmas morning unravelled itself, Leigh's father set up Professor Buggles, which also came with a podium, a desk and a box of small books.

"He's also a writer; you can have him do readings and get drunk at bars."

"So you bought me a toy made by a man in a mental institute?"

"Well, honey, he wasn't in a mental institute when he made it. You put the tapes in the back and he teaches you things about English literature. You can change his clothing and he's Stan Buggles, contemporary poet."

"So, its capacity to destroy my will to live is in fact infinite."

That night, Leigh put the plastic action figure (she refused to call him by his licensed name and referred to him as "it") on her desk and got ready for bed. She combed her hair in the mirror for a while, and eventually changed into the comfortable orange teddy her brother had bought her for Christmas. Her phone rang. It was her best friend Cindy from down the street. Like Leigh, Cindy was in first year at the University of Victoria and home for the gray and green Christmas break.

"Do you want to do something tomorrow? My Christmas stunk. I gave my demented family really sweet gift cards and they buy me lingerie and vibrating poetry dolls."

"What?"

"Do you want to meet at the mall tomorrow?"

"OK, how about ten?"

"Sure. At the bookstore, then we'll spread out from there."

"Sounds cool."

✲　　✲　　✲

The next morning Leigh grabbed a coffee and walked through the bustling innards of the Mayfair Shopping Centre until she found Coles. Leigh arrived early. She dug into her pocket for a mint and found one of Professor Buggles tiny books. "What the fuck?" She read the title and it said *"Goodbye, Limping Dog Biscuit*, poems by Stan Buggles." She shook her head in confusion. The buzz of caffeine coursed through her jaw and throat and arms, fingers, stomach, butt and down the backs of her legs. Feeling electric, she grazed through the aisles looking for a book to standout at her from their repetitive, stoic shelves.

I wonder, she thought, half chewing on her lip, and went to the poetry section and looked under the Bs. Between Emily Bischoff and Derek Busk were two slim volumes of poetry by Stan Buggles. Leigh balked, shaking her coffee cup, a habit she had accrued over the last few months as a new coffee drinker to see how much was left. This is weird, she thought, when her friend Cindy tapped her on the shoulder.

"Whadap?"

"Just browsing. I think I'm gonna get this," Leigh said, shaking the slim poetry book.

"I want to check out the magazines," and as quickly as she

sidled up to Leigh, Cindy veered off, her eyes zombie-ing towards the magazine stand.

After a thorough day of food-court excess—New York Fries, Bubble Tea and more coffee—the two friends parted ways with several small items in a couple of paper gift bags and headed home. "See you at school in a few days," Cindy said.

"Yeah, call me if you don't end up going away for the weekend."

"I will."

※   ※   ※

The house was empty and nothing remarkable stood out which would explain anything. Then Leigh came across a note that read: AT AUNT THELMA'S. BE BACK 8 PM. Leigh made herself a disgusting cheese and pickle sandwich with a dollop of mayonnaise on it and went to her bedroom and flipped on the radio. She placed her sandwich down on her desk and noticed Professor Buggles was face down with a tape inside his back. Dad must have lifted up his sweater and shirt and lodged the tape in there. What a creep, she thought.

"OK Dad, I get it, you want me to play with a fucking action figure made by a maniac: Merry Christmas to you too."

After a loud burp, which reverberated down the hallway, spooking her slightly, Leigh shut her bedroom door and opened her shopping bag. From beneath a pile of underwear and socks, some makeup and two bars of scented soap (goat's milk and chamomile), she pulled out the poetry book.

She read the author bio on the last page: Stan Buggles was born in Vancouver in 1957 and grew up in the borough of East

York. He began writing at a very young age and was first published at age eighteen by *The Crossbow Gang* (now *Owl Magazine*). He got his PhD in English Literature from The University of Toronto in 1984 and published his first book of poetry the following year called *Goodbye, Limping Dog Biscuit*, followed by *I Cut Your Mother's Toenails Yesterday* and the novel *Sheep In Virginia Wolf's Clothing* in 1992. Since 1995 he's been poetry editor of Jonestown Books and has edited over a thousand poetry titles including work from Stevie Sudds, Catherine Hart, Barbara Bentos, Damian Hadley, Jamie Simpson and Howie Cash. He lives in your basement next to a medieval crossbow and thousands of envelopes filled with unpublishable poetry submissions.

Leigh dropped the book on the ground. Howie Cash? And before she had time to question anything further, "GOOD EVENING, IT'S GREAT TO BE HERE. I'D LIKE TO READ YOU A POEM IF I MAY…" The crinkled voice was coming from the action figure.

Its cold plastic hands and legs began to move as if attempting to swim face down on Leigh's desk. "IT'S A POEM ABOUT A DOG WHO TRAVELS THE WORLD WHILE HIS MASTER IS KEPT IN A CAGE WITH SOME OTHER MASTERS AND THEY HAVE NO IDEA HOW LONG THEIR DOGS WILL BE AWAY. IT IS CALLED 'LET ME RUN THE WORLD.' I HAD A MASTER, HE WAS A GOOD MASTER AND WE LIVED IN A GOOD OLD HOUSE, BUT ONE DAY I GOT BORED, I OPENED THE REFRIGERATOR DOOR, THEN THE FRONT DOOR, FOR IT WAS WARM OUTSIDE, AND WITH MY PASSPORT IN MY MOUTH, SOME MILKBONES IN MY PANTS, SUMMONED THE COURAGE, SUMMONED A CAB…"

Leigh screamed and shuddered as pandemonium charged through the house. She ran from her bedroom bumping into things along the way (her dresser, a box of magazines, an empty bowl). She sprinted down the hallway into the kitchen, stepping in a bowl of cat food. She shook it off, stayed focused long enough to continue each gasping stride to the front door where she looked for her boots and jacket. She could still her Professor Buggles spewing off his poetry in his sarcastic voice; it grated on her the way he deliberately enunciated each word. From the basement, Leigh swore she heard a rustling. Passing a mirror in the hallway, she noticed that her eyes were bloodshot. And then someone or something cleared its throat.

❋　　❋　　❋

She had one boot on and with a scrunchy was putting her hair into a controllable ponytail when the front door opened and her heart began to cool with relief. It was her Christmas family, her meatloaf and potato family, her vcr rental of a family, the family that made popcorn and went ice skating and joked with her about her hair and clothes.

"Hi honey, how was the mall?"

"Dad, that fucking teacher toy . . . I, I . . . read about him and he's fucking real! I went to the mall and got his book and you wrote a book too! You were published by him! Jonestown Books, your name, in a list of other poets. Do you know him? Can you hear that fucking toy? It won't stop reciting poetry."

"Honey, calm down. What are you talking about?"

"The doll, Professor Buggles. Stan Buggles. He's a real poet." The rustling in the basement grew. The action figure continued to recite his incessant verse. Leigh's mother was still by the car gathering gifts and parcels. Howard Cash glanced at his wife in the driveway and then locked his gaze on his daughter.

"Many years ago I took a poetry workshop with Stan Buggles. Before you were even born. I was so excited about poetry because of it, and he was so encouraging, even publishing my first and only poetry book, you see, so I wanted to honour him in a very special way. The Atari craze was dying and I was in need of a serious career makeover. I stayed up for days marketing and designing the prototype for Professor Buggles. I pitched the action figure series to some regional toy manufacturers I knew and they rejected it. So I invested my own money into making the first batch. No one would sell it. I even tried to get Stan to buy some and sell them at his poetry events. He said that he didn't want them and that he was a serious poet and didn't need silly gimmicks.

"But is that his voice? Like on the tapes?"

"Yes, I recorded his readings and dubbed the tapes myself."

"Dad, this is insane."

"There's more."

"What, he lives in our basement next to a pile of poetry manuscripts?"

Howard Cash's face quickly froze.

"Dad!"

"He's lived downstairs for years. He keeps to himself."

Taking out his pipe, Howard Cash went on for a minute or so explaining how he had more action figures planned, and even action playsets where you could move Professor Buggles around his office and then into a cab and to a bar to give a reading. He exhaled the smoke from the left side of his mouth. The smoke moved across the left frame of his rather large bifocals.

"You're joking right? This is just a Christmas prank, right?"

"Leigh, sweetheart, calm down. Listen, he wants to meet you. I told him you write poetry."

"This is too much," Leigh shouted. "I want that thing out of my room."

Leigh was behaving like she didn't know reality anymore. Her father's face seemed to say, I'm sorry I didn't tell you I was a poet. But the truth was Leigh's anger ran far deeper and was far more fear-based than what Howard Cash surmised.

"You gave me this thing either hoping I would discover the truth about it or that I wouldn't. Either way, it's terrifying."

"I'll be right back."

"Where are you going?"

"To talk to Stan."

Leigh's mother was making her way inside the house now, setting down parcels and shaking snow from her shoulders when she noticed her daughter's face all contorted in teary horror and disappointment.

"How was the shopping?"

Leigh did not reply.

"Your father tell you about Stan?"

"You know about it?"

"Of course. I told him not to give you that stupid teacher action figure for Christmas. That nothing good would come of it."

"I didn't know Dad wrote a book of poetry."

"It's not very good. I think he wanted to encourage you, you know, creatively."

Just then a white-haired wizard of a man appeared at the top of the basement stairs beside the kitchen. Behind him was Leigh's father.

"Honey, this is Stan. He's the fellow I've been talking to you about."

"Heeee-llll-oooo … Leigh!" Stan Buggles said with a cantaloupe slice of a smile. "I heard your father introduced you to my littler incarnation. And I hear you like to write poetry. Mind if I read some?"

Leigh looked at her mother who was now wearing a Christmas apron and shaking flour into a large bowl. She looked at her father, mostly eclipsed by Stan's luminous white hair. He was nodding incessantly. She heard a rustling down the hallway and moved towards it, noticing the eyes of Stan and her parents following her like the odd times a set of eyes on a painting will follow you as you pass it.

In the hallway, Professor Buggles was on all fours, looking tragic as he attempted a normal set of footsteps. With whirling gears, Professor Buggles' neck began to turn from side to side, his arms and legs too began to move, and soon he was steadily crawling towards her, all the while reading a poem, "I HAVE A WOODEN UKULELE, I SMASH IT OVER THE HONEY TREES, I BEND THE WIRES OVER MY BROTHER'S KNEE, WON'T YOU GIVE ME ANOTHER CHANCE TO WIN THE LOTTERY?"

❄   ❄   ❄

Leigh Cash ran past her mother, whose face was now peppered in white flour. She grabbed her boots and coat and woolen toque. She tore down the front steps and ran down the street, never looking back. But if she did, what a Christmas portrait she would have seen. The kind you'd see in a YouTube video for some Bing Crosby endless playlist. A single image of a man with white hair holding a smaller version of himself, a woman in a Christmas apron, face blotched in flour, and another man in a brown sweater with glasses on with a pipe in his mouth. All of them smiling. All of them looking in the exact same direction, slightly out of focus, but focused nonetheless.

"'Gordon's Gold' exists in a fog, or a fugue, or a failure of the author's brain. But because that author is our beloved Nathaniel G. Moore, it is a strangely pleasurable experience. What can we learn from a long forgotten bit of celluloid, a far too revealing stretch of folksy skin, our modern ache for curating all things sallow and gone? You will learn nothing: this is not a Heritage Moment. But like the obscure crumbs of CanCon memory it recounts, it offers a kind of education of a place, a time, and of a singular artistic mind."

—Spencer Gordon, author of *Cosmo*

Gordon's Gold

The morning thunder orchestrated a deep romanticism inside Andrea as she awoke in slow motion: her phantom hands pulling the duvet down from her body, her feet gracefully traversing in their first steps across the bedroom floor. In her art-house loft with its large window and minimal décor, a mist appeared cinematic in scope. The overcast morning only added to the mystery-themed momentum she'd been egging on for days. It had been a week since Andrea watched her mom's old 8MM films, the ones she transferred onto a more contemporary medium at the school's video laboratory. The canister and its subsequent archive of rare gems—hippie footage and other garbs of celluloid her mother shot between 1969 and 1982—was a gift for Andrea's twentieth birthday, which they'd spent together, her mother flying from Montreal to Toronto for the weekend and holing up in Andrea's cozy loft. Sixteen small rolls found in a coffee canister in a large metal trunk Andrea was thinking of using as a coffee table were compiled into a single digital file.

Of all the footage, that together totalled seventy-three minutes, Andrea coveted the b-roll footage from a CBC in-house interview with legendary national treasure Gordon Lightfoot. For six of the thirty-two minutes of footage, Gord wore nothing but a toque, galoshes, his guitar and a pair of crisp, tea-coloured men's briefs. For whatever reason, a reason she could not squeeze out of her mother, Gordon had done a portion of his performance slash interview with his boot on a stool, guitar over his knee and very little else.

Of course this b-roll of crotch-level curiosity and the jungle coils of Gordon's stomach-hair footage never made it into CBC's iconic membrane, and those who were there to witness this out-of-clothing experience were precious few: a female interviewer (Grace Evans, now deceased), an assistant camera operator (Andrea's mother, Theresa Warren, now sixty-eight, still very much alive) and a head-camera operator, Mike Ramsey (now seventy-eight, semi-senile, residing at Grey Oakes Lodge for the elderly in New Market). The image had suffused over time until Gordon's brief underpants prank became a half-tone ghost of its original form: a smudged slide under a telescope, a forgotten love letter, and a threadbare video-rental receipt used as a bookmark now sitting inside a book on a bookshelf no longer owned by the book's original buyer. I need a coffee, no, a cappuccino, Andrea sent information to her internal motors. She had been keeping a "creative journal"; her OCAD teacher, recently dismissed, had encouraged her to "write shit down," and Andrea, ever the organized chaos-free student, despite trying her hat at an arts major, a major economic meltdown in the normative scheme of things, referred to it as her "creative journal," which documented any ideas or opinions about life or art that might enter her brain long enough to jot down. This is what she'd tell boyfriends and prospective friends and muses as she trotted through her days.

❋   ❋   ❋

For an entire summer and part of one fall she hung out with a boy who was vegan, didn't bathe a lot (or at least not with the leading-brand, fragrant-ready conditioner) and who played the guitar. She got him to learn several Lightfoot songs and play them, just to hear the songs her mother used to play for her when she was little. As he'd play the songs and belt them out, she'd be cooking or drinking or staring into the space around her, all the while knowing the footage lay dormant a few feet away in hush-hush sleep and was key to her work-in-progress, the one she laboured over in her fountain mind, a found tableau of sorts—a national treasure in his underpants, a bit of his guitar in the frame and all the coiled actuality at play—was sheepishly hidden in the compartments she'd fashioned out of an old guitar case.

Now Andrea sits in Bentley Gallery. It's early morning and coffee fumes and the smell of fresh muffins snake through the large open concept space with its obvious white walls and sparse nooks. The curator is Diane Kraus, who has been called "a dynamo of bravado, daring and sensibility" by *ArtCrawl* journal. She is on the phone with a delivery truck carrying "all of Andrea's life in it!" she says, looking over at Andrea, shout-whispering the phrase again, adding a bit of cheekiness to her tone, not wanting to come off as a snooty curator, the type portrayed in contemporary films in which an artist discusses their problems and or dreams with a handler—known as a curator to the sophisticated shopper of mass-culture sound bites.

"The catalogue is coming back from the printers, well, the proofs, just the proofs, you have to sign off on it of course, and we have to add your interview as we discussed. Are you sure you want to go with this for the cover?" Diane says, holding up a slick print off of the male-in-briefs still. "I'm fine with it," Diane insists, "it's just, in previous discussions, on two or more occasions you were thinking of the crystal ball piece or the unicorn as the centrepiece."

"Yes, I recall that."

"No pressure, Andrea, I love the, hmmm, how do we refer to it then? The Untitled, 2001? Yes, I know, but it's so specifically cropped to feature the central torso and fuzzy, possibly muscular stomach, the antique underwear brief and a possible bulge, or shadow. Enigmatic."

Andrea says nothing: she's texting her daughter who is at grad school at Bard College, studying to become, of all things, a curator: no, an international curator. "Mom, the program places me in a gallery while I'm still finishing the program," she has told Andrea numerous times. Andrea's show is seven days away and for the occasion her daughter will be flying from New York state to Phoenix. Diane sighs and half-twirls. She shuffles her feet across the gallery floor and snaps her fingers. An assistant slugs towards her, perhaps her cousin, Andrea thinks, a lanky cousin doing a summer internship with his hyper aunt. "Bradley, I need you to call the printers to see if the proofs are ready to view; they haven't gotten back to me and they're supposed to be ready." Brad nods and drags his uneven appearance back into a corner office cut out of the wall like an explosion.

Andrea notices the tiny bits of drywall dust from drills and hangings and re-hangings and cover-ups in between shows and the rented nights the gallery puts itself through.

A large fifteen-piece retrospective in Phoenix. It's somewhere, Andrea decides, better than her hometown, one of her hometowns anyway—Toronto, Montreal, Kingston.

Andrea has a file on her flip-screen computer pad that will be added to the catalogue at the last minute. An interview of sorts describing her work in her own words. The interview was conducted by her daughter. And in it, the glistening still from prehistoric times, taken by her mother when Trudeau was paddling his canoe—OK, bad joke, she remembers telling her daughter, don't use that; he was always paddling his canoe, right up to the day he died.

Andrea knows she never had a plan to make a big deal of whom the man in the tea-coloured underpants was; for Andrea that seemed falsely sensational. In the light of his death three years ago, in 2020, and for the simple purpose of clarity to the overall vision she had as a twenty-two-year-old artist many moons ago, she wanted to provide both a revealing tidbit as to his identity, but also a context into why it was so special. He was neither a former lover nor a distant relative. It was not anything as exciting as friends and insiders liked to guess whenever she showed the piece, which was only in her own private home. This is Gordon's first and possibly only public appearance and perhaps the only time Andrea will showcase the Lightfoot piece and bring light to it because she never went out of her way to take the piece out of its enigma in the first place.

As she prepares the catalogue with her curator, she recalls the affair she had with a young musician and how the image she took from the footage made its way into its final form—the large 54" x 78" photo on enamel over-extending the glistening alcoves of the late singer's stomach, a stomach unfortunately ruptured by highways of coffee and excess, fatigue and life itself, that eventually wound up cancerous, leaving him destined to Royal Canadian memorial treatment beyond Canada Post stamps and a national day of mourning, celebrating his life on his death day—December 14, 2020, and how even then she didn't dare think of revealing the identity of the man in his briefs who wore a small gold bracelet on his left wrist and had a birthmark just between one of his nipples and the boisterous coils of dark brown chest hairs magnificently at bay, calmed in the still extract she conjured in her final year.

❄   ❄   ❄

The catalogue for *If You Could Read My Mind Love*—the show's current title, a title stealthily cribbed from a Gordon Lightfoot song, after several other titles including *The Last Unicorn, Jettison, The Andrea Papers,* and *D.D.T.*—has been copy-edited up to the point of the artist interview, which Diane is waiting with bated breath to read, right now on this day 17, 2033, six weeks before her solo retrospective at The "gorgeous Mom, it's such a great space!" Bentley Gallery in downtown Phoenix, Arizona, on June 3, 2033, at 7:00 p.m., catered by Chelsea's with music by Cinnamon Belles, and the following fall the same basic show again taking place in Vancouver's Project Space gallery, a gallery overlooking the harbour and featuring recent solo retrospective shows by Michael Turner, Douglas Coupland, Shary Boyle, Dustin Tinker and Grant Heaps.

Andrea is at the restaurant early in the day of her art show and her daughter is moments away, texting her from a cab. The weather is fragrant with night and spring and construction: a strange harsh bouquet of vibrancy.

"I think the mini-interview thing is awesome, Mom, and the catalogue looks gorgeous."

"I'm glad you like it, I'm a bit nervous. I'm glad you're here."

Andrea orders the sea bass with asparagus and an arugula salad with cashews. Her daughter has the steak with roasted potatoes. They wash it all down with a 2025 bottle of merlot, which costs nearly as much as their entries combined. Andrea is more than grateful that this moment exists: her daughter's presence and the memory of her own mother's death and how her daughter stayed with her every weekend that fall until she was whole again.

"You should come to a talk at Bard, they'd totally cover your costs. I could make it happen."

"You could make it happen. You sound like you run the Yankees."

"Plus there's lots of hunky profs there; they'd love to chat you up."

"Oh yeah, I'm so sure," Andrea says, taking a half-swig of wine and eyeing a couple who walked into the mellow lighting the restaurant has clearly been perfecting for years. The show starts in twenty minutes. Andrea reminds her daughter that they have to stop at a convenience store for milk and eggs because there is no breakfast food in her refrigerator. "I know you never wanted to connect the dots with that crotch piece of Gordon Lightfoot OK, and nothing like this is happening at your show tonight. There won't be any secret fumblings of iPods or music projections, but I did something that is about to happen and I dedicate this moment to you Mom, because you are the coolest chick I know."

And with that a string bean of a male violinist and a woman with an acoustic guitar sidle up and begin a rendition of Gordon Lightfoot's sad-core anthem *If You Could Read My Mind Love*, which causes Andrea to tear just a bit at the halfway point.

"Oh who cares what I think; let's bring them to the show," Andrea says. "I thought you might say that," her daughter says with a vaudeville smirk. "And it's not like there's a stretch limo outside waiting to take us to your show," she says smugly, signalling for the bill.

"I read 'The Thorncliffe Strangler' expecting violence. The title, I thought, warranted it. Instead, Moore writes about a friendship. The memory of it, its nostalgia. There are funny moments and moments that point to deep wells of sadness, to the parts inside us either lost or absurd. Meanwhile, at the edge, an apoc-ryphal strangler hovers. What he represents to you will of course depend on your experience with stran-glers."

—Chelsea Rooney, author of *Pedal*

"The best part about reading a Nathaniel G. Moore story is that it's unlike anything else you have ever read; it's like making out with a stranger at a house party after taking some kind of pill, where you can't tell what is real and what is in your head. 'The Thorncliffe Strangler' is paean to adolescent friend ship as much as it is a meditation on the failings of memory and the shifting circumstances that make up a life. Formally it shifts from a kind of personal essay to an anonymous Internet article complete with troll-ish comments to an obscure Swedish poem, as its char-acters shift from hapless virgins to middle-aged fathers and husbands. The story, like its characters, wanders and meanders, and between the route markers and signposts lurks the threat of the Thorncliffe

Strangler, even when there are no victims to be found. Reading 'The Thorncliffe Strrangler' is like walking through a park at night: it's not until you emerge relatively unscathed that you even understand the thrilling danger you were just exposed to. Read it, and go on forever changed."

—Matthew J. Trafford,
The Divinity Gene

The Thorncliffe Strangler

"We live in general in our society with metaphors which belong
to the industrial and agricultural periods."

—Nicole Brossard, 1988

E veryone's had those friendships early on in life that
define a specific time period. They evoke a puerile
subjectivity within that is often hard to translate. So
difficult, in fact, that occasionally it might seem easier to never
bring them up at all. If attempted, these renderings can be seen
as fan fiction for a person no one but the author has even met:
that version of that person.

Tom Norden was such a friend. Tom grew up in our neighbourhood of slum apartments, crude "parkettes" (restrictive in
the bucolic sense; also in the sense of joy) and townhouses. He

would remain in the same building complex on Thorncliffe Drive up until two years ago when he married an older woman from his church and moved onto Danforth Avenue, known to some as "Greektown."

He was about as old and about as tall as me, but a head injury at twelve rendered him on the odd side. (I met him three years after the injury, one he suffered when climbing a rope in gym class and falling and landing on his head.) Just a bit slow and uncoordinated and to the untrained eye, completely dull. Yet, within the fitness of his substandard lucidity lay genuine comedy. And Tom being both the subject and enabler of this comedy made it all the more sustainable.

It was a time of great virginity, science fiction, sports: anything we could get our hands on that didn't require females. There was no point: neither of us was capable of getting women to stand within a sweaty leap of our proximity. We shadowed one another's social imperfections forming an all-dud team for the ages, stunt doubles for one another's turn at loneliness's cruel teen axis.

Tom's inability to drink water regularly made his face puffy and moon-like. On the hottest day you could see him quenching his thirst with coffee, followed by a can of Coke. Tom was even the subject of an entirely made-up article (transcribed below) about Puffitis, a facial disease for the dehydration fetishists worldwide. The disease's slogan was simple: "Water is popular for a reason."

❋   ❋   ❋

Your Face Is Not A Cactus

May is as good a time as any to kick off Puffitis awareness. And East York, that area of space bordered by Danforth Avenue and Laird and Eglinton is a superb choice for the cause's national headquarters. Over the last thirteen years, I have noticed increased facial girth in many of my contemporaries, mainly Tom Norden, who stopped drinking water directly (iced, hot, accidentally during rain or snow storms) in the mid-eighties. He enjoys drinking beer (Rickard's Red), black coffee and regular Coca-Cola, especially in the pedestrian cooking conditions known as global warming. Often I will find him wilted on a sunny patio in a long golf shirt a giant would wear, sweating in his puffy denim pants and putting sad pressure on his flat screen Frankenstein-fit orthopedic shoes, sweating into his beer like a Neanderthal on his lunch break.

Remember Pacey on *Dawson's Creek*? He got really puffy towards the show's last season, mainly because Josh Jackson, the actor who played Pacey, had no one in his life to tell him he needed to cleanse, drink water and cut down on the prevalence of beer/coffee throughout his day. Or Leonardo DiCaprio, the beloved silver men's watch model and the child star who was brought into *Growing Pains* in the early nineties to distract regular viewers from Ben Seaver's facial swell (played by Puffitis sufferer Jeremy Miller). Well, Leo too swelled in the face and got the globe girth in his cheeks as he entered his thirties. All due to a lack of water.

I have noticed occasional puffiness in my own face from time to time. I have to say that drinking water is the best thing about participating in glow trends and embracing pop culture.

Water is everywhere, a key ingredient for all. To celebrate Earth Day, I stood outside of a McDonald's and wished people a Happy Earth Day. They were grateful. They also saw me for who I was and didn't judge my lifestyle. I wish I could be an alcoholic but with water.

Water is probably my favourite thing. I like it in ice form. Clean white socks, ice, and world peace are my three all-time favourite things. So you can imagine what parties at my beach house are like! Hey guys, need some more ice? Take off your pants! Here, put these on! Don't contribute to your environmental footprint with facial girth!

Water: so refreshing, so loving and soft. You can swim in it, fuck in it, cook with it, and clean the stink off your body with it. You can cover each other in it and get all sloshie.

Without it, my face would be a lot puffier than the average thirty-four-year-old male living in circulatory oblivion. Like a sacrificed virgin, like ribbing someone with barbed dialogue or attending a barbecued funeral stinking of fecund awkwardness or unkempt drama, those who don't drink enough water will become as puffy as late-teen actors, seven seasons into their facial life sentence. So stop the cycle of facial inflation! Pretend every day is your ten-year high school reunion!

Drink water, but also jog or exercise regularly, and don't eat complex or single-file carbohydrates after 6:00 p.m. (Un-complex carbs always walk single file to hide their numbers). Burn loads of calories and don't swallow more than two tablespoons of sand a day. Did you know three tablespoons of sand can be found in a single cup of coffee? Extracted after dehydration, your average cup of joe contains enough sand to fill both your eyes! Don't wind up like Tom Norden, official poster monster for Puffitis. There is no cure for Tom, but that doesn't mean you can't drink an extra glass of water to honour him. Tom doesn't go on the Internet a lot so there is no way that he knows I'm making a social example out of him. But the fact that you are reading this shows me that you care about this tragic anti-beauty disease. If you want your corpse to be pretty, water it! *Your face is not a cactus!*

Recent Comments:
Bill83: Thanks for the tip, I'm going to drink a fish bowl of H_2O on the hour for the rest of my life.
19 days ago
SandyBeech: Whoa. Now I know what to get my boyfriend for his birthday! A case of H_2O!
205 days ago
JennaVenom123: Frig. Now I know why my parents' faces look like the two moons that orbit the planet of my nightmares. Thanks for this.

❋   ❋   ❋

I met Tom in the fall of 1989 when a slew of lanky grade tens invaded Hilary Talcum High from their junior high careers, which had expired. Everyone was staring at the vast student list, attempting to locate our homerooms for the semester. Tom approached me and said, "It's a day in itself," already overwhelmed by this new level of academia he was now facing head-on. His head injury required countless doctor appointments, pills and throughout his first three years of high school, various operations and scans on his brain. A brain operation seemed inevitable before graduation.

To cope with gaps in his availability in my lonely life, Tom and I both agreed that he was an alien from another planet, collecting data and posing as a high school student who mostly just stood in the hallway in his gray winter coat. A few kids in school would call him "Statue," which was apt since his coat was gray and he basically stood in the exact same place on the second floor for hours at a time. I developed his character further than any other known pedagogue at the time.

After his stint in high school fizzled in grade eleven, Tom was best known perhaps for wandering through Thorncliffe Park's concrete veins in daily walks to the Coca-Cola factory, the nearby train tracks, the decrepit plaza that boasted a Zellers and Pizza Pizza, as well as stops at the Thorncliffe Library, the gas station, Swiss Chalet and the thrift store.

We became friends reluctantly on my part simply because I knew that becoming friends with Tom would mean that I had abandoned all hope at social superficiality. There would be no parties or girls or mischief to speak of. Tom was strange, said strange things, always kept his coat on, his handwriting resembled that of a serial killer and it appeared as though he had no friends. But then again, I did all those things too.

We began our mirroring awkwardness with the perfect spin on nerd culture's rite of passage: Dungeons and Dragons—with one slight alteration: *Star Wars*. The role-playing version of sci-fi's greatest trilogy was a logical course for our arrested development. This proved frustrating, however, because neither of us could figure out how the game worked. The game had lost its luster considerably as the nineties ushered in higher resolution video games to preoccupy the hands of teen males everywhere. In fact, what once was a game near taboo and led a handful of young American men to murder people or kill themselves (Irving Pulling, an avid Dungeons & Dragons fan from Richmond, Virginia who killed himself, resulting in the boy's mother founding Bothered About Dungeons & Dragons AKA B.A.D.D. in 1982) was now completely associated as an accessory for lonely loser virgin nerds bereft of any edgy controversy.

One thing that Tom was very helpful with was signing out the school's video camera and getting me blank tapes. Together, during the winter of Grade 11, we built a series of props and sets, i.e., command centres, control panels and wooden guns painted black or gray. We also used a Count Dracula cape my mom had made for me in Grade 3 for a bounty-hunter costume for Tom, turning the inside out so the red lining was showcased in all its crimson glory. Adding to his outfit beyond his usual blue jeans and cement gray winter coat was a crude papier-mâché dome-shaped helmet with a slit for the eyes. He looked like a poor kid on Halloween who hadn't changed out of his clothing for five years.

※　　※　　※

So, with no blow jobs from the head blond cheerleader in sight for some time (read: lifetime), in a filmed segment in December 1990, Tom and I paraded around the driveway grinning and bad-acting our way through an inconceivable galactic hunt for a bounty hunter. I was in a hooded winter coat similar to that of Han Solo, worn ten years earlier in *Empire Strikes Back*, and Tom was hiding around the corner of our house waiting for his cue.

In the scene's most embarrassing moment, my then twelve-year-old brother heads to the car for a tennis lesson with my Dad, but not before laughing at us for our geek-riddled pantomime. With a combination of shame and method acting I rip Tom's bounty hunter mask off. "I'm exposed!" Tom cried in his best bounty hunter voice. When I begin to pad him down for more weapons I find a twenty-dollar bill and pocket it. "Hey! You're not going to take my bounty money!" Tom pleaded.

In another *Star Wars* vignette, I constructed a Stormtrooper helmet out of sunglasses, cloth and a discarded bucket of drywall cement. Tom wore a white turtleneck and, of course, blue jeans. It didn't help that the Stormtrooper footage was filmed in the beginning of spring with grass and driveway and other earth-based asides clearly in view. We tried to enhance the scene this time by using sparklers but that didn't seem to make anything more cohesive or believable. But we believed. I was concerned with Tom's appearance and took him shopping for a sport which was coming into vogue at the time. We settled on the sport—hockey—and now it was just up to Tom to pick a team to wear on his head and cover up his black hair, which appeared at times to be crawling off his skull. He settled on the Pittsburg Penguins. Six months later, the team would win their first of two back-to-back Stanley Cups.

"What are the chances of that happening?" became Tom's go-to saying for the strange coincidence that both frightened and enthralled me. In the summer of our sixteenth year, we both got paper routes delivering the *Toronto Sun*. Tom couldn't handle the in-person collecting the job required and was only required to deliver the papers once a week on Sundays. He told me one morning that while returning home with an empty shopping cart from his route, a car pulled up beside him and an arm jutted out with a crisp twenty-dollar bill. "I guess he thought I was homeless."

❋   ❋   ❋

In 1991, Tom got gold seats to a Finland vs. Sweden game during the Canada Cup tournament. In the comfort of Maple Leaf Gardens we witnessed his homeland lose to Finland by a score of 3-1. During the game I noticed Tom's lips had green scabs sprouting in a few places and, as the Zamboni drove past with a Roots logo (in green) on the side, we christened his alien lip guests as "Green Roots."

Years had passed and the alien storyline had run its course. Tom's appearance changed (he grew taller, his hairline began to recede and he walked with a hunch now); the two of us hinted at the notion that he was a local murderer—or at least someone in the neighbourhood who, minus the actual murdering of people, appeared to the public as a suspicious character with no civic motive other than to keep moving on foot and listen to Roxette (the platinum-selling Swedish pop group) on his yellow Sony Walkman, eating salmiakki—also known as salty licorice, a favourite family treat from his father's ancestral homeland.

I would imagine Tom's disappearance from the area in recent years has cooled off any suspicions, if ever any existed.

"The chief problem," says absolutely nobody, head of Friends of Thorncliffe Park, "is that we have no way of capturing someone who has no face. We have no record of what he actually looks like. If the so-called Thorncliffe Strangler actually ever existed, no one has really come forth with this claim." Let me just state this, however, I can assure you that if there was a "strangler" in the Thorncliffe neighbourhood, Tom would likely know this person by name.

In one of his last visits to our house, I had hooked up my video camera to my TV and Tom appeared "live" on the large screen watching himself. He was halfway through one of his epic four-hour walks around the neighbourhood and thought he'd stop by. Feedback growled as his voice hit the camera's microphone and this of course only fed into my theory that Tom's presence near human-made technology caused industrial distortion because he was, of course, an alien being. He gave me a smile, playing into the once red-hot myth we'd created. At this time I was entering my first year of university and Tom had all but forgotten about school; his mental health and continuous monitoring by doctors and technicians had taken up all his available hours. He now spent his days walking from Thorncliffe to his appointments some five kilometres to Sunnybrook Hospital and back.

Over the next two years, Tom would visit our house, usually in the midst of a family member's nervous breakdown, which would occur at dinnertime. Tom's face at our front door would cause my stepmother to use one of her standby sound bites Tom would often reenact: "We're eatin' supper!"

"It was a house of tears," Tom once remarked. "I remember coming over and your mom was upset because she had faxed something to the wrong person, and she started crying. Then your brother started to cry."

❋   ❋   ❋

In those trademark years, Tom had been known to wear blue jeans (on the baggy side), a spring jacket on the hottest of days, and regularly followed up a cup of black coffee with a can of Coke. He called these his "beverages." He had tiny glasses, a large forehead with an ever-receding hairline. He and his family regularly attended church. In fact, when, as a heathen such as I would call him early on Sundays, he would tell me that he had a church function. "Sunday, church all day!" I'd laugh into the phone in my best Tom impression.

By sheer luck I actually went to Tom's church one Sunday morning about a year ago. I was visiting an ex-stripper friend of mine named Lori who, like all professional sinners eventually found God after a string of affairs with blended juices, fitness, creativity, taxi cabs, welfare, jogging pants and celibacy. As we left the cathedral or whatever it's called (the inside part with the rows of hard seating), I was approached by Tom's seventy-year-old mother Barbara and a rotund woman who appeared to be the same age.

"Hi Bradley," Barbara said.

"Hi," I replied.

The rotund woman who turned out to be Tom's wife looked at her mother-in-law who continued her polite parlance saying, "Tom will be so disappointed he didn't come this morning."

"He's sick," Tom's wife said to me.

Eventually the stripper and I left the conversation and headed back to her apartment to see if we felt any better about ourselves. I have often imagined the Baptist church folks gathering a collection for a social field trip. A middle-aged woman wearing a blouse with controlled but noticeable *epaulettes* would take out a business-size envelope with several bills and coins inside, hand it over to the New York Fries manager at a food court who would then proceed to signal for three pimply assistants wearing the appropriate attire to assist in fashioning a rubber hose to the gravy machine. The hose would empty out into three small plastic pools and the whole congregation would get baptized in curds and whey, so to speak. The group's leader would cry, "We're here for you my lord, my Christy guy! Cheese curds from the goats of protection! Deliver us from Satan, let us all here in our makeshift *casse-croûte* pledge allegiance to your wonderous ways. As we are covered in the thickening earth-toned bath, your sacred gift to us, we rejoice and are nourished simultaneously! Oh my Lordo, please keep that fanatic, sluggish, timeshare-vacationing Satan at bay by throwing bad stew into his eyes so that he goes blind and wades deeper into nearby naval traffic! Oh Lord Jesus Christ, we invited the Latter-day Saints, the hobbled, the meagerly, the averagely-skilled at bingo, and the irreversibly old to this dessert offering, made from flour or bread crumbs, as we submerge and cleanse, as this bubbling crude keeps us warm! Yes we are stout, protein-poor and yes we are humble before our mighty caretaker which is you, our generous babysitter. We take the leftovers from the holy farm of life, we take what was once unappetizing and with your blessing, resurrect our hunger, and unite once again with you oh Holy, mighty Jesus!"

❋　❋　❋

You may detect a hint of trepidation on my part when it comes to organized religion. Don't be foolish. Any group activity that forces its participants to perform with repetition, use timing and what I like to call "behaviour restraint" (or uses a code for moral and ethical passion for that matter) betrays my sense of justice. Any organized social activity involving more than two people, which requires tickets with numerical sequencing... well, this bizarre vision of religious gluttony I've just reenacted with the food court and the carbo-loaded fire hose is a metaphor, if you will, for this fear, expounded by the two-fold effect of seeing malnourished Baptists sitting in a huddle at a food court with a stack of elastic-bound sinner pamphlets (the top one stamped in a big gravy thumbprint) and not being able to play with my friend on Sundays.

Tom hasn't said much about his new wife. He moved out of Thorncliffe Park where he had lived with his parents and brother for nearly forty years. At a recent meet up for coffee and cola, he skirted around the topic with diligence, countering my query with his own about my own romantic makeup.

I called his new place only once, asking for Tom and his wife answered, startled, sounding as if I had woke her from a two-week nap. Now awake, she spoke with a bright, panicked voice—as though just now noticing her house was on fire. I hope Tom is happy, and that he finds his life less stressful than when he was having constant surgeries or dressing up as Stormtroopers simply because I couldn't get laid.

❋　　❋　　❋

Nothing (outside of this writing and Östen Sjöstrand's 2003 poem "Strypa Grannskap Thorncliffe," translated and transcribed in full below, usually performed with an accordion by vissångare i.e., the Swedish troubadours) suggests that Tom

Norden (now forty-three) is the Thorncliffe Strangler. The poem was inspired by the 1956 Harry Martinson poem *Aniara : en revy om människan i tid och rum* about a failed voyage to Mars and something about existentialism. Sjöstrand said of his poem, "It's very sad, despairing even" and like the dejected spaceship passengers themselves, now lost forever, Tom's wandering is "a metaphor for the lost individual in the modern world of global depression."

The Thorncliffe Strangler
by Östen Sjöstrand

His receding hairline was prominent, even at fifteen.
He'd often walk long and slow on Laird Drive towards
Overlea (or the reverse) as the Leaside 56 passed on either side,
always home for supper in his gloomy stale-aged apartment
complex 49 Thorncliffe Park Drive, twelfth floor.
His facial girth exceeded normative expectations as he chewed
while his voice smacked hard against ninety-seven coats of paint
on the steel and brick and plaster and those sad and heavy doors.
The next day came and he piled on the hours: train watching,
library grazing, magazine-buying, hot coffee and a tingly Coke
on the hottest days, while on the coldest, lost in a too-large dark
winter coat, ropes, maps and plastic bags of milk in his hands.
Never knew what he was doing with all those civic components
as his puffy moon face orbited the neighbourhood never chasing
a simple glass of water—it held a deep ledger of every street,
every house where he observed a dusty, nothing at all.

Tom's likeness as I knew it was no invention: if I were to have invented a friend from my teen years he'd have a car and a lot of money, great taste in music and a social network he was willing to share. Tom's legacy, however, is partially based on desperate muse measures, limited resources as a teenager to find comfort, and a general "guilty pleasure" feeling that lacquered me in a strange excitement. Hanging out with Tom and making papier-mâché space helmets and watching episodes of *Cheers* in between rounds of incomprehensible sci-fi Dungeons and Dragons was better than not doing those things. And for this I have gratitude.

He was eccentric, polite, and had no social or fashion-based goals. The Thorncliffe Strangler remains an affectionate nickname that encompasses the sum of Tom's enigma: an unsolved friendship from a time destroyed by life itself. That he hugged lovingly, with every shoe and sock in his body, that urban stretch makes him, in my mind, an unsung subject in one of those hefty, nationalistic A Part of Our Heritage commercials.

Sitting on the Don Mills 25, the narrator rings the bell, noticing the 7-Eleven up in the distance at Flemington Park. He exits, inhaling several drops of heavy rain. Through the wet, late afternoon sky, about a kilometre west, he sees the iconic Thorncliffe apartment complexes jutting out like proud teeth facing one another, in a permanent setting, with no sign of decay.

"If a human dreams of electric sheep, does that make the human emotionally dead? What if their shrink turns out to be a robot? Can robots love? Or for that matter, can humans?"

—Craig Francis Power, author of
Blood Relatives

"Nathaniel G. Moore understands that people in love are strange, vulnerable dinguses. Like a wafting breeze of pheromones 'Blade Runner' is a story that seduces and enthralls. With tenderness, humour and pop-culture punches, NGM shows us how love and heartbreak can change us and give us so many feels."

—Dina Del Bucchia, co author
of *Rom Com*

"This story is great but you should definitely track down the three-disc Director's Cut Blu-ray."

—Brian Joseph Davis, author
of *Ronald Reagan, My Father*

Blade Runner

"Whom the gods would destroy, they first make mad."
—*The Masque of Pandora*, Henry
Wadsworth Longfellow (1875)

One morning, when Gabe Samsung woke from uneven dreams—dreams in which he both remembered and repressed key romantic impressions, characters, guilty imagery and symbolic refuges—he found himself transformed in his bed into a horrible cliché. He lay on his male-like back, and if he lifted his head a little, he could see his growing belly, slightly hairy and divided by swatches of morning sun. The bedding was hardly able to cover it and seemed ready to slide off at any second. His many papers, pitifully stained in rain, hot sauce and boot prints, wavered on the floor like coral garbage as he looked at their sad accruement.

"What's happened to me?" he thought. It wasn't a good time to be Gabe Samsung.

Just three months earlier he had it all, or so it seemed: Claire, a young concubine, co-escapee from a terribly misguided summer and autumn of sexual mind games and feeble lies who, despite the terrible back-story, continued to give him the time of day which included sleepovers with sex, showers full of mascara smears and winter morning make-outs, and movie marathons in which she'd inevitably fall into a big, soft, mushy sleep: sealed for the night behind two giant eyelids.

Those dead cold days and nights of winter were jam-packed with subjective interiors, anecdotal riffs, bed-quarantined meals with healthy side dishes, as if an esoteric play was unfurling from the quill of a disjointed bard (a real belletrist) who wore long robes and ate nothing but figs and was somehow rendering real his lexical theatrics through a wormhole of time and space. He served her green beans constantly. This was no bard, and calling him eccentric was a stretch. Somewhere between clown and crude, he came off as incomplete.

This morning just described was so long ago from where Gabe Samsung woke as cliché as a sunset or toe-clipping moon, surrounded by waving pages of stained paper scattered along the floor. So long ago now from that morning he was mid-monologue in the cold air before him, unaware for sure if Claire herself was even awake to listen. They had once again slept without closing the window properly.

Gabe spoke: "If the LORD had meant to kill us with this love, he would not have accepted all this bread and all these burned-out cigarettes as offerings, for we are the demented derelicts of his glory." He said this gazing tired-eyed out Claire's attic bedroom window one billowy, winter school-day morning; a red balloon, tied to a tree across the street, dangled in a disturbing way.

Claire had an eye cocked now. "Told us what?"

Gabe stretched and yawned and as he did so his knuckles grazed the lowest part of Claire's bedroom ceiling.

"What do you want for breakfast?"

"The same thing I always have: bagel and cheese, orange juice and coffee. At that place."

"The place we went yesterday and you almost got hit by a car and I pulled you back?"

"I don't think it was that close."

But Gabe thought she would have been killed—the truck was fast and she was a slow deer—he felt her denial for his perceived heroics as a form of cruelty.

Claire and Gabe walked towards the crummy breakfast nook on St. Clair just west of Oakwood Avenue.

"It's so cold," Claire said.

Gabe shivered, then added, "It's cold enough to make a skating rink." Claire's big eyes made it appear as though she knew what he was talking about. They moved in that way someone would move them to suggest acceptance. "When I was like eighteen, I was obsessed with hockey. I think it was because I had to fill up my time with something because all I could think about was sex and I wasn't having any sex." Claire laughed and Gabe could see the tops of her cheeks poking out from her scarf. "So I paid for a league session, right, but I wasn't good enough during the warm-up to even continue so I mostly sat on the bench and felt really embarrassed. I had played the year before in a league, but with much younger kids. This was a house league for men and I was still pretty small. So instead of refunding my money the guy somehow roped me in to run the time-keeping for the games and help sharpen the skates for the players. It paid around $140 a month and I only worked once a week. I got to hang out with the referees who smoked in the dressing room. Players would bring me their skates and I'd take them to get sharpened and then run them back to the players."

※　※　※

Today Gabe Samsung sits in a psychiatrist's office staring shamefully at the ground. It is a cold day years from any he shared with Claire and her attic room with the red balloon caught in a tree across the street, which he recalls was dangling there for weeks on end until it shrunk and resembled a withered heart, having softly imploded into a piece of worthless garbage. The psychiatrist is busy jotting down words in blue ink and getting ready to reveal the panacea for his deep psycho-malaise.

Gabe speaks up, "Listen to me; I'm not going to sign my life over to some wonder drug you and your golf buddies pop on weekends. I'm sure you get paid plenty to jet-ski in commercials to promote Frankenspiritan or Christorval, whatever it's called, but I know just as well as you that it's not like I'm going to wake up tomorrow with job security and a hot wife and two kids after taking this pill."

"I see," the doctor says. Gabe begins to sweat, a panic hatches deep within; he looks at her as if she holds the keys to a control centre aboard a large battle station which can elevate his pain, his mistrust, anxiety and dependency issues, fantasizing she is not the assisted-suicide doctor he perceives her to be.

Attempting placation, the doctor inquires, "Gabe, what makes you think the pills won't work?"

"I have never enjoyed them," Gabe infers. "Also what if the side effect is something like temporary motor skill shutdown or blindness or numbness in my limbs? What if my stupid roommates ask me a question in the hall and I'm drooling. Or I lose control of my body or mind while I'm on the stairs."

Gabe begins discussing key figures who continue to plague his psyche on a regular basis. "Can't you remove them, with lasers or something? Like part of a constellation you know, or a set of unwanted freckles. Just zap them off?"

"The first thing you must ask yourself is why do you continue to dwell on these people?"

Gabe sculpts his entire face with his fingernail and sighs heavily like he does most every day. The psychiatrist continues prodding, but it is the next comment however that infuriates Gabe the most: "Have you ever had any tragedy that caused you great pain in your past?"

Knowing no doctor was that stupid, Gabe stands up and pulls on the psychiatrist's head, revealing that it has all been a ruse: nothing more than a flimsy latex mask covering the metallic skeletal properties of late-twentieth-century cyborg robotics.

"I'm so embarrassed," it says to Gabe, who gets up to leave, but not before stealing a box of printer paper. The last thing he sees while exiting the office in a blur of rage is the robot placing its hands over its lowering head.

Pathetic, Gabe thinks to himself, frantically jostling down the hall carrying his boots, hat, paper and other winter drag-downs.

In the elevator, he puts his boots on. As he leaves the building, Gabe comes up with a wordy voiceover that suits an ad for a robotic psychiatrist and this pleases him considerably.

Latex-covered mental health robotics! Not just for a futuristic cutaway in a science fiction franchise! You don't have to pay them, simply pay for them once and pre-record general aesthetical mental health questions of quotidian concern and watch the profits roll in! Comes in over eighteen likenesses. Oh, man, now I really have seen it all, Gabe thinks to himself.

❋   ❋   ❋

Way back then, before the steely-eyed, hardware-hearted therapy, Gabe did what he always did with Claire since they first began tangling in the sweaty July moonlight and rain-stained sheets: he disappeared. She had done it to him, though not as long. The first time he did it was well after the summer and autumn sexual blockbusters had burned them both out so very much and it was getting colder—and not just the weather, mind you, and so in this second round of secretly dating—or trying to at least—Gabe Samsung said he got pneumonia and couldn't reply to her or phone her because he was so bedridden and ill he didn't even know where he was or how to speak. It had taken ten days off his life.

Ten days later he valiantly mustered the strength and reached out with his familiar outer-space voice on her messaging service something that sounded an awful lot like this—cue the Horror Product Placement Super Bowl Commercial cinematography!

"I was and am in hospital. I am truly sorry…My eyes watery…something gray and ratty…it is awful what has happened. To see you in the state I am in, would be death."

Claire wouldn't receive the message until well after Christmas. And, as far as she was concerned, he had stopped talking to her because she had rejected a social offer one night and that cruelty was something she couldn't forgive. Just two days before the pneumonia asteroid allegedly hit his front lawn, the silly Gabe Samsung had walked the streets with ratty old VHS tapes in his backpack hitting up payphones, attempting like a hobo in love to catch Claire coming out of her post-secondary school for good-girls-who-know-better and see if she wanted to have a sleepover and watch some flicks. But she had tired of his continuous cancellation of plans and no-showings and when she answered, curtly rejected him by saying she was hanging with another man that night.

The raw stink of night at the payphone played on a loop in both their minds. For Gabe it was a humiliating vignette with the sad sack of VHS tapes and how she would not see him and said she was going to another man's house instead. But Gabe had VHS tapes in his bag to watch on her crummy VCR! But he forgot to tell her in his anxiety, as it was always shocking when he could actually get through to her on her cellphone with its Right Said Fred I'm Too Sexy answering service greeting. He felt like a madman, walking payphone to payphone carrying Jean Claude Van Damme bootlegs in his sack.

But because Gabe Samsung was poor and unprepared for life's endless grocery bill, he did not have a similar answering service as Claire did. He could not in fact receive a message— the one she desperately wanted to send. So she wrote it out in a letter, which of course she never sent because Gabe Samsung didn't have a fixed address at this time in his filthy life.

This lengthy missive piled up in her consciousness, eventually expunged into a spiral-ring notebook and was then typed

out via her word processor. However, even emailing it immediately was impossible as Claire's dial-up Internet service was
down (something wrong with her modem, which was always
"on the fritz" Gabe heard her say).

Gabe. No. I hope that's not it. I thought it was, but I need
to say goodbye. Don't just leave like this; I want to see you first.
I miss you, I do. I had a long day and it's hard. I was tired, and
assumed we wouldn't get to hang out again. It's hard to
communicate with you when I get these panicked conference-
call payphone meltdowns that sound terrible, and worry me,
and then I can't see you and you say don't worry. It's hard when
you don't let me understand, and when I see you, you say "I
don't want to talk about it right now"—it bums you out. How
can I know what to do when you say this and then leave me
messages that sound like you don't want to be anymore? I just,
I was frustrated tonight, and not with you but with how this is.
How we are, and aren't, and can never be. But how much I
care for you and want the best for you and want to give the
best to you. When you hung up the phone, I felt so awful. I
don't want you to think I don't want to see you. I do . . . and I
think about you all the time and just want to lie with you and
talk to you and love you. I listened to your phone message after
and felt worse. I'm sorry—you should have told me you had
the movies because it's all I wanted to do with you all day
today. And I'm sorry. I even had my cell on me at work hoping
you would call. I just got home and put on *Freedom*, and then
got your message, which says you're gone and I'm so upset. I
know it's over. I feel it. But you're upset and I need to be there
for you, if nothing else, to say goodbye—for now. Don't do this
to me, I understand—and of course can never fully—what is

happening and how hard things are for you right now, but I deserve a goodbye. I want you to know how much I do love you. I read your letters and laughed and loved remembering all the moments we've had: the bicycle thief, and you singing *Nothing Compares to You* to me and the shark that brought me in from the rain. I will be so hurt if you leave without seeing me first. I will have my cell on me all night tonight and all day tomorrow. Please call me. Or come. Of course I wanted to see you; I even have tomorrow off and thought we could spend the morning together. I just, like you, was frustrated with how we have created such a complicated relationship. Please call me when you get this. I'm home tomorrow until 5:00 p.m., then a rehearsal at Glendon. I will get into Glendon early to help build our set if I don't hear from you or see you before then. Don't worry, just know that I won't forgive you if you don't do me this one favour and that is to say goodbye.

—*Claire Marie*

With no way to send the letter, it floated from her hands to a standstill on her desk. Claire (like hundreds of others wearing scarves, trying to therapize, cut hair, serve coffee) was preprogrammed with a distinct and believable emotionality that was hidden on her person like subwoofers. Claire was running her finger across the button that would end all things Gabe at once. And despite yet another disappearing act from the going nowhere lover of the moment, despite his absence over the romance that was Christmas, she never detonated. And she could have. And so too could have Gabe, had he of course known of this service.

It was all explained in the *New York Times* a few years ago. And in a BBC documentary that begins with The Kink's strumming away *Lola*. The article and the documentary both said essentially the same thing, it was a memorable voice-over, performed by Richard E. Grant: "Because so many people claimed to be mentally ill because of mental illness's fashionable boom in mainstream and civic culture in the mid-to-late nineties, and to save money on hospital fees, medication and music rights to soundtracks for movies dealing with mental health issues, the governments of the First World assigned a large population of each country, what some dubbed as 'synthetic emotion buddies,' varying in intensity, to be administered as a vaccine. Over the course of a year, for example, a standard dosage would give you a new friendship at a café, laundromat or bar, and these would be relatively light-hearted, easy-to-maintain friendships. Heavier emotional burdens would come throughout the year, as well as hellish romantic ones, passionate lust, dedicated love, and bitter envy. So what the patient perceives to be a toxic relationship is actually the equivalent of a bad acid trip."

The *New York Times* article also courageously summed things up with panache: "It's just easier on everyone and doesn't cost anyone anything because you don't actually have to break up with anyone or get angry with anyone. It's like a safety-word system in dangerous or experimental sex, only this covers all aspects of dating and social interactions. It's universal social healthcare. No need for anxiety, you see. You say the word and we just pull the plug and your hockey coach or lover or cousin disappears into static and pixel dust."

Again, to contextualize things for the protagonist's sake, and yours, Gabe Samsung never read the article in the *New York Times*, nor did he see the BBC documentary. (And to be fair, not everyone has tried Viagra, seen *Dancing With Wolves* or eaten lobster-fried rice or those beads of clay that burble around in that weird cold-fusion tea served with dome lids and the too-thick straws.)

Meanwhile, deep in the recesses of a mental ward, Gabe did everything he could do to keep the phantom images of Claire thick and real within his aging mind. He recalled the night she came over to his apartment partially soaked in the rain. She was going through her bag for something when she came across her underpants. "I got hot, it's kind of gross," she said, wrinkling up her micro-slop nose. He was drowning in his hospital sheets and thinking—I am here to escape all that had confused and upset me in the great void I had created in the real world. In the days leading up to his hospitalization he quit his job and packed up his apartment, leaving instructional notes to his landlord and friends.

❋   ❋   ❋

The night Gabe went into the hospital—December 13—Jaro Novak recorded the first six-point game of his career. Five assists, one goal. Gabe didn't have pneumonia as he would originally and eventually tell Claire. Instead he had found himself losing his mind, completely, unable to determine where he would live, work or enjoy the rest of his life. He talked his way into the tenth floor of CAMH (Canadian Association for Mental Health), a three-star hotel for those dabbling in the mental fringe.

The next morning, Gabe watched the sports highlights in the main lounge for sad men on the tenth floor of the institute, a stone's throw from the University of Toronto and various horrible dive bars and of course the always entertaining live-crab district they call Chinatown. The nurse asked him if he liked hockey. He nodded groggily. He was clutching the sports section. He waved an imaginary foam finger in the air.

Ten days before Christmas he sat and watched the sports highlights. It was after a five-and-a-half-month cocaine-doing, co-ed screwing, lie-juggling, pussy-eating, ass-slapping, bra-unfastening and bed-unmaking marathon. He went to the emergency room and said that he could not live another day without destroying himself. He didn't say anything about the drugs because the last time he mentioned dope he wasn't admitted and had to spend twenty-five dollars for a cab back to his friend's place while listening to a sad Gordon Lightfoot song about mind-reading and ghosts and paperback novels, the kind the drugstore sell.

So this time he simply said he was "sleeping around" a lot and had six girlfriends this past summer and some still remain with him now. He wanted to suggest that perhaps being sexually insane was on a shortlist of symptoms of a larger career-spanning problem for which he only had one foot in the door. In short, as his wife would later synopsize with sexual abjection, Gabe Samsung was hospitalized for "being awesome."

Even though everything he claimed to have done to wind up in the hospital could have been explained by scientists as part of a harm reduction program that everyone knew about because of the New York Times article and that BBC documentary and how this over-the-counter-glow trend had in fact been part of an alternative, normative and mainstream lifestyle just as much as virtual reality had made its way into online gaming, sitcoms and science-fiction erotica, Gabe wasn't having any of it. He knew what he saw, what he endured and how emotional it all was for him. He knew Claire was real and had squishy curves and as a Canadian citizen, living in Ontario, he had certain rights as it pertained to his mental health. I mean, just because Viagra exists that doesn't negate the responsibility one's general practitioner has to discuss erectile dysfunction, or sexual hallucination, mental ward incarceration, Oedipal issues or concerns of cerebral deterioration.

Gabe couldn't access the memory stick in his mental caverns when the news hit about the emotional alternative lifestyle chemical campaign, in which a simple injection, months earlier, could have been administrated by a professional, law-abiding nurse and these sorts of real life issues, while feeling entirely real, could be aborted with the right instructions.

From the sixteen-minute mark of the BBC documentary: "Over the years, people change their minds about people who wronged them—or whom they cherished. Sometimes they abandon a likeness altogether, using a sort of comfort-induced amnesia." Then it cuts to a shot of Emma Haines, forty-one, an artist and advocate—nay, spokeswoman—for the program. "My actions one summer were the catalyst for my decision to use the program."

As it relates to a tryst with a young man that summer, Emma shares the following journal entry, addressing, we assume, the young man she had the affair with:

"I talked about you in therapy yesterday. My therapist asked me what my responsibility in all of this Amy and Evan mess was. I said I lost my vigilance about the relationship, I let him slip away, I felt neglected and didn't give a shit about rock records or tours or how we were becoming apart from each other. I told her I started seeing a boy with a cut on his eye and poetry dripping from his electronic letters who was poor and sad and beautiful. And I fucked him behind bushes in public parks and held his hands beside mugs of wine and hot chocolate. I told her I felt in love/lust with this boy and didn't much care about anything else and how, I guess, it showed." Emma went on to discuss the benefits of being able to walk about from any situation at any given time. She says, at forty-one, she has earned the right to jettison destructive situations and personalities from her life. "I can't imagine living any other way," she tells the documentarian before it cuts to another voice-over and a final shot of Emma holding up a photo of herself as a teenager eating a piece of corn on the cob.

Gabe's emotional tropes had all built up inside him in this one way. Throughout his auditioning interviews that night, he was queried with different versions of "Are you going to hurt yourself or others?"

And for what felt like the third or fourth time Gabe responded, "I don't know, probably. I'll probably start in a few minutes if you don't help me," he said.

He hated all that he had done. And as he sat, awaiting his admission fate, imagining himself in a fancy new psych-ward gown and not having to worry about making his own meals, he heard Claire admonishing him about his sexual appetite.

"You ate all our pussies," Claire said to him sharply, back in September, when his litter of girlfriends was discovered during a raid of sorts. "And we're all friends," she reminded him. For

Gabe it painted a strange tableau: a perverse dorm-room black-and-white poster with three pantless women and the word FRIENDSHIP along their nude feet.

The mob hadn't made him do it but they certainly helped with their slippery cocaine and that's about it. (You see, he wasn't a user, this was anomalous, the entirety of his thirtieth year.) Every corner a naked twenty-year-old, another unbelievable night, bathtubs and hot sex, cocaine and, yes, the mafia was, in a way, sponsoring this pro-debauchery fantasy camp with their drugs.

The rest Gabe orchestrated with the help of a geo-atmospheric climate change that placed him in the right vocational hazard and neighbourhood at the right time, a sexual alignment in the second quarter of that given year. And the universe said, Do your worst, your best, do it for the next sixty days or so and then we'll evaluate your progress.

His birthday was in May that year as it always was and the sexual torrential downpour all started soon after that. If one of his sex slaves didn't want to come over, another one did— usually by way of bicycle.

※　※　※

Oh, they must have known what was going on, Gabe often thought at the time. At one point, one of them in the know, only slightly disgusted by his communal status, turned to him and laughed at what she perceived to be the hilarity of it all, "It's like we are cats howling on your front lawn!"

But back to Claire, the one Gabe coveted. She had not taken well to his radio silence heading into the holidays, never knowing where he was, and for the time being, put him out of her mind.

I've been in the hospital, he wrote to her on a postcard, but had no stamp and couldn't remember her address. And as the new year rolled from zero to one on a countdown of days, Claire still cared. It was the phone that finally brought them together after ten frosty days of introspection and double pouting.

"I've been in the hospital," he told her. Gabe couldn't remember why he waited so long to finally call her. He ate sponge cake every day at five thirty. Each day he convinced himself he would call her. For nearly two weeks he did this. Each day he'd wake up and say to himself, I will call her tomorrow at four o'clock.

"Merry Christmas and Happy New Year," Claire said into the phone. She had been away for the holidays, visiting her family in the small town where she grew up.

"Can I visit you?"

"I wish you were here," he said. "Right now," he said, and Gabe gave Claire the proper coordinates. "I'll come see you tomorrow after class at two," she told him. He prepared his room as best he could. The bed he slept on was rather rickety, so he dragged the mattress off and folded the metal frame up as much as he could until it resembled a crouching robot. He liked his new floor bed immensely and found great comfort now in lounging about. Claire arrived at 2:00 p.m. as she promised. Her hair was tied back and the makeup she wore accentuated her large eyes and shrinking rose of a mouth.

Now she was here and it was a brand new year. First they kissed and squeezed. He got her underwear down around her ankles and was fingering her asshole and kissing her intensely. He gave her a spanking and she shot her head as if to say, you old pervert. Her eyes opened even bigger in the darkness and the radio growled in static waves. Gabe and Claire were on the floor in a big make-out-reunion New Year's special and he was in heaven. Another girl he had been spanking and kissing in between the reefs of his secret affair with Claire left him in the bed days earlier saying, "I can't do this," and burst into tears, gathering up her things and ran down the hallway from his room.

Somehow these girls still found him, despite his being in an institution and unable to pay for dinner or a movie. Maybe he put up posters in the neighbourhood. Gabe just couldn't remember it all.

So Claire was sitting on his mattress on the floor and they were listening to oldies radio just like they used to in his apartment before he lost his mind from starvation, cocaine and intercourse and the otherwise boring room smelled of lust and sweat and perfume. He turned on a small lamp he had found in a hallway.

"What's that?" Gabe said, noticing a series of small bruises along her inner thighs.

"Oh, you know, I bruise easily," Claire said. "Best not to ask."

The lights in three rooms they could see from his window went out. The city was quieting down. Claire ran a finger along two tiny freckles on her hip and Gabe thought they'd be perfect places for electronic plugs to go. He did not mention this thought to Claire, for he wanted her to stay a while longer. The nurse came by and found them in the dark sitting on the floor.

She glanced in and nodded a greeting, then shut the door.

Together, congealed in antiseptic air they were still listening to oldies.

"I'm going to need a few more minutes with this patient," Claire said, bursting into laughter, imagining the nurse was still there. Gabe kissed her and stared into her big dumb eyes which is not to say he thought she or the eyes themselves were "dumb," but dumb as if it were the word "fat" or "bad" or "sick" and meant something different in the urbane sense, a universal colloquialism if you will, which only he could speak and hear. Outside the snow came down and some of it went into the room because the window was open. Claire covered up her hip with the electronic sockets.

After the fingering and kissing and listening to the old songs, they smoked a cigarette outside. The security guard who rode down the elevator with them was now standing a few feet away and watched their every move.

"It's so nice to see you," Claire said. "You seem to be doing well." He rolled his eyes in agreement as if to say, Yes, clearly things are going swimmingly.

"They're going to drill a hole in my head tomorrow."

"No they're not. Don't say that."

"You're right. Might give them ideas," he said, looking at the security guard who laughed coolly. A swelling briefly entered his mental flow, the medication, not now he thought, not now. Things slowed down. The guard couldn't stop looking real. Gabe began to speak, but stopped, as if pixilated in a slow download.

Claire paused as well, not blinking or moving and then everything flowed again, free from chaotic introspection.

"I'll come visit you after class on Tuesday."

The chief administrator of all things crazy and pill and rental slippers now raised her voice. "Mr. Samzan," she called to him. "What is wrong? You barricade yourself in your room, give us no more than yes or no for an answer, take apart your bed; you are causing serious concern to your friends and family and you fail your required eating duties in a way that is quite unheard of. I really must request a clear and immediate explanation. I am astonished, quite astonished. You seem to be showing off peculiar whims of insubordination." To this Gabe said, "My mother is narcissistic, and I feel hopeless and these drugs don't do anything but make me slow and stiff. How will I find housing and employment and reality in this state? How is fuzzy scrambled eggs and sharp apple juice going to help me with that?"

When he was released from the hospital in mid-January, Gabe stayed with a friend in Montreal who he promised to go see when he was released. He was nearly six hundred miles away from Claire. It was cold and pointless and the pills the hospital had given him were making him unable to sleep or, more specifically, unable to dream. "I ran into my friend and I was so fucked up on these pills I don't even think I said anything to him," he told Claire on the phone. "I miss you," Claire said.

He returned to Toronto after only a week in Montreal.

Upon his return, Gabe went to Claire's house with a bag full of specific gifts, along with sparse groceries. "I am going to make you pork chops and green beans. There is some vodka too. And a celebrity magazine. I also got you a Disney book about Bambi and wrote stuff in it for you." She took the bag and began to investigate. She flipped through the Disney book, noticing the plethora of enhancements on Bambi's behind.

"Is this what you did in the hospital?"

"No. I didn't have this in the hospital. I found it with my stuff. From when I moved out of my apartment. I remember getting you that book when I worked at the bookstore. Because you are my Bambi."

With the flare of a masturbating teenage boy in detention, Gabe had accentuated the animals' furry rear regions, adding curves and innuendo and written Claire's name like a maniac stranded in the tundra with bits of cardboard and a pencil crayon that only worked if spelling out her name. He drew hearts in the animals' eyes, dirty limericks. Each page crammed with filth and animalistic reassignment. "I'm worried about you and the animals," she said, face engulfed with manic laughter and big, golf-ball-sized eyes rolling around in her face. He played with her butt.

"Don't hurt the animals, OK?"

"I don't want to have sex with animals." Claire looked stern then changed her face into a lavish explosion of teeth and the whites of her eyes.

"I'm just teasing you."

Gabe and Claire downed a pair of Loose Tequila Zombies (blended pineapple, crushed ice, sea salt and maple syrup) and watched television in sweatpants. He kept playing with her butt. He heard gears and motors whirling about.

"You love that thing," Claire said. He felt as though he was about to cry, his fundamental antipathy to logic seemed to ooze and pulse throughout the evening, ever aware of the new ticks and twitches his post-release medications were capable of. It was as though he saw jump-cuts in real time; his arm would extend fully from a bent starting point without transition. He paddled and squeezed away at her behind as she fondled the remote.

"Do you spank all the girls?"

Gabe couldn't believe this was the way she was talking. Before he'd just spank her and that would be it. Now she knew everything. And, yes, he spanked all the girls. He felt criminal. But it was. She knew all his dirty deeds yet still invited him over. He had to answer her. "I guess so," he said. Someone named Mark was phoning her. She looked at his name on her phone and huffed.

"I don't want to date him." Mark is the name of the dude that girls always fuck but never stay with, Gabe thought. It is what he will think for a hundred years.

She had slept with Mark the previous week when Gabe was in Montreal. She later said, "I knew when you got on the bus to Montreal it wasn't over."

"I missed you," Claire said, and handed Gabe a four-page note. It said that she had slept with Mark the boy from her drama class who was directing her play and that she wasn't sure why, other than he had just broken up with his girlfriend.

"Sometimes I think with my pussy," she actually said. Her phone buzzed loudly on the coffee table. It rested on a magazine Gabe had bought her. He continued reading her note. The note said things about choking up when they would meet on the subway platform and the lump in her chest, her heart in her throat and things like that. The note also said that she wanted to do other things. To have sex with other people, different kinds of sex. He waited for the car chase part of the note to end. The slow motion explosions and the sex montage, the tequila shots and playful semi-nude mattress rolls, the champagne spraying across her torso, the whip cream wiped up by a production assistant.

"Like threesomes?"

"Yes."

"Have you had one?"

"Not yet," she said. He wondered when she would leave him for good. When she would assemble the team to replace him.

You never acted this way before, he thought to say but didn't. The night before he told her how he wanted to be a college-level home economics teacher.

"You'd sleep with all your students," she said. Gabe began to speak and suggested that maybe he could teach gym instead. Or coach hockey. Work in a library. He then discussed a fact about his life, which spanned several weeks in the early nineties. "When I was eighteen I worked at Rogers Sports and filmed girls' basketball. They were like a year or so older than me. I would film the cutaway shots from behind their benches, you know, like the coach telling them things."

She shook her head. "Perv." Claire told him about a teacher's assistant who really helped her out in second year. "I was going through a tough time; he was really supportive, this was about two years ago." He had no idea what she was talking about and later feared the worst. He never understood he could have at any time cancelled things with Claire and the psychiatrist. When things get too weird and you just don't believe things are happening to you the way you are seeing them, that's when you use your safety word. But only if you've

274 » JETTISON

been taking the supplement. If you haven't, this terrible thing befalling you is most likely really occurring.

✳   ✳   ✳

Later that week she flapped an essay in his face as she told him about it. "Look, I got an A and I didn't have to sleep with the teacher!"

"Yes I heard you, great," Gabe said. And that's when he put that one together. That real supportive teacher's assistant was a man she slept with and bragged about to him in a not-so-subtle way like a towel-slapping football jock. Gabe toiled and surmised that the experience gave Claire confidence, pleasure, a friend and a secret sexual high as she transitioned out of dumped-by-her-boyfriend mode into something else.

He now knew he was not enough. Each night he took a weird pill that made him twitch and stop talking. He had to take this pill at eleven or so each night. Then it would be a weird body undulation into sleep. "Don't take your pill tonight," she said.

He was not enough for what she wanted. He was a woolen hat all crazy and wet. He was Long John Crazy.

Gabe told her how much he loved the way she tasted. Her face dipped into darkness, and then her face came back when some moonlight found its way through the curtain.

"You can eat other girls," Claire said thoughtfully.

Gabe and Claire did the familiar reflection, the post-obsession sigh; they had become an award-winning synchronized team for the sexual afterlife.

※ ※ ※

It had been four days since they last saw each other when Gabe tumbled down another slope of what he would later coin as Mount Psychosis. She had admonished him for not reacting to her sleeping with Mark. They quarreled on the phone and for this Gabe didn't feel the need to change into clothes from pajamas.

"You didn't even get upset."

"You're young," he said in her defence. And in saying so, his lack of passion registered.

And Gabe disappeared again for several days while Claire, needing the security of a reliable boyfriend yet professing her independence, succumbed to the former and reached out into the ethereal plains of communication, scribbling away on the backs of her university essays: You really hurt me this time. I dunno if that's why you're doing this. To get me back or whatever. I really needed to talk to you. I haven't talked to my brother in two weeks since he freaked out on me. It's tearing me up inside. I found out Tuesday that Melissa slept with him, which is totally the most hurtful thing she has ever done to me. I can't see her and I'm really hurt. I specifically told her not to; I think I need to move out. They're turning off my phone and shit 'cause a payment didn't go through and I owe four hundred bucks before Monday or it's gone. I think I'm possibly pregnant. Really could've used your support there. Whatever. Do your disappearing act. Just remember we were at one point really good friends above anything else and you really aren't showing me that you care. At least one phone call. I've been crying alone in my house all week with no one to talk to. I can't even talk to Melissa because I'm so shocked with her. Thanks for all your help.

❉　❉　❉

"I got my period."

"I'm sorry I didn't call. I felt really sick. It's the pills and worried about money and just feeling crazy all the time." He wondered aloud if the baby would have been his or Mark's and Claire insisted it would have been his since her and Mark had used protection.

"I've got a job interview in four hours; if you want we can go back to my place and nap."

Gabe smiled as best he could, and hoped his face said something encouraging such as "Of course." His body language— all itch and numb—was *épater le bourgeois* and Frankenstein rides the bus.

❉　❉　❉

"Do you want to watch the hockey game for a bit tonight?" Gabe asked Claire, who playfully rolled her big dumb eyes up into her head and shook her head side to side along with her arms that moved an imaginary hockey stick. She also could have been pantomiming someone minigolfing. Her desire to watch the game it seemed was equally imaginary.

"I guess that's a no?" She scampered down the hall to the tiny washroom. "I'm taking a shower if you want to come."

Gabe joined her and noticed a cut on her leg.

"It's from shaving. I cut myself," she said, looking at his wrist

MOORE » *277*

where three antique scars rested in shameful permanence. "Not like you." He had told her about the time he cut himself like he always did with girlfriends. It always made him feel the same way—just a bit depressed.

Gabe wanted to tell her about the hospital—how he was almost mugged, how this one guy came into his room and saw a magazine with Paris Hilton on it and taunted him about it. How another patient on his floor would talk to his mother for hours on the hall phone and speak in NHL prophecy. That the guy was like Cassandra and would tell his mother things that were going to happen to him, or maybe that had already happened to him. He warned her about upcoming trades and point spreads in the NHL. He kept using Pat Lafontaine in a sentence. "Pat Lafontaine, Bill Masterton Trophy 1994, and in 1997 Mom, post-concussion syndrome, 1983 drafted first round, third pick overall, career points are 1013, not Luc Robitaille, not Sergei Fedorov, New York Islanders, New York Rangers, Buffalo Sabres, not Detroit, not Los Angeles. 1992-1993 with Buffalo he had ninety-five assists, no Stanley Cup. No, you are not listening; I don't want Calgary Flames defense, but maybe Pittsburg Penguins left-winger."

Gabe was terrified by the hockey-card prophet. To Gabe the young man was muddled and his words were owned and licensed by the NHL. It made Gabe feel even crazier every time he tried to imagine this man's poor mother on the other end writing it all down on a dressing-room strategy whiteboard.

❈   ❈   ❈

One terrible morning Gabe tried to have sex with Claire but

couldn't keep himself hard. Any form of sexual confidence was an unreasonable request to his psyche. The false couple had been waning in and out of each other's frequency for weeks at this point.

In the cold seconds following the embarrassing body-fail, Gabe kept imagining a giant glass of orange juice being handed to him but shattering to the ground in slow motion just as his body and mind agreed to give up on this physical plot point forever.

Claire turned the shower on. "I am going to be late for work. I gotta hurry. No more funny business," she said and headed down the hall. He watched her from the bedroom and saw how her eyes froze on him. She put her lips together under the stream and closed her eyes. A flash of light boomed through the whole house accompanied by a loud series of high pitch squeaks. He waited for her to calm him with an explanation, but this never materialized.

She hopped naked from the shower like a big fuzzy wet bunny. Looking at her big alarm clock she said to him stiffly, "We have twenty minutes."

"OK."

"Gabe," Claire said, closing her dresser drawer loudly as introduction to a new subject, "we can't do this anymore. Maybe you can't see it, but I can. I don't want to call this sad monster love, all I can say is we have to try and get rid of it. We've done all that's humanly possible to look after this love and we've been patient. I don't think anyone could accuse us of doing anything wrong."

"You're absolutely right," said Gabe, his heart now racing with worry and in general feeling self-critical. The idea of separating filled him with panic. Finding his way back to Claire, even in the remotest of conditions was a small comfort he cherished. The present tense in all its authenticity weighed a lot. He began to cough dully, as if an itch from some part-time smoking he'd been dabbling in was now catching up to his body.

She got dressed in another room, huffing off with her hands held out behind her carrying a pair of pants and concealing her semi-naked behind.

Upon re-entry into her bedroom, the once frenzied expression in her eyes had been replaced by a no-nonsense look. It was this new precise visage she sported that ushered in an era of realism for Gabe.

"The only way we can stop this is if we stop hanging out," Claire said, level-headedly.

He sat upright, reaching for his winter toque between the plates left after their meal. Beside her bed a small machine with asthmatic bellows breathed loudly and clicked in staccato every so often, giving off an air of insectoid malice. He surveyed her messy bedroom floor for his winter boots which lay there—somewhere—immobile, like those found at a hellish crime scene.

❋   ❋   ❋

One night years later, Gabe saw Claire with a giant man, six-foot-four. They were getting into a cab on Front Street, near the Hockey Hall of Fame. Later he found out from a mutual friend that she was engaged to a hockey player. He told the friend he was not surprised, that he had seen them near the trophy museum for great hockey players.

Gabe imagined Claire doing that bratty invisible hockey stick routine and laughing at log-cabin retreats with several other hockey players and their blond wives or blond girlfriends, and Claire the brunette would hear from each woman separately, "I just love your hair," and sometimes even touch it, or hold it up to their own hair while commenting on her 'Hang in There' cat charm given to her by her lifelong best friend from the small town she hatched from even though she was a dog person.

And Claire would say, "Don't mind if I do," when asked if she wanted another white-wine spritzer. The whole fantasy Gabe was completing resembled a big, dumb *Playboy Girls of the Jock Strap* special issue. He was happy for her though. Gabe wanted her to be happy for him and his lifestyle choices too. But he knew she didn't know about him anymore. He was doing almost all the recollecting. "All right!" Gabe said to himself after a big silent sigh.

He knew she was in a toque and mittens, cheering, her finger bedazzled with a pricey jewel. He thought that if he was a girl he would want to fuck a hockey player at least once, just for the jokes and also because they would probably be very strong and do a good job.

❋   ❋   ❋

For a year Gabe drank what he now believes was semi-poisonous coffee. He now didn't care what Claire thought of him. The memories had evaporated, the way a mint shrinks in a hot mouth. He just remembered a microbe of memories from that difficult thirtieth year: the hospital nights, the bed on the floor, the psych patient who spoke in NHL, and her joke about his suicidal scars. It was part of his life on the back of his trading card, along with his height and weight and position and place of birth. He watched an old commercial he had on vhs from taping television on the family vcr. It was a dramatization of Montreal Canadiens' goalie Jacques Plante and his facial injury, the one that took place the day after Halloween in 1959 in Madison Square Garden where Plante finally donned the face mask he'd been using in practices. And Gabe always taped the commercial when it came on because he was obsessed with Jacques Plante and the Montreal Canadiens from the 1950s and 1960s. This obsession with Jacques Plante and the Montreal Canadiens occurred during Operation Desert Storm in 1990-91.

"Just think about it," Gabe could have said to Claire on the couch watching the hockey game they never watched together, "there would be no Jason Voorhees without him." Then what? Then what would he have said?

And so Gabe crunched down on the last sliver of breath mint that had been lounging on his fat tongue for what seemed like eons.

AFTERFOREWORD: LINER NOTES

"Also By Douglas Coupland" was written and arranged by Nathaniel G. Moore. It was mastered at Protection Island Mansion with additional samplings from the blog *Critical Crushes*. Montreal fans will certainly identify Warren Auld as the muse for Douglas Coupland's future novel *2 1/2* with the looping "half a club sandwich" refrain in the actual book and this popular line, responsible for so many memes worldwide, can be attributed in the anecdote in which Nathaniel took Warren to Reggie's Sports Bar a number of times and only bought him half a club sandwich to which Warren finally charged, "It's not enough food!" Additional conceptual advice from Michael J. Fox came hours before the final draft was autosaved.

"The Catullus Chainsaw Massacre" appeared first in the 1999 zine *Flesh Jukebox*. All rights secured. Additional takes include CIUT 89.5 in the fall of 1999. *Catullus* appears courtesy of Penguin Classic Records. Faint backing vocals by Leonard Cohen, Henry Miller, and Kathy Acker were recorded, but eventually dubbed over, but appear in early drafts courtesy of Amazon.ca. Narrative arc consultation from Michael J. Fox proved to be invaluable. As we all know, the original script for *Back To The Future* was rejected forty times and in a private viewing, then President Ronald Reagan asked the projectionist to "rewind" to the scene where his name was mentioned in the first meeting between 1955 Doc Brown and Marty McFly. The use of blindfolds in the story is a metaphor of some kind about denial. The original story had terrorists in it who were after Catullus and Henry for stealing plutonium. When it came to the characterizations, Fox suggested not worrying about who was going to be Marty and who was going to be Doc Brown. "Let Catullus stumble around, let Henry help him out and see which one of them snaps first in a Canadian winter." According to an interview with *Rolling Stone* in 1985, Michael J. Fox failed drama because he wasn't there one day "to put a paper bag over my head and crawl backwards on stage." Tim's Ink Cartridge Refill owner Tim Blends said this: "And then you have Catullus right, who wrote once, that he was 'The worst poet of all' and Fox, right, biggest star in Hollywood for a time and he fails drama in high school! Fails! So I think that's what the story is about in a nutshell, without giving too much away. It's a way to say, 'See, I may have failed and call myself the worst poet of all but, look society, I can make this really cool chainsaw out of cardboard!' Something along those lines." This story was published in Joyland Magazine in September 2016.

"Son of Zodiac" was originally titled "The Hillbilly and the Bar of Soap" and was given a Writers Reserve Grant in 2003 by Coach House Books via the Ontario Arts Council. Thanks to Alana Wilcox. The line "The mass-produced lowbrow props stinking up my bedroom collection during those days—stale board games, worn-out comic books, ceramic garage sale commemorative dishes and the torn plastic sheen from the binding of expired bikini calendars—is now handsome landfill or has been recycled into a pregnant-looking cashier's bra." was originally more brand specific, with the cashier in question working at WalMart. The corporation's willingness to sell firearms, however, has made this author retract their nominal prominence.

"The Magic ~~Kingdom~~ Empire" was written by Nathaniel G. Moore in the summer of 2014 and contains a faint dusting of lyrics and narrative linchpins from Consumer Blvd © 2003 Proper Concern. "So many things resemble products out on the street / I find it hard / I find it weird / these things compete / with my need for a sense / of a well-being / and adjustment / nutrients / fibre-optics / perhaps a little splash of Tabasco" (Music by Warren Auld, lyrics by Nathaniel G. Moore). Please contact your local Toys 'R' Us cashier for more information on the app and the foundation. "Banjo," the fictional surfing Disney character appears courtesy of the author.

"A Higher Power" was written and choreographed by Nathaniel G.

Moore in Toronto and on Protection Island and later in Madeira Park/ Pender Harbour. An earlier version appeared at *Lies With Occasional Truth* (Ottawa). The editors emailed him to tell him his story was recently read by a search for "Paul Newman Penis Size." All footage of Paul Martin referenced in the story appears courtesy of the Canadian Broadcasting Corporation (CBC). Special thanks to the innumerous charitable organizations who use the dance-a-thon method to raise money and awareness. Thanks to Oshawa mayor Renee Sampears. Paul Martin was invaluable in the completion of this story as well as the entire Alcoholics Anonymous ™ organization. One Day At A Time Folks. A recipe for The Chicoutimi Free-Range Potato salad dressing is available by emailing the author.

"The Amazing Spiderman" was originally a fashion article about the prevalence of Goth culture in Northern Florida cities. In Gainesville, for example, young Goths in the late nineties rebelled against formed stereotypes of Floridian fashion (e.g., beachwear, white, old people with pants up to their Adam's apple, the aged keeling over, fricasseed in the crimson sun, etc.) It has long been believed that these strong images of clothed Florida citizens greatly contributed to the voluminous amount of "undead" hipsters walking the lizard-infested streets of Northern Florida. Goth deodorant has yet to catch on as a marketed flavour amongst leading "anti-stink" corporeal business models. The food at Panda Express was average and oily. Taco John's franchise information hotline is the toll-free numerical sequence of: 1-800-TACO-JOHN.

"American Psycho" was written by Nathaniel G. Moore. An earlier version of the story appeared in the *National Post* in late 2013. Things weren't always a glib, balls in the blender, "Did you put a bomb in my potato?" level of madness when it came to relations in the Toronto literary community. The 2003 song by Green Day "Or Were They?" for example, has an enduring message of pain but also admiration and acceptance towards lost love and was based on a Rower's Reading Series drink and dash goodbye kiss. "She kissed me on the lips goodbye / it was soft / crushing / like pulling hot bread out of my shoulders and the bread was my arms / soul crushing. / am I going to be all right?" Interesting to note: "The Pepsi Generation" fostered an entire all-star team of sociopathic blood-thirsty white male misogynists in the twentieth century with Zodiac being their star left guard and Ted Bundy being the team's empathetic water boy. Twenty-odd years later, "A whole new generation" was the soft drink company's lobotomized jingle in the fizzy eighties, led by Michael Jackson.

"Gordon's Gold" was written in August 2014 on Protection Island by Nathaniel G. Moore. A spoken-word version is in development. The tightie-whitie (actually tea-coloured tightie-whitie underpants, so tightie-tea-coloured") print sold later that night for $17,430.00 US. Several pairs of ripped underpants appeared originally in no less than three stories in *Jettison*. The reason for their threadbare condition was never fully explained in editorial meetings so they were removed.

"Jaws" was originally mastered by *Forget Magazine* in 2003 as "The Nightmare Lover." That title was developed from a letter the lead love interest Louise got from her sister about Benjamin. The letter is truncated for dramatic purposes, "Maybe this is the first time that I've ever felt some amiability towards your dearest dead friend [Benjamin] Nathaniel G. Moore. It's hard not to, but sardonic wit and a true attempt to love oneself? Yup, he's doing a great job at life, so cheers to him and his beautiful words. Are you being hard on him? I do feel he's holding this thing over your head to make you feel bad about your twenty-seventh break-up with would-be nightmare-lover Nathaniel. He knows that love lies in the depths of the dragon's cave and that all dragons need pretty princesses to devour, or the dragons get angry and ravage the towns and villages nearby. Nathaniel isn't a dragon or a princess and he failed at being the prince so where is he now? Who's going to love him if he's been ignored/denied by the myth of his own tragedy?" Eventually repackaged as simply "Jaws," the story was also inspired by the song *Gotchaman Love Song* © 2003 Proper Concern.

"Professor Buggles" was first a seedling podcast experiment in sound called *Gar Wilson*, a 7:16 YouTube clip of auditory gibberish (a faux interview with the infamous action adventure novelist) by Proper Concern recorded and mixed in Montreal in February 2011. All rights reserved. Listener discretion advised: may cause Gar Wilson addiction.

"The Thorncliffe Strangler" was written in Toronto and on Protection Island with further mixes taking place from prerecorded celluloid data vis-à-vis VHS tapes and the recollections of their 1990, 1991, 1992, 1993, and 2000 contents. Puffitis is an actual dehydration disease prevalent in many moon-faced members of society. If you think you're a carrier of said condition, visit your local walk-in clinic or drinking fountain.

"Blade Runner" was written in Toronto, Protection Island and at Madeira Park. An earlier version of the story called "That Time That You Made It with the Whole Hockey Team" was published in 2013 by The Barnstormer with additional edits by Michael Spry. It has since gone missing from the web, so perhaps it knew it had to grow up. A deleted exchange of dialogue referencing George Michael's music (including *Father Figure, I Want Your Sex, Cowboys and Angels* and his cover of New Order's *True Faith*) was deleted. "We're like…this song," Claire muses while she and Gabe listened to *Father Figure*. The evening continues on its narcissistic way via George and ends with the comical New Order *True Faith* cover as both lovers fall asleep, destined for romantic failure. Former New Order bassist Peter Hook told the BBC Michael's version was a "beautiful" interpretation but admitted it was "not exactly to my taste." According to Hook, the band became friends with the former Wham! singer in the eighties when they would attend the same parties in the US.

ABOUT THE AUTHOR

Nathaniel G. Moore is the author five previous books including, most recently, *Savage 1986-2011* (Anvil Press), winner of the 2014 ReLit Award for best novel. He is the lead singer of the non-fiction electro-folk band Proper Concern with Warren Auld. His fiction has appeared in *subTerrain, Joyland, Taddle Creek*, and *Verbicide* magazine. He currently lives on BC's Sunshine Coast with his partner and daughter and works as a book publicist full time.

[PHOTO: Amber McMillan]